HOGGE

WILD

KAREN SIRABIAN

ISBN: 979-8-218-00515-3

Logo designed by Christopher Lynk

This book was published with the assistance of Self-Publishing Relief, a
division of Writer's Relief.

For my diamonds and rubies…

This much the pigs do for each other
If one squeals they all come in droves...
—Francois Villon

CHAPTER 1

The water taxi from Palm Point marina finally got under way for its Thursday morning run to the relief of everyone sweltering on board under the strong August sun. It was headed for Hogge, a barrier island off the Florida coast in the Gulf of Mexico, and carried an eclectic mix of passengers— residents, tourists, workers and, on this particular morning, a man in a blue silk shirt who was none of these.

A combination of transport and supply boat, the water taxi was a lifeline for those who called the bridgeless island home. A pod of dolphin accompanied the boat on its five mile hop across the blue green bay, leaping and playing in its wake. Passengers laughed at their antics and crowded the stern to take photographs, the banal strip malls and dreary landscape of the mainland already forgotten.

The man in the blue silk shirt sitting expressionless and apart from the rest took advantage of the distraction to make two calls. If anyone had overheard the first, it was a simple exchange giving notice of his arrival. If they'd overheard the second, a great deal of trouble might have been avoided. Brief, tense and menacing, it consisted of three words: "Time is up."

The dolphin veered off to enthusiastic cheers as the captain cut his speed and motored into the channel leading to the Hogge Island landing. Passengers milled about gathering their possessions, chatting, and generally impeding the work of the captain and his mate as they struggled to secure the lines and dock the boat. One by one they filed off and waited on the pier for their belongings to be handed down by the crew. They took no notice of the man in the blue silk shirt, carrying only a briefcase, who shouldered roughly past them in the bright sunlight.

CHAPTER 2

Thursday afternoon on the east end of Hogge Island, building contractor Richard Sharpe gave a loud whistle to his crew indicating quitting time. The workers made their way down off the roofs and decks of the luxury home they were working on, eager for a cold beer and respite from the sun they'd been baking under for hours. He watched them climb down. Backlit against the strong rays, they looked like an army of insects swarming down the white Tyvek-wrapped sides of the house. It was five o'clock but the sky still blazed with the intensity of mid-day. With nowhere left to go, the waves of heat hung in the air, became visible, shimmering. It seemed entirely possible that the sun would never set again.

Richard stepped into the shade of a giant banyan tree and lit a cigarette, waving away the smoke that hung around him in the breezeless air. They were already a month behind and this week was the final kick in the ass. Two days lost to boat trouble, supplies warping on the mainland dock, and now days of unbearable heat, grinding the already slow pace of work to a dead crawl. The owner, a self-important big-time banker out of Miami, was leaning on him good. *No more money*, he'd said, *until the job is done*. They liked to play hardball like that, the big shots. It made them feel like they were getting their money's worth. Particularly this big shot.

Richard was twelve grand out of pocket and there were already three contractor liens out on the job, with more to come. And today was payday for the crew, a fact not lost on the men coming toward him. He waved them toward his golf cart and the cooler of iced beer on its trailer. He could manage half a week's pay with the promise of the rest next week, news they could swallow better on the heels of a few cold ones. And where was next week's money going to come from? Sweat bathed the leather cord hanging around his neck, and it had nothing to do with heat or sun.

A golf cart was almost on him before he heard it pull up with a hushed whine of tires in the sand. The man behind the wheel peered at the house, shading his eyes against the glare, an arm raised to his gelled black hair. He wore a perfectly tailored short-sleeved shirt without a hint of a sweat stain. Max. The son of a bitch himself, on another of his incessant surprise inspections.

Sharpe forced a smile he didn't feel. "Max! When did you roll in? Good to see you," he said, swallowing hard. His mouth was so dry that his teeth were sticking to the inside of his lips.

"Sharpe," Max's tone was acid. He walked over to Richard who was leaning against his golf cart under the graceful limbs of the banyan. For a guy with a slight build, Max had tremendous swagger. "What the fuck have you guys been doing for a week? Looks exactly the same as the last time I came out. Oh I know," Max said, cutting off any reply, "boat trouble, heat, the usual crap." He laughed, which was never a good sign. "I came out here *intending* to give you the next installment."

The word "bullshit" came into his head so strongly that Richard wondered for a moment if he had said it aloud.

Max was talking again in his short, staccato hyena barks. "But this…." He waved dismissively at the house rising above the palms, with its expansive dock and breathtaking views of open blue water. Then he turned and nodded toward the crew. The men, shirts off, were raising beers and taking turns pouring icy water from the cooler over their heads and lanky tattooed bodies, snatches of weekend plans rising and falling in heavily twanged accents. "They—and you," he said pointedly, "would last about a week in Miami before they shut your asses down." Max tapped a manicured finger against Richard's chest and let it linger there. A gold Rolex blinked in the sunlight on his arm. "You should be building doghouses," he said, the words thick with insult. "And you're lucky if I pay you at all."

Richard had endured Max's taunts for months without pushback. But this time—maybe a combination of the unrelenting heat, worry, and the sheer frustration of being someone's whipping boy—he lost control.

"You bastard!" Richard slapped Max's hand away. His sudden snarl of anger took even his crew, used to his erratic temper, by surprise. He reached behind him into his cart and instinctively grabbed one of the scrap two by fours piled on the back seat. A few of the crew started forward, nervously.

"You know damned well no one else on this island would put up with your crap." An ugly vein bulged on his forehead. He grabbed Max's shirtfront and raised the two-by-four. "How about I jam those sunglasses right through your skull, huh? You think anyone would stop me?"

"Richard!" one of the crew yelled his name, "Put it down, Sharpe—he's not worth it!"

Max loosened Richard's grip on his shirt gently, brushing at the lapel, and took off his sunglasses. "He's right, Sharpe." Max said, coolly, eyes coal-black, piercing. "Not worth it to go through all that. *Again*."

As if the word "again" was a magic incantation, Richard lowered the piece of wood to the ground. He looked shaky, disoriented. "I need money to pay the crew," he said, licking his upper lip. "They're working hard here and you know it." No anger now. Just pleading.

"Four grand," Max peeled the hundreds from a stack bulging under a gold money clip that gleamed in sunlight.

"You owe me twelve thousand," Richard countered, but his tone was dull with defeat.

"Owe? You want to talk about owe?" Max tucked the money in Richard's damp shirt pocket with offensive care. He spit his words out like bullets. "Don't forget how you got this job. Or why a a shit like you is working anywhere. At all."

His voice carried clearly to the men who'd returned to the cooler, and they grew silent over their beers. The sun had started its slow descent to the water. It was deep and liquid: the color of blood.

CHAPTER 3

At his customary table in *Gordon's*, the restaurant bearing his name, Gordon Strange was enjoying his second breakfast bourbon in between the last bites of Marvelita's delicious baked eggs. Dawn was making an appearance slowly this morning. Sunlight glowed under a heavy layer of cloud, infusing the water with rose and gold tones that carried him on the long years of memory to other sunrises on other shores. Wind blew steadily and warm from the southeast. It would be a busy Friday, he thought, with plenty of boat traffic before the weather turned.

Overhead, a clutch of turkey vultures took advantage of the high thermals and made wide circles, great black wings spread ominously against the sky. Opening time was just over an hour away and tantalizing whiffs of Marvelita's *pan cubano* wafted steadily out of the kitchen, a siren call to man and beast alike.

Gordon lit one of his two daily cognac-dipped cigars and, through a trail of sweet smoke, watched a small skiff navigate the bay and bump to a landing at one of his docks. The single occupant climbed out, threw a couple of ropes around the piling, and walked carefully down the narrow slip carrying a bucket. *Lattie Mainstay*, he registered mentally—the island's inveterate fisherwoman and busybody. He was slightly surprised to find her out this early, and alone. Normally she'd have Doris Killgalen with her. Twenty-eight year veterans of Hogge, they shared a small bungalow and were generally inseparable. Lattie was making a beeline for him, holding up the bucket.

"Trout, Gordon, nice ones—five of 'em," she sat down opposite him, slightly out of breath, and plunked the bucket down next to his bare feet. Water splashed the hem of his pants and over his toes. Her comment wasn't so much a statement as an inquiry. Gordon smiled.

"Marvelita," he called out, and a petite woman with glossy black hair piled high into a tight bun came out from the restaurant. She was incongruously dressed in a white chef's apron over a bright blue and white patterned sarong and moved with a deliberation some might mistake for languor.

"Fresh trout," Gordon said, indicating the bucket. "Lattie just brought them in."

Marvelita gave a faint smile and bent down, pulling a fish out of the murky water to inspect it. "They are a decent size. I will give you two dollars for each," she said to Lattie.

"Five each," countered Lattie. "Come on, Marvelita. You'd pay twice that and they wouldn't be half as fresh if they came from the mainland," she said, eying the basket of bread leftover from Gordon's breakfast. "Hard to find in August," she added, reaching over and slathering butter on a slice with Gordon's knife.

"Four," said Marvelita firmly. She picked up the bucket even before Lattie, chewing, nodded her acceptance. "You can come for the money this afternoon," she added. "Fish and grits special—they'll like that," she said to Gordon, gesturing toward the sandy road where dozens of workmen were gathering to get their morning assignments. "Beni," she called, and an equally small man came running from inside, white apron flapping. "Filleto—no bones!—rapido." She followed him calling out further instructions in Spanish as he hurried into the kitchen with the prizes.

Lattie watched them disappear and laughed. "She's amazing, Gordon. An alchemist in the kitchen and one hell of a businesswoman."

"And beautiful. And my best friend, as odd as that may seem." Gordon said, brushing ash from his blazer. His shirt was half open and a gold anchor on a heavy chain glinted against the expanse of his massive chest in the breaking light. Lattie looked at him inquiringly but he didn't elaborate. Instead, he looked at her keenly and asked, "What got you going so early, Lattie? Trying to beat the heat? And where's Doris?" He leaned over and gently brushed a few crumbs off Lattie's chin. A white hair or two sprouting, he couldn't help but notice.

Lattie helped herself to another piece of bread. "Someday I wish you'd tell me how you and Marvelita met. I'll bet that's a story worth hearing." She looked at him hopefully.

"Someday I might. So where *is* Doris?" He repeated his original question. He had no desire to go down the path of "what makes Gordon tick." Everyone's favorite pastime since his arrival on Hogge more than a decade ago.

Lattie brushed a few crumbs off her fishing shirt self-consciously. "Doris is out turtle monitoring. I thought I'd get some fishing in early." She didn't sound very convincing. "And by the way, can we borrow a cup of sugar? We seem to have run out."

"Sure," he said, watching the ever-efficient Marvelita pull out her "specials" board, with "Fish & Grits Breakfast $5" chalked in bright red. Lattie was right in more ways than she realized. In fact, Gordon thought, she'd be surprised to know just how amazing Marvelita was. He turned his attention back to the woman spontaneously sharing his breakfast. "So you're up at dawn just to sell me some fish and borrow a cup of sugar?" He flashed her a wide grin.

Lattie's face creased into a weathered frown. "Oh all right. I want to get down that canal and have a good look around before anyone is up and about. You know as well as I do Hollow's is up to something."

Ah, now we're coming to it, Gordon thought. And why not? Why should Hogge Island and its little band of contrarians treat him any differently than the half dozen other places he'd tied up at along the course of a misspent life. Meanwhile, Lattie was giving voice to his suspicions about this particular early morning visit of hers.

"Something's got to be done, Gordon. Someone's got to stop him before he destroys this place." She threw an angry nod toward a cove in the distance, home of the Hogge Island Resort and Club and its owner, Alan Hollows. "He's not even waiting for a hearing. They've dug up half the mangroves and there's a bunch of heavy equipment in place. He's paid someone off and got the permits, must have. He's going to do it." She was as angry as he'd ever seen her. "He's going to build his damned so-called community hall. Community hall!" She said contemptuously "That's how he got his permits you know. As if he's ever going to let anyone from this community in!"

"I wouldn't hold my breath waiting for an invitation," Gordon agreed, spearing his last piece of ham.

"He's already cleared a road from the bay to the beach. I hate that man." She tore a chunk off the last piece of bread, stuffed it in her mouth and leaned forward glaring at him, jaw working furiously, waiting.

Gordon stubbed out the end of the small cigar ruefully— no more until nighttime. He recognized in Lattie's outburst the signaling of yet another "Island Issue." There had been at least half a dozen since he'd first come to Hogge. Most were petty grievances whose outcomes didn't amount to much, except to feed the seemingly insatiable demand for drama in the tiny place. This one was the first to threaten the very existence of what was left of the unique island lifestyle the inhabitants, including himself, originally came for. Still, he had not come to take up battles a la Don Quixote—he made that clear from the get-go. He eyed Lattie warily. A warning not to look for trouble might save him from the quicksand of personal involvement.

"I figured you weren't out this early just fishing." Gordon shifted back in his chair, straining the flimsy resin. "Look, you need to be careful. Hollows owns the property and that's a tough bunch with a lot of money at stake." He kept his voice low, willing her to pay attention. "Things are changing, Lattie, you're right about that. But you and Doris—you're out alone, all the time. Everyone knows it. Don't forget what happened to the Grandersons."

Rudy Granderson, veteran County Commissioner and conservationist, had come, along with his wife Selda, to Hogge seven years ago when the powerful sugar lobby spent millions to get him out of office and out of their hair. He lost the election but not his dedication to public service. He was a regular on the front lines of any protest organized in Tallahassee or Tampa involving run-off, water diversion and the sugar industry. Two years after his arrival on Hogge, he, his wife, and his neighbors awoke to the sound of an explosion. Almost instantly, the Granderson's deck burst into flames and the two barely escaped the conflagration that consumed the entire house within a half an hour. In time, the verdict was arson, but by the time the Sheriff and mainland fire departments arrived nearly two hours hour later, both the house and any perpetrators were long gone. The investigation was still open and, most residents suspected, would remain so in perpetuity.

Gordon picked up his broad white hat from the table so he could shade his eyes, see Lattie's face more clearly. *Had his words sunk in?* He was not reassured by her set and stubborn face, and the look of pure fury she directed toward the gay pink and green Resort awning in the distance that peeked over the top of the island's canopy.

"I don't care about the Grandersons. This is Hogge, not Tallahassee. We've got to stop him," she said vehemently. "The wildlife is already beginning to suffer. Doris told me he's disrupted sea turtle nests—five of them already."

"You can't prove that and you know it. He'll just blame it on the high tide or storms."

Lattie bristled. "Well, you can sit here and hold court at this table and drink bourbon, but Doris and I are going to do something about it. Everyone knows he's planning a lot more than a damned community hall." She was becoming more agitated and the whole situation threatened to become an emotional firestorm just as the restaurant opened. "Please Gordon. You have to help us."

There it was: the all too familiar cry of distress. He could ignore it or respond. Either way it meant trouble. Not for the first time in his life the rescue doctrine, the Good Samaritan's friend came to mind. *The cry of distress is the summons to relief.* Only, Gordon reflected wearily, they were a long way from a court of law on Hogge Island, or from any law at all for that matter. Good Samaritans fared well in aiding island wildlife and hapless tourists. In other matters, they generally ended up hospitalized.

Not for the first time, Gordon cursed the genetic fortune that endowed him with towering height and a build to match. The combination seemed to peg him as the go-to man in any emergency. Only this man had done with all that a long time ago and thought he'd at last found the place where his greatest worry would be the day's menu. Of course, Fate had its own ideas. He didn't look for trouble, he was done with that. But trouble seemed to follow him. It was that simple.

The smell of frying fish and grits mingled with the scent of *pan cubano* was already drawing dusty looking workmen to the take-out counter like flies. As golf carts rattled up outside heralding the arrival of the hungry, Gordon threw back the remains of his bourbon in exasperation and signaled to Marvelita for an espresso. He gazed over Lattie's shoulder at the stand of ficus trees at water's edge. Brooding like hooded judges in the far limbs were the turkey vultures that had been circling overhead earlier. They seemed to be watching him. "I'll see what I can find out," he finally said.

Lattie nodded in satisfaction, got up and headed for her skiff. Frowning, Gordon watched her ample backside retreat toward the dock. He recalled, with some irritation, the first part of the doctrine: *Danger invites rescue.*

CHAPTER 4

After Lattie put off the dock in her skiff, Gordon checked his watch. Lunch service didn't start for a few hours. Enough time to take a quick trip around the island and see what he could find out, like he'd promised. He ducked into the kitchen to have a quick word with Marvelita about the day's specials. Like a clairvoyant, she was waiting for him, menu in hand.

"Grilled fish taco and triple-tail with mango habanero," she said, pointing to the illegible scrawl on the stained sheet before her. "And that *vieja* will get you in trouble, I tell you this," she warned him, shaking her head. It was clear she had overheard Lattie's plea.

Gordon sighed and gently took the sheet from her hand. She was right, of course, she always was. "Let me write this over and get it copied before tonight," he said, running his eye over it. "Where'd you get the tripletail?" he asked quickly, to forestall further discussion about Lattie.

"Fletcher brought it earlier." Marvelita wasn't so easily sidetracked. "That *vieja* is one big nose," she pulled at her own upturned one, "and someone will cut it soon." Behind the annoyance in her voice was a good deal of concern. "And $15 would have been enough for her trout, but," she brightened momentarily, "we are doing very well for breakfast!"

"Tell Fletcher I said thank you," Gordon laughed, making a mental note to congratulate his friend on this rare show of work ethic. Fletcher James was rarely up before 10a.m, unless he had a fishing charter. On his days off, he usually wasn't sober. "Don't worry, Marvelita—I'm just going to have a look around—for myself."

Marvelita remained unconvinced. "This is not her island," she said darkly, and turned abruptly back to the kitchen.

Actually, Gordon reflected, climbing into his custom black golf cart, Hogge was as much Lattie's as anyone's island. Two centuries back the Indians who populated it were wiped out by conquering Spaniards, who in turn lost it to malaria, mangrove fever and outlaws of one stripe or another. It remained uninhabited for a century except by "pirates"— largely invented, it would seem, by the tourist board.

According to the History of Hogge, a poorly printed monograph that was more pamphlet than paperback, around 1965 a few stragglers boated out and discovered it was a pretty good place to disappear from the impoverished sprawl that was becoming the Florida mainland. Their numbers increased by ones and twos and, by the 1970s, about thirty of them had paid their $10 homestead claim for title and lived there, almost invisible to each other under the dense canopy and outnumbered by wild pigs, from which the island largely got its name. The last two letters were bestowed much later in a moment of Chamber of Commerce inspiration and remained a source of division on the island, which remained "Hog" or "Hogge" depending on which camp you were in. With no bridge or roads, the island stayed under the radar. Florida claimed it but rather halfheartedly—it didn't appear on official maps, had no zip code, no governing body, no law of any kind. Its residents were close-knit by necessity and Robinson Crusoe by nature. The community they formed was one of stubborn individuals, which was to say no community at all. To those who stayed, this was its chief attraction.

Gordon's first impression of Hogge on his arrival over a decade back was a scattering of small cottages, modest, home-grown efforts, low profile, like the people living in them. The largely one-story, Old Florida frame bungalows were set deep in a canopy of vegetation and cabbage palms. Dense green tangles of invasive pepper fought to choke out the native seagrapes. White shell paths were scattered here and there, scraped lines stretching off the rutted sand roads. The early residents were a colorful collection of hardy retirees and others fleeing cold Northern winters, remittance men, and folks who for one reason or another found living under the radar and off the grid a desirable prospect. They made do with two, maybe three bedrooms, propane for cooking and generators for what little electricity was used. Devoid of cars or commerce, the island had a harmonious quiet in the daytime broken only by the cry of osprey, the clear notes of migrating songbirds, the rustle of snakes and gopher tortoises making their way through the undergrowth, or the thrum of a distant boat engine. At night, the rhythmic lapping of the Gulf soothed when it was at peace or served up waves promising a shift in the weather. The perfect place to disappear into, in fact, as long as you could tolerate the mosquitos and humidity.

Change reached Hogge slowly, but when it finally got there, it came like an avalanche. The first building boom in the late '90s spilled out into the Gulf in a relentless claim for anything with a sand beach as a likely spot in paradise. Electrical service of a sort was established, and two-story houses sprang up, replacing quaint island cottages. The internet brought a stream of visitors who quickly became both sought after and loathed in the fashion of island communities everywhere. In five short years, the island residents found themselves outnumbered by tourists. A sort of grudging acceptance took hold that masked the underlying tension of such disparate populations. But you didn't have to scratch far beneath the surface for a problem to erupt.

Oddly enough, it was Hurricane Charley that, although it first threatened to wipe Hogge off the map, actually transformed it completely. In its wake, speculators descended on the island grabbing up properties and lots. When Florida went bust along with the rest of the country in 2008, the boom halted. Properties again began to change hands, but this time in the form of short sales and foreclosures.

Hogge Island real estate eventually rose from the ashes and money once again flowed in construction, only now it was on an even grander scale. Fueled by Alan Hollows' club, his pockets well-lined after the storm, more rental houses went up, most three stories, not two—with elevators and private pools. Now, at high season and low, the island was swollen with families and toddlers and roaming bands of what seemed like 1950s beach-party-movie refugees. A collective sigh of relief went up each September when the island returned, Brigadoon-like, to its meager 40 or so residents, attendant bugs, fauna and quiet vegetable population.

Where some people saw disaster others found opportunity, Gordon thought. How they found it was something he wondered at the time, but he was too busy trying to resurrect his own place from the wreckage to pursue it. But with the Hogge Island Club's latest expansion plans, the question returned to him. Likely too late, he thought with a tinge of regret, as he navigated the rutted path leading out from the restaurant slowly, trying to avoid the deep pools of water that invariably formed at high tide.

On his right was one of the more recent additions to island blight, Van Cross's home, if home is what the sprawling structure with its dock lifts and turrets reaching to the sky could be called. Rumor was, Vanderbilt Cross was a washed up hotshot Navy pilot who lost his commission years ago owing to nerves or insubordination. In any event, for the past decade he worked for Protiex, a corporation with headquarters in Tampa, as a fish spotter. At some point there had been a wife, but she was gone before Cross ever got to Hogge.

Protiex touted itself as a green company and friend of the sea, but in reality, Gordon's researches revealed, they were almost single-handedly responsible for destroying the ecosystem of the Chesapeake Bay through the overfishing of menhadden. In the highly competitive spotter business, Van was damned good at what he did, which was to spend hours at a time over the Gulf trying to spot the enormous schools of menhadden, or pogie as the natives called them, so he could radio the scrambled coordinates to the fleet of purse seiners as to where exactly to deploy their 1500 foot nets. The pogies didn't have a chance, as Rudy Granderson belligerently pointed out to Van at every opportunity. The animosity between them was so well-known that Van was briefly a suspect in the arson fire that took Rudy's house, until it could be established that he actually wasn't on the island at the time.

Aside from his house, Cross was a man of fairly simple tastes: he liked people with money, power, and whom he could control. Since Gordon put little value on any of those things—he preferred the eclectic to the elite—they were natural antagonists.

As Gordon passed by Cross's compound he turned partially into the driveway, marveling, once again, at what one man's ego could produce. A mistake.

"Strange!" Van's voice rang out, imperious as ever, from the shade of a giant bismarckia tree. Possibly the most difficult resident on the island, Van was on a last name basis with those he held in contempt. He was always careful to pronounce Gordon's name correctly, S-T-R-A-N-G, once he learned its mid-15th century English origins. He also always managed to make it sound like an insult.

Gordon nudged the cart back out onto the road. "Morning, Cross," he said, touching his hat. Van looked more worked up than his usual state of righteous indignation, he thought.

"You're trespassing!"

"Just admiring your house, Van," Gordon said, disingenuously.

"Can't you keep decent hours at that roadhouse you're running, Strange?"

"You need a road for a roadhouse, Cross. We close at 11. You have an issue with that?" His tone was mild but menacing. He removed his hat and placed it on the seat beside him with deliberation.

"You've got the scum of four continents coming and going from that place at all hours. I've had three drunks run over my property in the past two weeks. You don't know what you're bringing in there. Drifters, thieves. Murderers, even. You should be shut down."

"You left out terrorists." With a surge of irritation, Gordon considered the man standing on the other side of the low wall. So far, he'd tolerated Cross's insufferable comments and had wasted a lot of time defending himself against a steady stream of complaints and reports of so-called violations. His temper, usually well under control, got the better of him. Van would look better, he thought, with a black eye. Maybe two. Without really thinking about it, Gordon started to climb down from the cart.

Cross lurched back toward the tree and whipped a shotgun out of the shadows. "You come on my property and I'll shoot you, Strange." He spit out the words. The gun shook slightly in his hands. He waved Gordon away. "Get out of here. I'm warning you."

Gordon was momentarily stunned. Even for Cross this was bizarre behavior. Then, he shrugged and heaved himself back on his cart. However satisfying it would be to wipe the yard with Van's ass, it wasn't worth it. "You're coming unglued, Cross," was all he said, driving away slowly. But he wondered as he bumped the cart along the worn path, about the look in Van's wild blue eyes. Despite Cross's angry bluster, Gordon knew fear when he saw it. Over what he couldn't imagine.

Gordon mulled it all over as he went down the road, maneuvering around the mud puddles—miniature lakes in the deep gouges worn into the sand. Van could be charming, as long as you agreed with him, he'd give him that. But disagree with him and he'd turn on you like a pit viper. Privately, Gordon chalked him up as one of the "not quite sane."

Although he would have cheerfully knocked Van out, if it came to it, he tried his best to remain intimidating from a distance. So far, so good. Van stayed out of his restaurant, contenting himself with snide remarks, and Gordon pretty much ignored the man altogether. But the gun and the threat could change all that.

Yes, if Cross really *has* lost it, Gordon reflected, he might need a course correction. On the heels of this thought, his cellphone rang.

CHAPTER 5

Doris Killgalen wheeled her cruiser bicycle with its practical fat tires onto the beach, her "turtle nesting patrol" sign hanging prominently from the wicker basket on the handlebars. She usually got up before Lattie, but today Lattie had beaten her to it, saying she wanted to do some fishing and then stop in at *Gordon's*. The sun was just poking through the cloud cover, coloring the eastern horizon with faint pink light. A freshening breeze from the overcast Gulf blew Doris's gray short cropped hair back from her face. Rain today, perhaps— just not, she prayed, one of those violent sudden storms that would churn up the sea and threaten the tentative nests on shore. But this was no time for ruminating on the weather. She had a mile and a half of beach to cover. She was eager to count the nests, shore them up with wire, check them for signs of predators.

The island was truly a paradise at this time of day. The beach was practically empty. Gazing toward the horizon you might have been alone in the world. About a quarter mile down, she passed two early risers, a mother and toddler. The little girl carried a pink bucket and the two stooped and picked their way along the shore, sifting through the occasional shell mound looking for this or that to complete their collection: a cat's paw, perhaps, or a large perfect scallop shell. A rumble of thunder over the water made the woman glance up and pull the little girl back from the edge of the lapping waves. They hurried up the path through the sea oats toward home and safety.

Doris hesitated but decided to push on. Pedaling down the beach on the firm wet sand she counted off the "streets" barely visible through the scrubby dunes with a practiced eye. First the fish streets—Mullet, Grouper, Mackerel, Flounder. Then on to First Fifth, Second Fifth. How odd, she thought, as she always did, that someone felt the need to name them, these sand paths meandering through Hogge. At Fifth Fifth, she spotted the first nest. It looked unmolested, despite the wedding canopy not fifteen feet away that Alan Hollows' club had set up illegally. The wedding party, it seemed, had chosen to stay by the—also illegal—temporary dance floor. Irritated, she made a mental note to lodge a complaint about it. Nothing would come of it, of course. The man was impossible.

Pressing on, Doris passed the last little house, an odd angular one bedroom cottage fronting the sea. Glancing east to check on the progress of the sun, she could see, even at this distance, the framework of the newest luxury house, towering four stories high. It had all the charm of a Miami office building and the sight of it never failed to depress her. Richard Sharpe, the contractor, was building it for some banking mogul from South Florida and rumor had it that it was ruining him along with the landscape it dominated.

A menacing rumble of thunder suddenly sounded, fairly close overhead, precluding any thought of going farther. Storms came without much warning on Hogge. As if in emphasis, a bolt of lightning struck the water not a hundred yards in front of her. Time to head for cover. Doris quickly wheeled her bike back up to the little house and ducked under the deck.

"Just in time" Doris thought, leaning the bike over and flopping down heavily next to it. The sand was damp and a few drops fell on her from the slatted deck above. Odd. It wasn't raining yet. She brushed at her shirt and her fingers came away sticky. Not really wanting to, she looked up and saw that it was raining after all. Blood drip drip dripping through the boards of the deck above.

CHAPTER 6

Five miles across the bay from Hogge Island in a neat two bedroom Old Florida house on the mainland of Palm Point, Sheriff Jackson Fitz woke later than planned. It was already eight o'clock on Friday morning but the sunlight that generally brought him to his feet at seven was sluggish today. Only a haze of light came through the gaudy yellow and lime green curtains his wife, Marly, had insisted on hanging in the bedroom. ("It'll cheer the place up, give it a little color," she'd said over his tentative objections). He looked out the window. A fairly good line of clouds was thick on the horizon. Probably an overcast day.

Good fishing weather, was his first happy thought. *Marly will be pissed*, was the immediate depressing second. He could hear her in the kitchen, banging dishes around. Give Marly the chance to sunbathe on the deck of his Grady White and she was happy as a clam. Fishing she had about as much use for as she had for his first wife's furniture.

As if he'd spoken his thoughts aloud, Marly appeared in the doorway, hands on hips, her face already set for a fight.

"Dammit, Jacko, your one day off and the weather sucks. You're not still planning taking that boat out, are you?" Storm clouds of another sort were brewing behind thick mascara.

"It'll be fine, honey," he said, forcing cheerfulness. "It'll burn off by noon, you'll see."

"That's bullshit and you know it. I'm not going out and getting trapped on that smelly sardine can all day in the fog."

For a woman with plenty of curves she could be all angles, Fitz thought glumly.

"I'm unpacking the cooler." It was her final statement.

Flitz had a fleeting vision of cold beer, potato salad, fried chicken wings, macaroni salad and a quiet day on the water. Now to be replaced by a trip to the mall or, worse, Naples. It was no use. This was not an argument he could win or, if he did win, would enjoy winning. When had things changed so much between them? Where was the bubbly upbeat blonde downing Yegermeister and beer boilermakers in the Rat Snake Saloon, who fingered his uniform and said "we could have fun together, you know?" Before he could pursue this depressing line of thought, his emergency phone rang. He answered it with guilty relief.

The woman on the other end was almost incoherent, words tumbling over themselves.

"Dead? Who is this and where are you calling from" Professionalism exerted itself as Fitz, phone to his ear, struggled into the uniform he'd ripped from the closet. He got a location and her name. Details poured out in a hysterical jumble. Blood everywhere—dead or likely dying. "Okay, Doris. Don't touch anything and please leave the area and get to a safe place." *Jesus. Hogge-- it'll take an hour to get there,* he thought, *and every person on the island will be all over the place like flies.*

Marly was signaling from the doorway impatiently. He waved her away.

"Go to *Gordon's*. Yeah, the restaurant. Stay there until the authorities come," he said into the phone. *Authorities! What a joke—he was it.* Emergency services, yes, that would be his next call. "GO TO *GORDON'S*," he commanded. "NOW." *Gordon Strange. The only man competent enough to keep control until he, Fitz, got there.*

Marly started in from the doorway, "Jacko, what the hell?"

"Not now," Fitz said, grabbing his vest and weapons. He pushed past her brusquely, dialing Gordon's cellphone number as he grabbed his official boat keys and headed out the door.

"Gordon." *Thank god the man had reception.* "Get over to the "angle" house, whatever the hell they call it—the last one on the beach. Someone's been hurt. Doris Killgalen— yeah, the turtle lady—put in the call. No. No details. Keep everyone out until I get there with the Medevac. I'm not asking you, I'm telling you," he shouted into the phone. "I DON'T GIVE A DAMN ABOUT YOUR LUNCH CROWD!" He hung up, vaguely aware of Marly bleating after him like an indignant sheep.

Backing out of the driveway, Fitz called emergency services. "HOGGE ISLAND," he enunciated clearly into the phone after they finally answered after four rings. Budget cuts effected by the new Lee County officials drunk on Tea Party politics had eliminated the local Medevac service. "Palm Point Sheriff's office. I need a Medevac chopper, STAT, on Hogge.

Someone's been..." he hesitated for a moment..."critically injured." *That much seemed certain.*

An unruffled voice asked him to hold. After three maddening minutes, it came back. "We've dispatched the chopper out of Tampa," the young voice breathed happily. "It should be there in an hour and twenty minutes."

"Wonderful!" Fitz snapped back, as he careened the car into the marina where the Sheriff's boat was moored. "Maybe it'll be in time to handle an autopsy!" He rang off, boarded the boat and put in another call, to Deputy Joe Harris, filling him in quickly on what details he had. Harris agreed to come out on the next water taxi and meet him on Hogge.

Maybe a trip to the mall wouldn't have been so bad, Fitz thought twenty minutes later, as the boat bounced full throttle through the chop toward that godforsaken spit of land called Hogge. On the other hand, he conceded, as the island appeared in the haze, it had spared him a trip to Naples.

CHAPTER 7

Gordon got back to his restaurant just before noon, fresh from the frenzied staging area that had overtaken the normally quiet end of the island abutting the State Preserve.

When he arrived at the house Fitz directed him to, he immediately found himself with an armful of hysterical housekeeper who had unfortunately gotten there before him. She'd discovered, as far as he could make out from the girl's machine gun bursts of Spanish interspersed with wails, that there was a man if not *muerte* then clearly dying, bleeding on the deck like a gutted sheep. Or at least that's what he thought she said. Gordon got her into his cart with some difficulty and told her to stay put until the *policia* got there, which statement sent her into a fresh round of wails.

He took a quick look around but saw no signs of anyone else around. Grabbing his cart key he headed for the stairs. He could just make out a slumped figure on the deck above, jammed up against gaily painted pickets. At that moment, Fitz arrived to take charge of the scene. The next hour was a blur of officialdom arriving by boat, chopper, golf cart and even on foot—it seemed the local National Guard chapter was holding a training session a mile down in the preserve and they arrived in full regalia, adding to the surreal atmosphere of violent disturbance amidst the swaying palms.

The victim turned out to be badly injured—clearly as a result of some sort of attack. But he was alive, if not conscious. The Medevac EMTs—the last to arrive—carried him to the chopper and he left the island in a tornadic swirl of sand amidst the roar of rotors. As the gurney went by Gordon recognized him, with considerable surprise, as a German tourist with whom he'd had a few brief words the night before at the restaurant. As unlikely a victim as you could imagine, if, in fact you could imagine the word "victim" and "Hogge" in the same sentence. It didn't make a bit of sense, but there was no point in hanging around the chaotic scene any longer than he had to. Fitz would fill him in later. Meanwhile, it was lunch hour and unless he missed his guess, *Gorden's* would be ground zero for the brush fire of gossip and rumor that had by now, he was certain, swept the island.

He wasn't wrong. The restaurant's cart park area was overflowing, vehicles stacked against the mangroves and jammed against the wooden gate three deep. Reduced to parking by the dumpsters around back, Gorden ducked in through the kitchen. Marvelita was in command but even so it was clear the staff—including a bevy of temps that she had apparently conjured up—was on overload. The savory smoke and patois of Spanish and English hit like a time machine, sending a little thrill of alarm up Gorden's spine. It passed in an instant, and the world righted itself. Hogge. This was Hogge Island. Not Iquitos. And he was the proprietor. Not a twenty-four year-old adventurer awaiting a visit from the *policia.*

"Gordon, *que paso?*" Marvelita was doing her best to sound casual, but her eyes were dark with anxiety. "The *vieja* with the bicycle is in there and so is everyone else. No more rolls, fish, meat for the hamburger," she was ticking the items on her fingers. "And tomorrow is Saturday, when all the boats will come…" She broke off suddenly. "Your jacket is dirty," she came closer and pulled the sleeve so he could see. "This is blood. *Dios mio*, what the *vieja* said, someone is dead?" Eyebrows arched, she looked the rest of the question at him rather than spoke it.

Gordon hastened to reassure her. They'd known each other a long time. "I wasn't involved," he said, pulling his sleeve loose with a slight shake, "and the gentleman's not dead. Beaten up. Badly." He recalled, a little sadly, the man who'd come into his restaurant the night before. Tall and trim, neatly clipped beard, intelligent eyes taking in the scene and Gordon himself with quick, birdlike movements. He'd been casually dressed in shorts like any other tourist, but Gordon noted at once the "European signature" of sandals worn with black socks and the small leather purse at his side. The man's "hello" pegged him as German and Gordon took some pleasure in the delighted surprise that lit up the man's face when he answered in his best Hochdeusche. Hermann, he'd said his name was and he clearly would have relished a longer talk, but it was a busy night and, with a sensitivity rare in tourists, he'd had the tact to see it.

Gordon had expected to see him again—but not battered to a pulp lying on a stretcher, eyes swollen shut and covered in blood. The attack baffled him, and the only one more perplexed than himself was Sheriff Fitz, who would be coming to speak to him, a harassed Fitz said, as soon as the circus at the end of the island was under control.

"Marvelita, can you manage out here alone for a bit more? Have to change my jacket." Gordon gave a nod in the direction his small office behind the kitchen. "And don't worry, Lita. I won't be mixed up in this." There would have been a time when he would have been, of course, and with more than just blood on his sleeve. But that time had long passed. Whatever this attack was it was a police matter—home invasion, likely. There'd been a rash of them on the mainland. And while that was shocking on bucolic Hogge Island, the times were bound to catch up even in a place like this. However tempting it was not his business. Thirty years and four continents in to comfortable middle age, he'd lost the appetite for roughhousing. Besides, the fifty or so extra pounds he'd picked up along the way were no longer conducive to strenuous physical activity.

He emerged in a fresh linen jacket and, in deference to the gravity of the occasion, a black raw silk Tommy Bahama shirt, size XXL. He swapped his dusty blue slacks for black ones but drew the line at shoes. The man left the island alive, after all. Marvelita was waiting for him outside the office with a thousand questions.

"Not now, Lita—I don't know much. Wait until Fitz gets here; he'll have the full story." He looked around the crowded restaurant. "Where's Doris? The one with the bicycle?" To Marvelita, people's names were irrelevant—only their props distinguished them.

"In there—Fletch is with her." Marvelita nodded in the direction of the main dining room, indicating Fletcher James, reprobate boat captain and Gordon's good friend. "Calming her." This last with a hint of sarcasm.

Gordon suppressed a smile—she might be rattled, but she hadn't lost her bite. No doubt this bit of "calming" was liquid in form, knowing Fletch.

"We are running out of everything," Marvelita insisted, returning to her chief concern.

"Make a list of what we need—I'll send Fletch by boat this afternoon." Business was business, after all, and by the sound of things in the next room, business was going to be booming for a while.

"Two boats, probably" she called at him as he crossed the kitchen. "And I told you those *viejas* would bring trouble!"

Gordon ceded the last word to her, as usual, and ducked through the low door leading to the main dining area, which was packed. Conversation ebbed and swirled as it always did, but with an edge. It was clear word of the attack had gotten around, trumping any of the normal discussions that would have been taking place about fishing and the latest island rumors. A number of people tried to hail him, but he waved them off and made for a back table where he spied Doris and Fletch. They were alone. Doris had a half a glass of whiskey in front of her. There was a fuller one in front of Fletch and a half empty bottle between the two, Gordon noted wryly. So much for the morning's industrious sobriety.

He lowered himself into a chair and joined them, signaling to Beni for another glass. He suddenly felt tired. "Fitz is on his way over. He told me she was the one who found the guy and made the call," he addressed Fletch. "An ugly scene."

Fletch nodded slightly and looked significantly in Doris's direction. "Been here with her about two hours. She looked like a mile of bad road when she got here. Still does. Nice shirt," he added as an afterthought.

Gordon ignored the jab and sized up the condition of the woman sitting next to him. At the moment, she looked considerably older than her seventy-five plus years, her normally pleasant, broad face, pinched and pale despite its tan, hazel eyes fixed on nothing in particular. The familiar island uniform of shorts and a t-shirt was marred by dark rust-like patches that stained one shoulder and the front of the shirt. Dried blood, no doubt. How had that happened? Unless she'd fallen on the man or tried to revive him, which was possible, or had attacked him herself which, frankly, wasn't. All in all she looked lousy. She was no youngster and shock was taking its toll.

"Doris," he reassured her, "They got the fellow off, he's—"

She burst in before he finished the sentence. "He's dead, isn't he? Who was he?" She didn't wait for an answer. "Blood. Dripping. I thought it was rain, I thought it was rain and then I saw—" her words were tumbling over themselves as she rubbed and rubbed her shoulder, Lady-Macbeth-like. "I went up on the deck and he was lying there, blood everywhere. I was just checking on the nests," her voice broke and her eyes filled up. She shook her head and stared in the distance at something they couldn't see.

"It was a renter, but he's alive, Doris. Hurt bad, but they got to him in time." Gordon reassured her again. "You're probably the reason he's alive. He wouldn't have made it if you hadn't turned up." That seemed to help. At least she looked at him. He hesitated but asked anyway. "How exactly is it that you found him anyhow? He would have been hard to spot from the beach."

Doris wiped her face and took a little sip from the glass, pulling herself together. "I was on the beach, for the nests—"

"You said you were checking on them," Gordon urged, nodding.

"I heard thunder and it looked like rain any minute. So I pulled up under the deck to ride it out. Then it started to rain. Or at least I thought it started to rain. Only it wasn't— and when I looked up..." She shivered and the kind hazel eyes welled up again, tears magnifying the remembered terror.

Although he himself was not terrified Gordon could well understand it. Blood and violence were personal in a way other crimes were not—a thing you felt in your throat, in your gut. They had no place on Hogge, and yet, here they were.

"Is Lattie here?" He scanned the room quickly but saw no sign of that stout figure.

"No, no—she went out early in the boat." She gripped his arm as this new terror took hold. "Oh God. You don't think...?"

"I'm sure she's fine. She was here early this morning, brought me some fish. She probably took the boat back out," he said with a confidence he didn't feel. Was anything probable at this point? Where was the woman? And where was Fitz?

As if on cue, Fitz came through the entrance. He spotted them in the back and made his way through the crowded room, the hectic buzz of conversation dying down in his wake.

"They think he's going to make it," he said to no one in particular. Then to Doris "I need to get a full statement." He hesitated, eying her. "You okay to get on the boat?" From his tone it was obvious he didn't much relish the ride and return trip to the mainland but had no choice.

"Use my office. Behind the kitchen," Gordon countered. The last thing the woman needed was a half hour boat ride to the Sheriff's office.

"That'll do fine," Fitz said, grateful, as he helped Doris out of the chair. She followed him a little unsteadily toward the kitchen, the two of them weaving through the tables as the now silent patrons eyed them like zoo exhibits instead of the familiar faces they were.

"Reality doesn't sit well in a place like this," Gordon remarked to Fletch and picked up the bottle. "Fortified yourself?"

Fletch gave him a lopsided smile, more of a grimace. He was a lanky man about halfway through his fifties, a once handsome face weathered by sun and booze framed by receding hair that was blonde or gray or brown, depending on how the light hit it. Some people didn't give him the time of day but Gordon knew him to be one of the best charter captains on the water. He'd put you onto fish when others couldn't find bait. And he could navigate the tricky waters around Hogge night or day, in weather other captains wouldn't be caught dead in. When he was sober. Even drunk his brain was better than most, as one look into his red-rimmed gimlet eyes would tell you. And his brain was working now, despite the half bottle of whiskey Gordon suspected Fletch was largely responsible for disposing of.

"What the hell went down out there?" Fletch demanded, as soon as Fitz and Doris were out of earshot.

"Tourist was attacked—beaten pretty badly," Gordon said, aware that at nearby tables patrons were straining to hear his every word. No matter—there were no secrets on Hogge, at least, not for long. "A German fellow who was in here last night."

"He have a fight with someone?"

"No. He was a nice, quiet man. Here alone," Gordon said, reflecting. "And now he's in a hospital with his head cracked open. I'd say it was a robbery gone bad, as ridiculous as that sounds." Even as he said it, he was trying to picture which one of the Hogge Island regulars might be cast in the role of robber gone berserk. It wasn't working.

Fletch looked incredulous as well. "Which house was he in?"

"That small cottage, down at the end. On the beach."

"That was Costello's house," Fletch put in.

Gordon swallowed some of his drink, thoughtfully. "Never had dealings with him, but I heard Costello was a shit heel. Wouldn't have minded if this had happened to him. But he's been gone for years."

"He was a piece of work," Fletch agreed. "Didn't mind hounding you to death to do work for him but try and get your money." He shook his head. "Told him if he wanted anything out of me, he could pay up front."

"And how'd that work out for you?" Gordon caught Beni's eye and made "something to eat" motions. The lunch crowd had moved on to the serious business of eating and the steady flow of plates from the kitchen made Gordon realize he was famished. Breakfast was six hours ago.

"Never heard from the bastard again." Fletch's grin was malicious. "Suited me just fine. He sold the place—or did the bank take it?"

"Don't know. Place changed hands a couple of times. Far as I know Hollows rents the place out now. For one of his cronies."

"So nothing's really changed," Fletch said cynically.

Beni arrived and set two plates of grouper fragrant with cilantro and lime and Marvelita's famous plaintains and salsa verde in front of the two men.

"*De Marvelita*," he said, handing Gordon a grease-stained sheet of paper. A list of supplies.

Gordon pushed it across the table to Fletch, who'd already tucked into his fish. "You sober enough to boat over to the mainland and bring me some supplies?" Gordon asked. "See if you can read this."

Fletch looked over the list, frowning. "Pretty much. What's she mean, two bricks of beef?" he asked through a mouthful of grouper.

"Briskets. Briskets of beef," Gordon said, taking out his billfold. "Put it all on account. Here's a hundred for gas." He slid the bill to Fletch, who folded it into the list and pocketed both.

"If I leave now I should be back by about six," Fletch said. He finished the last bite of fish and pushed back from the table. "Delicious." He wiped his mouth, looked toward the office, then back at Gordon. "You'll see that Doris gets home when the Sheriff's done with her?" He pronounced it "Shurff."

Gordon nodded. "Yeah. I'll fill you in on what I find out from Fitz when you get back." As if Fitz would have any more information than either of them at this point. On the mainland it wouldn't even be unusual. Just another violent crime in a sea of violent crimes. *We think we're immune, but we're not. Civilization is catching up,* he thought. It was the most rational explanation, even if it was a bit depressing. He became aware of silence once again falling over the restaurant and glanced over at the office, expecting to see Fitz and Doris. But everyone was looking in the opposite direction, at the entrance.

In the doorway stood Alan Hollows, owner of the Hogge Island Resort, making his first appearance in *Gordon's* since it opened. Apparently oblivious to the stir he'd created, he stood, hands on fleshy hips, scanning the room impatiently.

What brought him to the restaurant Gordon couldn't fathom, but he was fairly certain it wasn't for lunch.

CHAPTER 8

Gordon watched Hollows with interest as the man stood in the doorway, assessing the place. He seemed to be unaware of the stir he had created. It was clear from his expression that Hollows didn't think much of Gordon's style of restaurant. His eyes said as much as they took in the bare wooden tables, paper and plastic cutlery, resin chairs. The giant mosaic wall Gordon had spent two years creating seemed to offend him outright: a lifesized, barebreasted mermaid with curling raven hair (who bore a striking resemblance to a younger edition of Marvelita), arms outstretched amidst a school of fish swimming in a magnificent sea constructed of every shade of blue that the eye could conjur.

By contrast, the Hogge Island Bistro featured white walls, linen tablecloths, polished silverware, an expensive wine list and an even more expensive menu. Unfortunately, the fish was often three days old, the wine poorly housed, and the service lackadaisical, even belligerent on occasion. On any given day or night, the Bistro boasted three, perhaps four tables of customers. It rarely had repeat ones. Rumor had it the longest any particular chef lasted at the Bistro was about three months.

Well, whatever Hollows was doing here it certainly wasn't to size up the place, Gordon decided. He'd had almost ten years to do that and had never set foot in the place. He sat back in his chair and motioned to Beni for another drink. Hollows had spotted him and was walking to his table purposefully.

"Strange." Hollows grunted the greeting and pulled out a chair without being asked to sit down. "They told me I'd find Fitz at your place. Is he here?"

Gordon nodded, sipping.

"You could offer me a drink," Hollows spoke casually, but his mint green polo shirt had damp patches under both arms, and the scar that ran from his ear to his collarbone was unusually prominent. A man under pressure.

"I could do that," Gordon said, making no move to do so. "Fitz is in the back room taking a statement. He'll be out soon. Why don't you find yourself a table?" He looked around. "Or a seat at the bar?"

Hollows flushed but didn't get up. Instead, catching the eye of one of the waiters, he signaled her over. She nodded at him but disappeared into the kitchen.

"Why don't you wait for Fitz at his boat—it's tied up outside." Gordon suggested. There had been enough tension for one day, and now he was fighting the urge to haul the insolent bastard out the door by the collar of his Izod shirt.

Just about the time he'd made up his mind to do so, Fitz came out of the kitchen with Doris. They stopped by an elderly couple—the Marsteins—and after some brief words, Doris left with them. Fitz returned to Gordon's table.

"Do something with the air conditioning in there," Fitz said, wiping his face with a napkin. "Must be 90 degrees. Those people—Marstein, they said—are going to see her home," he addressed himself to Gordon. He nodded to Hollows but didn't seem surprised to see him.

"Well," Fitz said to Hollows, taking out his phone. "I got your calls. Two of 'em. Urgent, you said. What about it?"

Hollows threw Gordon a sour look. "Don't you have something to do?"

"No," Gordon said ungraciously. "If you want privacy, find your own. You invited yourself to this party. *And* to this table."

Hollows glared at him.

"Awright," said Fitz. He took out a small notepad, thumbed through a few pages. "I need to talk to this housekeeper, Carmen. She one of yours?" He looked up at Hollows, who nodded yes.

"That's not what I called you about." Hollows glanced at Gordon, weighing whether to speak, deciding. "It's personal," he finally said.

"Don't have time for personal right now. I'm trying to figure out who beat the crap out of this tourist." Fitz glanced at the notepad, "Hermann Gottschalk. German. Know anything about him?" He waited.

Hollows got up. "I probably have the information in my office—the Resort rented the house to him. I'll round up Carmen and you can speak to her, too. I'm not going to say anything with him sitting there," he pointed to Gordon.

Fitz looked exasperated. "Suit yourself," he said snapping the notepad shut. "Wait in your office. I'll be along in a bit. Have to finish up here—with him," he indicated Gordon.

"Don't be too long about it," Hollows rose, scraping back his chair as noisily as possible. "I said it was urgent. It is." He strode toward the entrance. An important man in a hurry.

Fitz shook his head, watched the man leave. "A regular snake charmer, he is. Where does he get the attitude? Guess it's the money."

"More like a Mister Kurtz complex," Gordon said, more to himself than to Fitz.

"Mister Kurtz?" Fitz was puzzled.

"*Heart of Darkness*—a book. A lot like this place, actually," Gordon said reflectively. "It's not so much the money. It's the power." He sat pondering Alan Hollows' unexpected visit, wondering what was so urgent that the man would come to a place he had publicly announced, on several occasions, he would never set foot in. Of course, Hollows had sent employees over to secretly (or so he thought) check the place out numerous times. Gordon made it pretty clear from the start—the man had suggested not so much a partnership as collusion when he first got to Hogge—what he thought of Hollows, his restaurant, his whole operation. He was a martinet running a fiefdom. In return he got as much loyalty as one would expect. The place was a revolving door of employees, the best of whom found their way to *Gordon's*.

Fitz, who was pursuing his own train of thought, now turned his attention back to Gordon. The notepad came out again, open to a fresh page. "I have a few questions for you," he said. "First, you told me you recognized this tourist from your restaurant last night, spoke to him. Right?"

"That's correct. Just 'hello,' 'good evening,' that sort of thing."

"You said you spoke German to him. I didn't know you spoke German."

"Some," Gordon said. "Also a little French, Italian, Spanish, and Russian."

Fitz looked suitably impressed. "So did you know him before?"

"No. Met him for the first time last night. Is this leading somewhere?" Gordon asked, aware that the line of questioning had taken a formal tone.

"When I called you this morning and told you to go over to that house, where were you? Here?"

"No. I was in my cart on the other side of the island, mixing it up with Van Cross." Gordon said testily, briefly explained his run-in with that gentleman, leaving out the part about the gun. "Am I suspected of something?" He tried to keep the annoyance that flared up out of his tone. Succeeded partially.

"Look, I'm gonna be asked, so I gotta ask," Fitz said doggedly. "You're, what are you? Six foot five? Six? At your weight, I'll bet you'd have a punch like a steam hammer. I'm not the only one that might occur to. Strange—" now there was an impatient edge to his voice—"If I thought you had anything to do with this I wouldn't have called on you in the first place. But before we get on with this I had to get the whole picture clear."

"Get on with this?" Gordon pounced on the phrase and looked hard at Fitz, aware that the Sheriff was pursuing something other than establishing his whereabouts. "Get on with what? What gives?"

"Just this," the Sheriff shifted in his chair, stared at his notepad. "Look, I don't understand you," his gesture took in everything from Gordon to Marvelita to the restaurant itself. "Hell, I'm not even sure I like you." He stopped. "But I trust you. And there's damned few out here I trust."

"Why me in particular?" Gordon asked, suspicious.

Fitz grimaced. "Mostly because you don't give a damn what anyone thinks, you have no axe to grind. A man like you can't hide, so you don't try to. Besides, people, well, not so much like you, but they come to you," he finished. "And that's something to consider in a place like this."

"Thanks for that lukewarm endorsement," Gordon said sardonically, "but I still don't understand what we're talking about. Why am I getting your vote of confidence just now?"

"Because I'm deputizing you, that's why." Fitz grinned faintly.

Gordon met this announcement with stunned silence. The man was joking, had to be. He looked up.

Fitz seemed to read his mind. "No joke. I mean it. And you can't refuse." He was no longer smiling.

CHAPTER 9

"You can't be serious," Gordon finally said, after the prolonged silence with which he'd met Fitz's statement.

"Serious as a heart attack," Fitz said wearily. "Look, I can't keep running back and forth to Hogge in a boat. I can leave Deputy Harris out here for a day or two; three, tops. It costs money to house people and we don't have it. I need someone reliable out here and you're the best suited." He sucked in his lower lip and looked up at the ceiling. "You can't refuse either. Law says so. I have the authority to deputize whoever I want in an emergency if they can help with the investigation."

"What law?" Gordon demanded. "And what makes me especially qualified?" He prepared himself for an argument. Thankfully the lunch crowd had thinned out. The two men had the place largely to themselves.

"I'll send you the statute when I get back to the office. Be reasonable, Strange. You see how it is. You're the only one for the job. Besides, it's only temporary. Once we get this thing sorted out you can resign. I could use a Coke," Fitz sighed.

Gordon waved for service, considered what Fitz said. The statute part was undoubtedly true. True, also, that he seemed to inherit most of the island's problems eventually. His conversation with Lattie in the morning came to mind. And where was she, by the way? Beni arrived with a Coke and placed it in front of Fitz, picked up Gordon's empty glass, raised his eyebrows, questioning.

Gordon nodded assent to a refill. Tried another tack. "You really don't know a damned thing about me, Fitz, any more than I do about you. Not even your first name."

"Jackson," Fitz offered. "I know enough. Checked you out. All the usual—no record, no outstanding warrants."

"Not in this country," Gordon conceded.

That got Fitz's attention. "Anything serious?"

"A few dust ups here and there," Gordon said vaguely. "Everyone's still around to curse about it."

"That's what I'd have figured," Fitz said, unexpectedly. "Doesn't change my mind about this here." He sat thinking for a moment. "Why no shoes? Just curious."

"They give me blisters," Gordon said curtly.

Fitz let the comment pass. "Well, shoes or no shoes, you're still the man for the job."

They seemed to have come to an impasse. Gordon shrugged, resigned. Fitz was dead set on his plan. There was no point in arguing. The sooner they got the whole debacle straightened out, the sooner he'd be well out of it. "Okay. You win. So what next? What d'you expect me to do?"

"I'll get to that but first, let me ask you…" Fitz hesitated. "Do you own a gun?"

Gordon just stared at him.

"Let me rephrase that." Fitz closed his eyes briefly, held up a hand. "Do you have *access* to a gun?"

"This is Florida. Everyone has access to a gun. Do you expect me to carry a gun around? What's next? Going to pin a silver star on me and suggest I ride around on horseback?" "Blazing Saddles," came to mind, only instead of a black man he'd be the barefoot deputy.

Fitz ignored the sarcasm and continued. "Look, this is an island, a handful of people in close quarters. You all know each other. Or think you do." He reached for his glass, swirled the cubes around. "Now, thing like this happens, people start looking at each other funny." He paused. "I've seen it before. Until the picture's clear, people get jumpy. You've got plenty of characters out here. Just saw one of them," he jerked a thumb at the door, referring to Hollows. "Have to be ready for anything and I don't have to remind you how long it takes to get the law out here."

He continued after a pause. "I need eyes here until we figure this out. I realize that puts you in the middle of things but my guess is," he eyed Gordon speculatively, "you're used to that."

Unfortunately, he was right. For the second time that day Gordon reluctantly accepted the mantle he seemed unable to avoid. Unable or unwilling, a cynical voice in his head asked. He shook off the thought and nodded, resigned. "Okay. So fill me in." *Marvelita—she was going to have a field day*, he thought.

The Sheriff grunted, satisfied, and looked at his pad, reading from his notes. "This is what I've got so far. At 8:05 this morning an emergency call from Doris Killgalen reporting a man—she thought he was dead—on Hogge Island, last house on the beach before State land." He looked up at Gordon. "When I interviewed her just now she said there were no other carts, least far as she could see, and she didn't see or hear anyone. Walked up onto the deck but didn't go in the house. Man turned out to be Hermann Gottschalk, German tourist, early 70s roughly, lying on the deck, attacked by person or persons unknown."

Gordon nodded, recalling the details of the scene.

"The house had been entered but wallet intact, money, passport etc., all there," Fitz continued. "Search of house and grounds yielded—nada. Until he comes to, were not going to know much more." He pulled out a pen. "You said he was in here for dinner? What time?" Pen poised, he waited.

"That's right. It was late. He was the last customer. About 9 or so." Gordon said. "Quiet guy, didn't speak to anyone except me, had his dinner, left. Nothing remarkable."

"Has he been to Hogge before?"

"Not since I've been here. I think I would have remembered him, since he was German. But a lot of people come and go—"

"Yes." Fitz tapped the pad. "You've got, what? Fifty or so residents here in August? Who else?"

"Tourists like him—give or take sixty a week. Then there are the people who work in a couple of places, like Hollow's crew. Contractors and their people. There are two builders on the island right now—Delmar Lampkins and Richard Sharpe. I've known Del a long time. He's a good man."

Fitz considered the omission. "What about Sharpe?"

"Don't have much to do with him. I get the impression there's something off there. Just an impression." Gordon didn't offer any more.

"What about the altercation you had this morning with," Fitz consulted his notes, "Cross. Vanderbilt Cross."

"It was odd," Gordon said slowly. "He's always a cantankerous son of a bitch, but this morning he seemed more worked up than usual." Gordon paused. Normally, he wouldn't have reported the incident but in light of recent events it seemed worth mentioning. "I got off the cart to speak to him and he pulled a gun on me. He was beyond agitated, yelling for me to get off his property." He sloshed his drink around, looked at it. "Unusual, even for him. Just after that happened, I got your call."

Fitz looked up at him. "I haven't spent much time on Hogge but it doesn't strike me as the sort of place you'd encounter a guy waving you off his property with a gun. But you don't seem awfully surprised. Why?"

"Cross has been a pain in the ass since he got here. He's just getting worse." Gordon tried to explain. "He's an angry guy—over what I don't exactly know—with a short fuse that seems to be getting shorter. He has a very high opinion of himself. If you agree with him, he's charming. Disagree, and he bites."

Fitz made a note and continued. "Fletcher James. He's a friend of yours?"

"Fletch is a sometime drunk, but he was sober this morning. And fishing. Brought three tripletail in just after sunrise. Can't be in two places at once. He's running an errand for me in town. Be back here about six, he said, if you want to speak to him."

Fitz grunted but made no other comment. "There's a guy living out at Okum's End, Doris told me. Jervis Potts. What do you know about him?"

"Potts?" Gordon was surprised. Jervis Potts was, among a community of recluses, the chief recluse. A remittance man, it was said, living check to check, doing odd jobs and in his spare time searching Okum's End for sunken ships—not a complete nut, but close. He said as much to Fitz. "Other than that, I have no contact, or almost none, with him," he finished up. "I heard he does a few odd jobs for Hollows now and then. You might ask him about Potts." He watched Fitz write. "I should tell you—fellow's not all there, at least not all the time. That's the local take on it, anyhow."

Fitz grunted, paging through his notes. He finally pocketed his notepad and looked at Gordon. "This is a mighty odd place for a thing like this to happen," he said slowly. "Doesn't figure. Man beaten half to death...I mean, you have your coots and cranks, but...." his voice trailed off.

"There was that business with the Granderson's," Gordon said reflectively.

"Arson. That's way different. Could have been payback but even so—no one broke in and whacked them." Fitz drained his soda. "Never been violence here, not like this. Until now."

"Until now," Gordon agreed. *And that was the inescapable thing.*

"Guess I better go hunt up Hollows and find out what's eating him. Speak to that maid, too. How long had she been there before you showed up?"

"No idea," Gordon said, "but she came from the house, not the deck. I think she saw Hermann lying out there bloody and panicked. I didn't see a cart. You might ask him about that, how she got there. Are you planning on returning to town tonight?"

"Late, probably."

"Dinner starts at 6," Gordon said, "you're welcome to some. Besides," he sat back in his chair and looked at Fitz, "I'm curious. I want to know what brought Alan Hollows into this restaurant this afternoon. I'd say he wouldn't come in here unless his life depended on it."

CHAPTER 10

After Fitz left, Gordon sat at the table nursing his empty glass, thinking. It was just after two-thirty in the afternoon but it seemed later.

Marvelita appeared from the kitchen and made her way over to him slowly with a plate of food.

"Already eaten," he said, waving her off.

"I know. This is for me." She pulled out a chair and sat, staring at the plate in front of her. "So tell me what has happened," she said finally, waiting.

Gordon gave her a brief, precise accounting of events, starting with his encounter with Cross and ending with Fitz's uncompromising demand. There were no secrets between them. "I don't like it, but he gave me no choice," he finished, referring to his sudden affiliation with the police force.

Marvelita frowned, but her comment was unusually subdued. "It will be a problem, yes. But don't make it a bigger one. There are too many locos on this island." She sighed and picked up her fork. "I knew when the *vieja* came this morning trouble would start. I felt it. " She put a hand to the front of her chest. She concentrated on her food for a few minutes, then put down the fork. "So 'Senor Loco' is upset," she said, referring to Cross. She paused and gave him a catlike look. "He was here last night."

"I didn't see him," Gordon said, surprised. "Believe me, I would have noticed. Where did you see him? At the bar?" Cross was not an enthusiast of the restaurant. The pile of complaints he'd filed against it and Gordon personally with every licensing agency from Ft. Myers to Tallahassee took up its own drawer in Gordon's office. Gordon waited for an explanation, intrigued.

"He came in the back way, through the kitchen. He said he was going to have dinner, but I know he was just there to snoop," she said with contempt. "He looked around the dining room and kitchen. Trying to find something to make trouble about. Then he left. When you were busy out there, with the fight." she waved toward the restaurant's outdoor bar.

The fight. Gordon stared down at the table. He'd completely forgotten about that in the whirlwind events of the morning. Hadn't even mentioned it to Fitz, not that it had any bearing on all of this. Just a garden variety argument that escalated into a blowout between a couple of well-oiled patrons. It had threatened to get out of hand, but he'd taken care of it.

Two parties of boaters were involved. The most belligerent one, a florid, leathery-faced fellow with a shock of wavy, shoulder-length dark hair flecked with grey looked familiar, although Gordon didn't have the time to reflect on that as the guy looked like a bad science experiment. Wild unfocused eyes, flushed from his thick neck to his temples, he was doing his best to take the bar apart. His friend—a tattooed, stringy youth of about 25 or so looking out of his depth—was trying to calm him down without effect. With sudden speed, the drunk lunged at the guy he was arguing with and flung his drink in the man's face. Gordon wasted no time on conversation. He came up behind the drunk and, with a half a foot advantage, put him in a one-armed headlock and applied pressure. The guy staggered to his knees, almost passed out. His friend caught him and took advantage of the break in hostilities to haul him off, coughing, toward the dock.

The patron who was the drunk's target wiped his face with a napkin and flung the linen down on the bar. He, too, looked vaguely familiar, in his fifties maybe, shorter than Gordon by a head, stocky but muscular. He ran a hand—part of a hand, actually--over his close-cropped hair, fashionably gelled to hide the thinning and fixed Gordon with a belligerent stare. "Thanks but no thanks," he said unpleasantly. "I could've wiped the floor with that son of a bitch. Still might." He peered over Gordon's shoulder toward the dock, an ugly glint in his close-set eyes.

"You can do whatever you want with him on your own ground," Gordon said, staring down at him, unsmiling, "but not here. And not," he jerked a thumb at the dock behind him, "out there. I don't like trouble in my restaurant. I don't care whether you found it here or brought it with you. Time to go." He closed his hand around the man's arm, urging him toward the parking area, noting that the bicep under his grip felt like iron. With the advantage of height and at least sixty pounds, Gordon was certain he could take him, but frankly hoped he wouldn't have to. The guy was fit enough to cause a scene and ruin an otherwise pleasant evening.

The man shook Gordon's hand off abruptly, then changed his tune. "Look, I'm not out to cause trouble," he protested, looking furtively over Gordon's shoulder. "I'm meeting someone here. I can't help it if some drunk didn't like my face." His tried to sound friendly. "I'll just go inside and wait for my friend. Order dinner."

"Nope." Gordon shook his head. He had an ironclad rule: if trouble started, both parties got ejected. "House rules. You're involved in an altercation, you go. I don't care who started what. I don't need that guy coming back to look for you or find out that you're not as innocent as you seem." His tone made it clear he didn't believe this last statement, but the guy couldn't object without damning himself. "Drinks are on me," Gordon said in dismissal, reaching over and picking up the tab on the bar.

The tough's face had darkened and for a minute it looked like he was going to become a nuisance. Then he muttered something that sounded suspiciously like "shithouse," shouldered belligerently past Gordon and stalked toward the dock.

The whole episode took less than ten minutes. Another owner might have called in the law, but cops resented being dragged out to Hogge for skirmishes like these and besides, it was nothing Gordon couldn't handle. Remembering it now, however, he wondered what had led to the fracas and who the parties were.

He looked up at Marvelita. "I'd forgotten about the fight. Last night seems like three years ago." That, he thought, would explain Cross's outsized irritation and roadhouse comments of the morning. "Van would come here the one night something happens," he said, more to himself.

Marvelita nodded in agreement. "Naturally. He has a good nose for trouble, that one." She went back to her lunch, ate a few bites, then said, casually. "He saw the fight. He did not look happy. Then he left in a big hurry."

"Probably in a rush to get home and send in another complaint. Wonder what it'll be this time," Gordon said, shaking his head. Van Cross was not the only busybody on the island, he was just the most industrious one, and the most pernicious. Once he got a bug up his ass on some issue, it became a campaign. Letters and emails rained down on local and state officials in such volume that Gordon often wondered how the man managed to find time to work. Gordon seemed to be his primary target. The number of ordinances and statutes Cross could pull out of his armpit was endless. All had to be addressed, followed up on, responded to. And all, so far anyhow, amounted to nothing more than a colossal waste of time and—given the number of local and state officials chasing his complaints down—taxpayer money. Gordon was seriously entertaining bringing an island-wide class action against him for being a public nuisance. Either that or take up a collection to help him move to Oklahoma.

So last night's altercation would fuel the next round of paperwork, likely. Gordon sighed and figured he might as well get his facts straight to answer whatever preposterous charge he'd have to defend himself against this time. "Do you remember what time this was?"

Marvelita frowned in concentration. "I don't remember the time. But the restaurant was full. The last one who came in—"

"The German," Gordon put in.

"Yes, he had just ordered. The rest were already eating."

Marvelita continued with her lunch, letting her information sink in. After a bit she looked at him appraisingly and switched gears to more important matters. "The maid you saw at that house this morning, Carmen? I know who she is. She's *barco,* that one--unreliable. She will be afraid to say anything. But she will talk to me."

It was not a boast, merely a statement of fact. Speaking the lingua franca opened doors and erased barriers as if by magic. Gordon witnessed it himself many times in his travels over the globe. It was one of the reasons he kept himself open to new languages, new customs. Egalitarian in nature, he did alright on most levels of the pecking order—and there was a growing one on Hogge, despite what its residents might like to think. But among the workers who toiled to keep the machinery of life going, Marvelita seemed to have a sixth sense for making allies and drawing out confidences. There was little she would not know by the end of the day.

Gordon knew her too well to doubt her confidence. He nodded in agreement. "See what you can find out, then. I don't know how she got to that house. There was no cart. Fitz will ask her, but you're right, she'll probably lie just to be safe. He should be back here around six. I'll know more then." He changed the subject to more practical matters. "What are you doing about dinner tonight? Fletcher won't be back with supplies in time for that."

Marvelita waved off the supplies. "That is not a problem. Tonight is Friday—Paella night. I have everything for that. Bread, too." She finished her late lunch and got up, plate in hand. "I have to start now. What will you do?"

"Go home." Gordon said, getting up from the chair wearily. "Clear my head, take a shower. I'll be back around 5:30. Call me if Fitz gets here before that."

"Maybe no more whiskey," Marvelita called after him as he opened the front door and plunged into a cauldron of cloying heat, humidity and another not-too-distant rumble of thunder.

CHAPTER 11

Gordon drove the golf cart home as fast as the pitted, dusty path would allow without putting out a kidney. The heat had set up again preventing even a light breeze through the overgrown Brazilian pepper hanging over the road like a shroud. By the time he got home his shirt clung to him under his jacket like a second skin which did nothing to improve his mood. He wasn't generally given to a foul temper but he was in one now and—put out and put upon—entitled to it. A dull throbbing behind his left eye heralded the onset of a full-blown headache probably brought on by equal parts whiskey and aggravation. He planned to strip down, plunge himself into a cold shower, eat about four Advil, and sleep. Thinking could come later.

He parked on the little ramp leading to the modest two-story cottage he shared with Marvelita and plugged the cart into the charger. The house was nestled amidst tall palms and lush tropical plantings that made the Tiki-like lower deck inviting and cool. Constructed around the foundation of the house, the deck was open to all sides, its interior spaces hung with a hodgepodge of coconuts, palm fronds, shells and artifacts from Borneo and the Amazon. Low-slung deck chairs, plump with cushions, graced a large stone table. Refuge. Almost immediately his sense of peace—so violently shattered—returned. A few hours' sleep, he thought wearily, trudging up two flights of stairs to the main living quarters, would feel damn good.

Upstairs he passed through the airy kitchen, swiped a handful of Advil from a bottle on the granite counter. A glance at the ridiculously ornate little ormolu clock on the counter (the only possession he retained from his long dead mother) told him he had about an hour and a half before he had to go back to the restaurant. He set the cellphone alarm for 5:15p.m., tossed it on the bed and headed straight for the shower, peeling clothes into a heap on the floor.

The shower was oversized, comfortable enough for him to stretch out in. It took him almost a year to create the mosaic that blossomed like a many-colored sun from the farthest corner and spilled its pattern out over the transom onto the bathroom floor. He stepped inside and turned the faucet on "cold" full blast, relishing the gush of cool water that soaked his long hair and soothed his aching head. He opened his mouth to take a few gulps. When he'd had enough he shut the water, wrapped himself in an enormous white Turkish towel, padded into the bedroom and sank down on the luxurious bed. He'd never been so comfortable, Gordon thought drowsily, as he drifted almost at once into a delicious sleep.

He woke up dreaming of Angel Falls. Jimmy Angel, the pilot, looking for El Dorado and finding instead the great waterfall that fell from the sky. He could hear the roar of the cascade as it plunged thousands of feet from the mountain cliff, disappearing into mist in the river below. It took him a moment to realize it was his cellphone that had awakened him, not the magnificent cacophony of Angel Falls. And not his alarm, either. He'd only been asleep for twenty minutes, he realized bitterly, resisting the impulse to toss the phone across the room instead of answering it. On balance, he reflected later, he should have followed his first instinct.

"Gordon!" It was Fitz, sounding impatient. "I called the restaurant. Marvelita said you went home to rest." He made it sound like a dereliction of duty.

Gordon raised himself onto an elbow and spoke into the phone, groggy. "I was. Resting, actually. My alarm was set for 5:15. It's," he looked at the phone, "just after four." He tried not to sound aggrieved. Failed. "I had a headache," he added. "What couldn't wait until later?"

"Chopper is coming for me any minute. Hospital called and the tourist—"

"Hermann," Gordon put in, turning over heavily, sitting up.

"Yeah, him. He's come to, apparently, talking. I left Deputy Harris in charge of the crime scene. So that leaves you."

"Leaves me for what?"

"I don't want that woman, Doris, to be alone."

"She's not alone. She lives with a partner, Lattie. Lattie was out earlier but she should be home by now."

"I don't want either of them alone," Fitz cut in. "Look, I can't go into it now." He was shouting to make himself heard over the roar of the chopper landing. "If you have to, go get them and take them to the restaurant, around people."

"Why? What did you find out? What did Hollows have to say?" Gordon struggled to get dressed, juggling the one phone with one hand so he could talk. His questions went unanswered.

"Can't go into that now. I'll get with you later. Go get those women." The phone went dead.

CHAPTER 12

About a half mile northwest of Hogge lay Okum's End, a small spit of land home to an indeterminate number of feral pigs, numerous osprey, one eagle's nest and its sole human resident, Jervis Potts. No one on Hogge recalled when Potts arrived on the island or where he came from. Like the mangroves and melaleuca that ringed the dun-colored stretch of sand and shell, his stringy, gray-bearded figure seemed part of the landscape for as long as anyone could remember. The small, dilapidated shack he called home had once been an icehouse, the last vestige of a once thriving mullet fishing industry that vanished in a tangle of legal battles and the onset of refrigeration. Mullet and the men who hunted them were still in evidence around Hogge, particularly in December, when the roe that was still prized by Asian diners could be harvested. But Potts was not a fisherman, at least by trade.

True, he lived off the land and water but, it was rumored, his lifeline was the occasional check from far-off relations who were more than happy to throw a few dollars his way in exchange for the relief of not having to deal with him. That and a few jobs here and there—usually those nobody else would take on. Potts was a man more comfortable in shadows than sunlight. When he was spotted, it was usually at dusk or dawn, a solitary figure in a small rust-colored skiff—his only real possession—making his way across Okum Pass to or from Hogge.

On Friday evening, while dinner was in full swing at Gordon's, if anyone had gazed at the darkening sky toward Okum's End, they would have seen Potts in his little skiff bumping across the Pass, negotiating its deceptively strong current. But as it was, the curtain of evening had already come down on sunset. And so, while diners got down to the serious business of eating at *Gordon's*, and tourists filed back from the beach on foot or in golf carts full of evening plans, Jervis Potts made his way to Hogge, virtually unnoticed.

His ancient skiff rode low in the water under a heavy load as Potts silently drew up to shore, out on the unpopulated State land and the empty silver ribbon of beach that stretched south for four miles to Oyster Pass, beyond which lay the glittering condos of Captiva. Empty, that is, except for the crust of shells at high and low water marks the tourists and charter boats out of the mainland beat a path to daily.

Years of boat and foot traffic had taken their toll on Hogge's rich mollusk population. The more ordinary species of periwinkle and scallops were plentiful but uncommon varieties—the colorful lion's paw, giant conchs—were hard to find, intact or otherwise. The prized junonia had become a rumor more than a decade ago. Still, hopeful shellers made the hour trek by foot out to the State beach to mingle, with some chagrin, with equally hopeful tourists who paid $27 a pop to be carted out from Captiva for two hours of perspired shelling in the heat of a blistering sun.

That they continued to do so was largely owing to the efforts of Potts who, in one of the odder of his odd jobs, was secretly paid by interested parties to seed the beach. Twice a week in low season and more often in the high, he journeyed, shrouded in darkness, to Hogge's southern shores with sacks of shells culled—some legally, some not—from Okum's End and sprinkled them, a grizzled fairy godmother, among the more pedestrian leavings of the tide.

Potts was not troubled by the need for secrecy since, according to his peculiar ethic, shady arrangements that were not strictly illegal and kept the wheels of commerce moving—especially his own—were necessary, desirable even. He had a similar arrangement with a few fishing charter captains out of Palm Point during redfish season, when he could be found (but never was) surreptitiously "chumming" waters along banks of Hogge Island Bay just in advance of a charter to draw the fish out from under the mangroves. The arrangement served everyone—except possibly the redfish—well, from the ego of the successful fisherman to the reputation of the captain. The Florida Wildlife commission might not agree but they belonged to a world Jervis Potts had abandoned long ago and took care to avoid at all costs.

So on this particular night, as Jervis was reaching the end of his long trek down the beach, he found himself on the horns of a dilemma when he stumbled on a sodden figure face down on the shore. There was enough moonlight, despite the drifting cloud cover, to see that it was clearly a man, and he didn't appear to be breathing. He crouched down and heaved the man over, satisfied himself that he was, in fact dead—drowned, by the look of it. He had a familiar look, the way all tourists did, but Jervis didn't know him. Which was good, because what he didn't know couldn't hurt him.

He briefly considered getting hold of the police. But the man would likely be reported missing by someone and was dead anyhow. People did stupid things all the time on the island—got drunk, fell off piers, came to grief on boats. It was no business of his. There was, he reasoned, no call for him to involve himself with the authorities and be forced to explain what he was doing on this beach at night in the first place. It wouldn't help the man, and could only get him, Jervis Potts, into trouble. It would be best to forget he'd tripped over the body in the first place and just go on his way.

On the other hand, the man might have some money on him—he certainly wouldn't need that anymore. Jervis carefully checked the man's pockets for a wallet, but there was nothing—just a sodden book of matches, which he put back. A watch on the man's right arm glinted gold in a sudden shaft of moonlight. It looked expensive. It was likely waterlogged and would become more so by morning and besides, it was just another thing the dead man would no longer need. It might bring a fair price at pawn at some point in the future. In fact, it could easily have slipped off anyway and washed up on the beach. The sea was always bringing him one sort of treasure or another—sunglasses, shiny new lures that had broken free of whatever tangle they'd been snagged on, loose change. Once he found a twenty-dollar bill drying in the sun.

The watch, even the man himself in a way, came under Jervis's heading of beach treasure, and with that thought he slipped the prize off the dead man's wrist and pocketed it. Taking care to retrace his steps to the water quietly lapping at the edge of the shore, he made his way back to the skiff and pushed off, heading toward the murky pinprick of Okum's End. He gave no more thought to the curious jetsam on the beach. His night's work was done.

CHAPTER 13

By Friday night, the attack had ceased to be the main focus of the island's population, largely overshadowed by Paella Night, the one Friday a month phenomenon that Gordon introduced several years back. Residents and visitors alike flocked to the restaurant by cart, boat, foot—even the occasional small plane that put in on Hogge's private airstrip. The idea may have been Gordon's but the credit, he always pointed out, went to Marvelita—who had yet to encounter a dish she couldn't improve on. She supervised the cooking outdoors. Two enormous paelleras, each six feet in diameter, simmered on makeshift firepits and the aroma alone was better advertising than Gordon could ever hope to pay for. One held Paella Valenciana, featuring chicken and rabbit in the tradition of the Spanish coast. The other, a nod to Hogge's Gulf water bounty, was a seafood version, brimming with clams, mussels, shrimp.

The sun was going down by the time Gordon maneuvered his cart down the rutted path from Doris and Lattie's house to the restaurant. He'd spent a while there persuading them to join him for dinner, mindful of Fitz's instructions not to leave them alone, not that he understood why. Now, he stopped for a moment on the road where it came around the airstrip, offering an unimpeded view of the deepening flames of color streaking from the sun, which had just slipped below the horizon. The three of them watched in silence as the colorful palette transitioned gray to purple black, giving the sky a bruised look, ushering in the shadows of night. It was less than a quarter mile to the restaurant but by the time they reached it, it was already getting dark.

Gordon breathed in the fragrance of saffron and pimenton, took in the bright little lights ringing the outside bar and decks, the bustle of voices mingling with the strains of Valencian La Jota and was happy to forget there was any trouble in the world. Life was righting itself. He said as much to the women. Doris, who was sitting beside him, agreed. Lattie, riding in the back, muttered something he couldn't make out. She'd been unusually truculent, Gordon thought, both at the house and the ride over.

"I feel much better," Doris was saying now, hands pressed on the serviceable khaki skirt she'd changed into. "Hard to believe anything bad could really happen here." She peered ahead, sniffed eagerly at the air, like a terrier, leaned back in the cart and sighed. "It smells just wonderful. I don't think I've eaten anything since this morning." She was getting back to normal, Gordon was glad to see.

"Looking forward to it myself," Gordon said, absently, noting as they passed the docks that Fletcher's boat was there, alongside Fitz's green and white "Sheriff" boat. So Deputy Harris was still on the island and presumably Fitz wasn't. "How 'bout you, Lattie?" He again tried to draw a response.

She didn't engage. The vigorous, sharp-tongued woman he'd breakfasted in the morning with had retreated, and he couldn't quite figure it. Anger, outrage, even, he could deal with. Her silence and preoccupation puzzled him. Concern for Doris? He wondered. Maybe she'd loosen up once they were in the restaurant, among people, like Fitz suggested.

They found a space in the crowded lot and came in through the front door, greeted with friendly waves and "how-are-yous?" shouted above the din from various tables of regulars. The tourists among the diners threw the usual curious looks Gordon's way, recognizing him from description. Island regulars Helen Marstein and Nevada Campbell, dining with their husbands, rose and threaded their way through the crowded room, making "sit with us" motions at Doris and Lattie. Gordon handed the two women over and turned to his usual table by the door where Fletcher was already seated with, Gordon saw with some surprise, Sheriff Fitz.

"When did you get back? I didn't hear a chopper," Gordon said to Fitz, but his eyes were on the food the two men were clearly enjoying. God, he was hungry. He looked around for a waiter just as a lithe blonde he didn't recognize set a plate before him.

"Marvelita said you'd be starving," she said with a bright smile and hurried back to the kitchen.

"Nice," Fletcher said through a mouthful of food, "who is she?"

"No idea," Gordon said, inspecting his plate. Paella Valenciana. Excellent. "Marvelita finds them. So?" He looked the question at Fitz, inhaling a forkful of safron rice and succulent rabbit.

"I ran into Fletcher here at the Palm Point marina. Harris was going to bring the boat for me," Fitz explained, "but I wanted to talk to him anyhow," he indicated Fletcher, "so I hitched a ride with him instead. Faster."

"And? What's new?" Gordon said, not looking up from his plate.

"Plenty." Fitz put his fork down. "We need to talk, but I don't want to do it here," he gestured at the crowd. "When you're finished—which should be in about two seconds," he observed, watching Gordon eat, "we'll go into the office."

The office, not *your* office, Gordon registered with irritation. Another tentacle of the creeping officialdom that he seemed to have become ensnared in. "Get everything okay?" he asked more sharply than he intended of Fletcher, who, done eating, was carefully pouring a shot from the whiskey bottle on the table.

"Yup. Everything's already in the kitchen." As if reading his mind, Fletch winked, threw back the shot and washed it down with Fitz's coke. He paused a minute, then said to Gordon: "Word's already out on the mainland about the trouble, if you're interested. There were two reporters sniffing around the marina asking questions. Tried to get a ride out here with me. And they were grilling him," he jerked a thumb toward Fitz, "like a salmon. They looked about 18 years old, by the way. Thought they were kidding until they showed me press passes."

"I didn't make any statement," Fitz said gruffly, snatching back his empty coke glass. "Told 'em to come back in the morning and we'd have something official. Didn't surprise me they tried to get over here, though. Only a matter of time."

Gordon grimaced, finishing his last bite of rabbit. *Another thing they had to thank the Granderson arson for*, he thought. Before that, Hogge was invisible. Even after Charley, the worst hurricane in forty years to hit Southwest Florida, a storm that made landfall on Hogge, couldn't put the island on the map. Most accounts still said it landed in Punta Gorda. But the fire got everyone's attention from Palm Point to Estero. Even then, no one had a clue where Hogge was. Hell, the news crews rushing to cover it spent hours racing around Sanibel and Captiva before they realized they were in the wrong place entirely. But they eventually found the island and descended in droves, delighted at having breached a place that made some claim on privacy which, in the last ten years, seemed to have become a dirty word.

Gordon tossed his napkin on the table and looked around, catching Beni's watchful eye on him from the kitchen door. "Let's go to *my* office (the emphasis wasn't subtle). We'll have coffee there."

"Just us," Fitz said, "I'm done with Mr. James here for the time being. But," he skewed a glance at Fletch, "hang around in case I need you again?"

"Sure thing," Fletch said lazily. He got up from the table and collared the whiskey bottle. "I'll be at the bar. Maybe the young lady with the sunny smile will get a break soon."

"And what if I need you sober?" Fitz demanded.

"I will be. In the morning." Fletch grinned at the two men and half raised the bottle in salute as he left them.

They watched his lanky form weave gracefully through the crowd in the direction of the outdoor bar. Their own progress toward Gordon's office, with Gordon leading, was more like the parting of the Red Sea, as diners hastily shifted their chairs to let them by.

The office was hot despite the air conditioner humming loudly in the window. Gordon started to perspire the moment he closed the door. He switched on the light, walked over to adjust the controls, which were already at full throttle, and settled for peeling off his blazer, hanging the damp garment on the back of the closet door. He turned to find Fitz already seated behind his desk, entering notes from the small pad he carried onto his iPad. Irritation returned.

"Comfortable?"

"Not really. Can't you do something about the air conditioning in here? Don't know how you stand it."

"I'll take care of it first thing tomorrow." The sarcasm was lost on Fitz, who merely nodded and said, hospitably, "Sit down. We've got a lot of ground to cover."

Gordon gave up and sat uncomfortably in a small wooden chair in front of the desk. "What happened at the hospital?" He shifted his weight on the chair, gingerly, so as not to reduce it to splinters.

"Victim was a German tourist, Hermann Gottschalk, age 76, from Hamburg," Fitz intoned, reading from his iPad, "in the U.S. on business. Came to Hogge for a few days' vacation before returning home."

Gordon nodded impatiently. "Don't give me the whole nine yards, Fitz, we're not in court. Just tell me what happened when he came to. What did he say?"

Fitz looked up. There was a considerable pause, as if he was weighing something. "He doesn't remember much about the attack. A stocky figure, black mask—very red lips. But" he watched Gordon carefully, "just before it all came down he was on the deck looking at the Gulf. He remembers seeing a small skiff pulled up on the beach. A light color, he says. Thought maybe it was people shelling but he doesn't remember seeing anyone on the beach." He stopped and let that sink in, consulted his notes.

"Someone could have come by boat. From the mainland?" Gordon said, quickly latching onto this information. So the problem was likely an outside one after all, a thing brought in by an unfortunate tide that would just as soon be washed onto other shores. The threads of suspicion that had been nagging at him all day, threatening to weave themselves into a web that would snare one of his friends or neighbors, began to dissipate.

Fitz didn't respond to this but continued summing up his notes on the victim. "He'd never been to Hogge before and didn't know anyone here. Only person he really spoke to was you, the night he came, when he had dinner here." He looked at Gordon questioningly.

"That's right, we've been over that. He came in late. The place was still pretty crowded, but he ate alone. Left alone, too. Europeans eat slowly. By the time he left the place was pretty empty. He looked over at me a few times, wanted to make conversation, I could see that. But…it was late.*" And he looked lonely, and I wasn't in the mood for conversation.* But all he said to Fitz was, "So what was it? Botched burglary?" Not a pleasant thought, but the island couldn't remain immune forever from the problems of the mainland. Still, burglary was far easier to deal with, he thought with relief, than the idea that someone he knew had come suddenly unhinged and was running around attacking people.

Fitz looked at him curiously. "No. We confirmed he wasn't robbed and nothing was taken from the house. Not a burglary."

"So it was personal? Someone with a beef?"

Fitz shook his head. "The man was a foreigner. He didn't know a soul on the island. No," he spoke slowly, "I'm pretty sure it was a case of being in the wrong place at the wrong time."

Gordon picked up a porcelain model of Blackbeard from his desk and absently ran a thick finger over the stylized beard. The uneasy feeling was returning. "You mean—"

"Mistaken identity," Fitz finished the thought for him.

"That place is one of Hollow's rentals," Gordon immediately pointed out, setting the figure down sharply. "I guess this puts the problem in his lap." Which is where it probably belongs, he thought. Still a shock but at least a digestible one. "Makes sense, too," he continued, making the case. "Unpleasant people like Hollows tended to attract unpleasant things." And, he thought but didn't say, that would explain Hollows' insistence on seeing Fitz earlier in the day. The pieces seemed to be falling in place nicely. Now the only thing left was to end his own involvement in this garden variety thuggery as soon as possible. He looked at his watch— eight thirty. Still an hour or so of dinner service left, tomorrow's menu to go over... . He pulled his scattering thoughts together. Fitz was speaking again.

"Could be, but here's the queer thing—" A soft knock on the door interrupted his train of thought. "Come in," he said, before Gordon had a chance to.

Beni came in with two steaming espressos on a plastic tray, and two plates of caramel glazed flan. "*Flan y café*," he said. He seemed startled to see Fitz sitting behind Gordon's desk but being well trained, set the tray down and slipped out again, unobtrusively.

Fitz looked appreciatively at the flan. "Looks fantastic," he said, picking up a fork.

"Never mind that," Gordon said sharply, washing his own mouthful of flan down with the entire espresso. "What's the queer thing?"

Fitz ignored him. Finally, after he'd devoured the flan and drank half his coffee, he leaned back, folded his hands over his stomach, and spoke. "Hollows wanted to see me this afternoon, you remember?"

Gordon nodded, disinterested, forking off another slice of flan.

"He claims the attack was meant for him." Fitz looked up at the ceiling.

"Not queer at all. That's exactly what I figured." Gordon set his espresso cup down in its saucer with a sharp click. He didn't really give a damn what happened to Hollows. That was Fitz's problem, not his. He was done here. He started to get up.

"Yeah," Fitz waved at him to sit, flipped open his notebook. "Then I had a call at 3:45 p.m. from Richard Sharpe, one of the contractors you told me about. The attack was meant for him, he says."

"What? Why?" Gordon demanded, sitting back down in the chair.

Fitz ignored the question. He spoke meditatively, apparently to the wall behind Gordon's left shoulder. "And when I got to the hospital I had a voicemail from a Max Lupes or Lopez, couldn't tell. Says he's a banker from Miami. Says he's building a house here. The minute he heard about the attack, he says, he knew it was meant for him." He slapped the notebook shut.

"Three of 'em, so far," Fitz said, leaning on one elbow, sipping the rest of his espresso. "You figure any of that?" he said curtly, breaking Gordon's astonished silence.

At that moment, with an ominous *clunk* from the air conditioner, the always capricious Hogge Island electricity cut out.

CHAPTER 14

"Hell!" Gordon said violently, reacting as much to Fitz's information as to the blackout. He was thinking hard. Relief was fading rapidly, but it was still likely a case of *on* the island, not *of* it, as it were. "Hold on. I've got a torch." He got up and groped for the powerful flashlight he kept hanging on the wall. The beam illuminated a startled looking Fitz. From the other room came the excited hum of the diners, plunged into sudden semi-darkness. Gordon stuck his head out the door and saw that Marvelita already had things in hand. Waitstaff were busy flitting between candlelit tables, assuring guests that service would be uninterrupted as all the cooking was done outdoors.

"What the hell happened? And how long is this going to last?" demanded Fitz, as Gordon spoke to Marvelita, who had appeared at the door and was conveying information in a low, urgent murmur.

"No telling," Gordon said, returning to the chair. "All the power comes in on one line from the mainland and gets distributed over the island. The lines were all put in piecemeal so the grid looks like spaghetti. Sometimes it's just in one area.

But Marvelita tells me the whole island is out. Someone must have knocked over a pole or something on Palm. Could be twelve hours, could be two. Never know." He switched on a hurricane lantern on the desk. It threw grotesque shadows on the walls of the small room which was growing noticeably warmer by the minute without the a/c. "If it's not up in two hours, I'll have them run the backup generator."

"Run it now—it's getting hot as hell in here." Fitz mopped his face unhappily.

"Not until I have to," Gordon said. "Might need the fuel if it's a long outage. I have a weekend's worth of food in there. I know the first two people pretty well," he said, steering Fitz back to the original problem, "the last one, Max whoever, not so much. If he's anything like the others…" He let the thought hang.

"Can you think of anyone who might have it in for any of them?" Fitz asked.

Gordon gave a snort. "I can think of about a dozen people, easy. Including myself," he said. If the situation weren't so serious, he thought, it would be laughable. It wasn't every day that you got men falling all over themselves insisting they were worthy of attack. A sort of perverse form of self-awareness?

"There's nothing funny about this, Strange," Fitz said testily. "You didn't see that poor bastard in the hospital. I did. This was no tap on the head. Someone was out for blood. They almost killed him. Now you're telling me it could be almost anyone on this island. And we're sitting here in a goddamned blackout while whoever it is, is roaming around."

"That's not what I meant," Gordon hastened to clarify his statement. "They're not particularly beloved here, that's all."

He went on seriously. "No one here would do something like this. They might think it, say it even, but try to kill them?" He shook his head. "No, Fitz—whoever you are after is long gone. Guys like these piss people off everywhere. You're better off taking this investigation to the mainland. Hired hit, that's my guess. People get hot over issues here but they usually settle things with words. Or in court." As he said it, he had a fleeting vision of Lattie's early morning visit, her vehemence, her unexplained sullenness. But no, he shook his head. Ridiculous, just like he said.

"What?" Fitz demanded. "You've thought of something."

The man was quicker on the uptake than Gordon had given him credit for. "I was wondering if that's all Hollows had to say. Can't see why he was so reluctant to speak in front of me."

"He had another problem," Fitz said, "more pressing than a beaten up guest. Apparently, some person or persons vandalized all his heavy equipment." He found his notes. "Two front-end loaders, a forklift and a backhoe. Gas tanks were compromised." He glanced up looking mildly amused, but his eyes were watchful. "He thought you might have something to do with it."

"ME? Sorry, that's more his style than mine," Gordon's tone was off hand, but felt his temper rising. "If I had a problem with him, I'd be more likely to pay him a visit and throw him in his canal. Which," he said lazily, starting to get up, "I may just do."

"Simmer down," Fitz waved him back. "I told him as much. Frankly, I think he was uncomfortable admitting someone dislikes him that much in front of you. Man has an ego twice his size," he shook his head. "Anyhow, that's neither here nor there. We'll get around to his vandalism eventually. Right now, I told him, finding out who tried to kill his guest takes precedence. Between you and me, I think he was more interested in filing a police report on the equipment so he could make an insurance claim," he confided.

"That would be his main interest," Gordon grumbled, his brief flare up over. "And also couldn't resist throwing a few stones at me while he was at it." He was still angry, but he wrenched his thoughts back to the issue at hand. "So to get back to the real problem, how about that third guy, Max Lopez? Have you spoken to him?"

"Not yet. I left him a message but he hasn't gotten back to me." Fitz's tone was bland. "Hollows says Lopez usually stays in that house, the one the German was in. He rents it when he comes to check on the house he's building, but the German reserved it before him."

"So obviously—"

"I know what you're going to say, but it isn't that easy," Fitz cut him off. "Hollows claims *he* stays overnight in that place sometimes, too, when he has a late night out here. Working, he says, but who would know in this place," he finished up disgustedly.

"So what's Sharpe's connection? Don't tell me he uses the place, too? What, is Hollows running a cathouse?"

"That's a little more complicated. Seems that the original owner of the place—guy named Costello—and Sharpe had several run-ins."

"Costello was a piece of work," Gordon cut in.

"Yeah, well to hear Sharpe tell it, he owed Sharpe thousands on work he'd done but was contesting it. Slapped him with a dozen liens, tried to go after his license. They finally settled, but Sharpe was vague on how or why. It wasn't a court case. That's all he'd say."

"Probably dug up some dirt on him. Costello had plenty to spare from the stories I've heard. But he sold that place a few years ago. Or the bank took it. I'll have to check on that."

"I have," Fitz said. "He sold it. To Hollows, for about half what it's worth." He let this sink in. "Anyhow, according to Hollows, Costello still has property on Hogge, so he visits. I don't know how that ties in yet, but I'll run it down once I get back to the mainland. Can't go tonight. Harris is out there alone in the dark guarding the place. Unless…" He looked at Gordon hopefully.

"Forget it. I've got my own problems here. You can borrow one of my carts if you want to go out there and hold Harris's hand. Besides," he pointed out, "you wanted me to stay with Doris. Why was that, by the way? Afraid the shock was too much for her?"

"Ye-ees but that wasn't the whole reason," Fitz got cagey again. "Doris was pretty early on the scene. She may have seen something or…" He hesitated.

"Someone may think she saw something." Gordon finished for him. He was wondering about that himself and despite the fact that he was pretty sure the attack was a grudge that had spilled over from the mainland to tiny Hogge, the thought nagged. Not to mention the cast of characters was growing and the damned island was in the dark for who knew how long. Which reminded him.

He fished out his cellphone and brought up a number. "Let me see if Palm Electric has any update on the power." He got the automated menu and jabbed zero until he finally got a human. "I'm calling from Hogge Island," he managed to say before the woman on the other end curtly told him that, yes, they were aware of the problem and, Yes!, technicians were working on it but had to get out to Hogge to check the main connection and, NO!, they wouldn't be out before daylight.

"Which means," Gordon said getting up and opening the door, "no power until tomorrow. Beni!" he shouted over to the waiter. "Start the generator. No power 'til morning. Tell Marvelita. And run the kitchen. Nothing else." This over Fitz's squawk of protest over the office a/c.

Marvelita's name brought something else to mind. "What did that housemaid Carmen say, the one who was at the house when I got there? You were going to Hollow's club to interview her when I left you this afternoon."

Fitz grunted. "She wasn't there. In fact, no one knows where she is. She's vanished. Hollows had no clue she'd gone and the other workers said she left suddenly because her mother was ill. There are a hundred and seventy Diaz's on Palm Point but no one of her description. It's like she never existed. The water taxi remembers taking her over on the twelve o'clock boat and that's the last time anyone saw her."

"Or ever will, unless I miss my guess."

"Looks suspicious," Fitz said, squinting down at his pad, making notes.

"Less than you think. Or," Gordon clarified, "I should say not for the reason you think. Half of Hollows employees are illegals, not that he'll admit that. They'd rather go hungry than get mixed up with the law, not that I can blame them." He shook his head. "You'll have one hell of a time finding her now. Marvelita may know something about her. I'll ask her after we close. But I'm pretty sure her running had nothing to do with your crime scene."

"How can you be sure? Do you know her personally?" Fitz asked.

"Not really. I've seen her around the island for, oh, about two or three years it seems like. Quiet but friendly, waves when she passes you. She looked fairly happy here. A shame." He felt a sudden wave of anger as he said it. Another casualty of some jerk's personal vendetta or grudge. The world could be an ugly place. The sooner it retreated from Hogge Island the better.

"So what's your plan now?" Gordon spoke more abruptly than he intended to. "You've got everything you need from that house at this point. Tide took care of any evidence on the beach. Hollows and Sharpe live on Palm, not here. You can follow up with them there." *And leave us in peace and me out of this mess.* He didn't say it but might as well have.

"Maybe." Fitz was noncommittal. "Hollows is putting Harris and me up in the house next door. It's empty at the moment. He's giving us a twenty percent break on the rate," he added sourly.

"Generous of him."

"Yeah. Isn't it though. I'll take the night shift and let Harris get some sleep. We'll go back over to the office in the morning. But," he jabbed a warning finger at Gordon, "that doesn't mean you're off the hook or that I won't be back here. Still plenty of loose ends to tie up and—" His harangue was cut short by the melodic tones of his cellphone. He answered it.

"Fitz here." His tone changed." Oh, it's you. Dear," he added as an afterthought. "I'm sorry, I haven't been able to— no, not even a minute to call. Yes, yes I got the messages. I realize that." He swallowed. "Look, sweetie, I won't be home tonight. Have to stay out on Hogge. There's been a power outage. Well of course it doesn't affect my running the boat but this is a crime scene and..."

Gordon, correctly sensing domestic trouble, decided this would be a good time to see how things were going in the restaurant, have a word with Marvelita. A fair number of tables were still occupied, as diners were in no particular hurry to get back to their dark, airless homes. Besides, Beni and the boys had the generator running and, in addition to the kitchen, they'd wisely (Marvelita's doing, no doubt) expended a few BTUs on running the large Casablanca fans that were providing a refreshing breeze—at least refreshing compared to the sweatbox he'd been sitting in with Fitz. He went out around back and found Marvelita, cool and composed in the humid darkness, supervising the staff tending to the paelleras, finishing up the cooking. It would take more, Gordon thought, than small things like a deadly attack and a power outage to throw her off her game. She spotted him and came over.

"We have good business tonight. They don't want to go home," she said with satisfaction. She slanted a look up at him. "The two *viejas* are still here, by the way. The bigger one doesn't look very happy."

"I didn't think so either," was all Gordon said.

Marvelita nodded and looked past him and watched two waiters ladle the last of the steaming paella into large serving platters. "I talked to the maid, Carmen, this afternoon. She was waiting for the boat."

"How did you know—" Gordon started, then smiled. She was Marvelita, after all. Should he be surprised?

Her look said as much. "I knew she would fly, that one. Only one way to go, so I waited for her. She was scared the police would come. So she left," she said simply.

"Doesn't want to get involved? Because they'd report her?"

"No—she is a citizen. Not that. She said it was the blood, the dead man—"

"He's not dead. He's going to be okay. Eventually."

"All that does not matter," Marvelita waved a hand dismissively, "She was lying. I could see. It is something else. She is afraid of someone."

"How could you tell?" Gordon demanded.

"She kept looking around. Every time a cart came she looked this way, that way—like a rabbit. I told her, don't worry, the police were busy with her boss. But she gave me a look. She did not say it, but it was not the police. Something else. Here, on this island."

Her last words dropped into Gordon's thoughts like lumps of ice.

Marvelita put a hand on his arm. "You must be careful, Gordon. This island is beautiful, yes, but it is an island. Islands have secrets. *Everyone* has secrets, not just you," her gesture took in the whole restaurant. Her grip tightened. "Secrets sleep. But you scratch one, they all wake up."

Gordon started to answer her, stopped. Instead, he gently removed her hand from his arm, bent low, and kissed her once on the forehead.

Sorcery? Second sight? Whatever. He'd learned long ago never to argue with Marvelita.

CHAPTER 15

With Marvelita's warning in his ears, Gordon went back inside. The place had largely cleared out. In the main room a dozen or so islanders had pushed four tables together and were having an animated conversation by candlelight, presided over by Jack Campbell, the island's oldest resident and chairman of the Hogge Island Community Association, or HICA as it was affectionately known. At 85, he'd lost none of the shrewd edge that had served him so well as a litigator. It would appear he was once again holding court as he often did in *Gordon's* on Friday nights. The subject under discussion was not the recent trouble, as Gordon expected, but the annual island Fall fundraiser, the aptly named Hogge Island "Hamboree."

A heated argument was underway between Jack's wife, Nevada, representing the old guard, and Renee Watkins, a real estate agent and Naples transplant whose ostentatious house had already been the subject of much debate. Rail thin, in a sleeveless blue linen sheath and pearls, hair perfectly highlighted to the tips of its blunt cut, she presented quite a contrast to Nevada, plump and comfortable in her camouflage shirt, HICA cap planted firmly on her grizzled gray hair. It was, Gordon felt, like watching a face-off between an Alsatian and a Bulldog—doomed from the start. Jack was attempting to moderate but gave up, calling for another martini. He liked them dry with three olives from the private stock Gordon cured especially for him.

"It's ridiculous," Nevada was saying heatedly as Gordon approached, "How can you change the menu to salmon? It's called the 'Hamboree' for a reason."

"What's ridiculous is that name," Renee said coolly, "I don't care how many years it's been running. It's time we changed things up around here. I mean a pig roast—really? Who even eats pork anymore. Salmon filets, a nice frisee salad, new potatoes. If you give the event a little class, I can get a dozen, two dozen people with money here from Naples, easily. Besides, if you're worried about the cost of salmon, charge more for the liquor—ten dollars a glass for wine isn't unreasonable." She paused, then added a little too casually, "I've spoken to Alan Hollows about it, and he agrees with me. In fact, he'd be willing to do a really nice event there for $50 a head."

A chorus of objections erupted out of which Jack's voice rose loudest. "Now wait a minute, wait a minute," he waved a gnarled hand to quiet things down. "Renee's new here," he said in a conciliatory tone. He could still exercise considerable influence. "What you don't understand, Renee, is that we like things quirky here. It's what gives Hogge its character. We can make a few changes, sure. But don't throw the baby out with the bath water." It was one of his favorite phrases.

Renee was unmoved. "Is it a fundraiser or isn't it?" she demanded. "You've been trying to raise money for a firehouse on the island for over ten years and where are you? Last I heard all you had was $55,000 in the bank." She lost patience. "At the rate you're going, half of you will be dead by the time the first brick is laid."

Breaking the stunned and offended silence that accompanied this remark, Gordon felt it was time to intercede. He pulled up a chair facing Renee and straddled it, dwarfing her. "You might want to reconsider that last comment," he said mildly. "And while you're at it, maybe you want to have this conversation someplace else. Like Hollow's place."

The shot went home. Renee looked at Gordon, reddening under her tan, as if she'd just recalled where she was. "I didn't mean to imply anything about you, Gordon, or the restaurant. I love *Gordon's*. I just meant we should try to mix things up a little, get a different crowd involved. Not that they wouldn't come here—" She broke off, flustered.

Gordon gave her no help. She'd dug this hole for herself. He watched her with a bemused expression until she looked away, fingered her pearls and finally squinted at her watch.

"I have to get home and see how the bird is doing," she finally said, rising, referring to her ancient, ill-tempered parakeet, Noah. It was hard to say whether the bird took after her, or she after him. They were perfectly suited, in any event. "I was only trying to be helpful," she said looking at Gordon reproachfully, as if he had let her in for this trouble. Then, to the rest of the gathering, "I guess we do things differently in Naples." She was affronted, as the underappreciated often are.

"You know, I've heard you say that a number of times, Renee." Jadyn Hayes, sitting a bit apart from the group smoking one of her long cigarettes, suddenly spoke up after being silent for much of the time. "And I have to wonder," she inhaled expansively, "why did you come here? I mean, why Hogge of all places? It's pretty obvious we're not your speed. At least not yet." The emphasis was slightly acid.

Renee bristled, but she had regained her composure. "I'm here for the same reason the rest of you are," she said pleasantly. "The views, the wildlife, the beaches, the lifestyle—it's a unique place." She sounded like a brochure. "I don't have to tell you that."

"And the real estate opportunities. Let's not forget that," Jadyn pointed out, tilting her angular face up, blowing smoke at the ceiling.

"Yes, that too." Renee's tone was icy. "And now," she glanced at her watch again, "I really must go."

As no one suggested she stay, she said goodnight with an annoyed wave and left. When the door closed behind her, everyone started to speak at once.

"Nothing but sheer gall!"

"Salmon and ten dollar wine, can you imagine?"

"—another word about how they do things in Naples, I'll scream!"

"Half of us'll be dead!"

It went on. Jadyn moved over and took a chair closer to Gordon. Watching her smoke, Gordon reached for his small pack of cigars—he hadn't had his nightly ration yet—and realized, infuriated, that he'd left them in the jacket hanging in his office.

"Have one of mine," Jadyn offered. "That woman gives me a pain." She swept a handful of sleek brown hair off her neck and wrapped it in one motion, fixing it into place with a pencil she fished out of her shirt pocket. "She's like the first wave of bad news. More sure to follow. Unique! How long will it stay that way if we keep getting Renees?"

Gordon shook his head. "It's like trying to stop the tide. Can't be done. I've seen it all before. They discover a place, fall in love with it because it's different, tell their friends, then—"

"Spend the next five years turning it into exactly what they left!" Jadyn finished grimly, reaching past him to grind out her cigarette on a plate. "And then wonder what happened when they've ironed the life out of the place." She sighed, bent her head closer to him, and spoke in an undertone. "Speaking of ironing life out, what's happening with that guy that was attacked? German tourist, they said. Is he going to make it?"

"He'll survive. He's pretty banged up. I really can't say much about it," Gordon began apologetically. He was spared further inquiry by a wordless summons from Fitz, who emerged, hot and unhappy looking, from the office. "Give Doris and Lattie a ride home, will you Jadyn?" Gordon said, getting up. "I'm concerned about those two."

He joined Fitz, who was headed outside, presumably to get hold of a cart.

"Everything okay?" Gordon asked as they walked around back, knowing it wasn't. He didn't really want to hear it, but you had to ask.

"You ever feel like you know someone and then all of a sudden, they turn into something else? And you wonder if you just dreamed up how they were before?" Fitz sounded depressed. "Marly's a great girl," he sighed, "at least, I keep reminding myself of that. She just doesn't understand priorities."

Gordon nodded sympathetically, said nothing. From what he knew of Marly, she understood priorities just fine. And they started with her. But he wasn't about to put that on the table. Instead, he said, drily, "I've woken up from several dreams. This is just the latest in a long line." Fitz looked at him, questioning.

"Do you need anything out there or are you all set?" Gordon said quickly, before the conversation threatened to become personal. "Because if we're done, I've got things to take care of here. I've asked Jadyn Hayes to take the women home, Doris and Lattie," he said. Then, anticipating Fitz's next question. "Jadyn's okay; knows how to handle herself." He looked at Fitz critically. "What you need is a good night's sleep."

Fitz sighed again and climbed into the cart. "Great. The one thing I'm absolutely not going to get." He started to back out, stopped. "We'll be leaving at first light. I'll park the cart by the dock in the morning. Okay to leave the key somewhere?"

"Leave it on the back tire," Gordon said. "Give me a call tomorrow when you get settled? Marvelita spoke to that maid, Carmen, while she was waiting for the boat. Yeah," he confirmed the question Fitz was forming, "she left the island. She said she was frightened by finding a dead man, by the blood—but Marvelita doesn't believe her. Thinks something else is scaring her. It's just her hunch," he said, forestalling further discussion. "We'll talk about it tomorrow. I may get more when we get home tonight. And you let me know what that third guy Max says when you reach him."

Three, three. The number reminded him of something. "Rub a dub dub, three men in a tub," he said aloud, inanely. It was the end of a long day. The heat was getting to him.

"Three wise guys, more like," Fitz said cynically, driving off.

CHAPTER 16

After Fitz took off, Gordon was relieved to see that the regulars—the only people left inside except for a few hangers-on at the bar—were preparing to leave. He told Beni to cut the generator output to run the freezers and fridge only, preserving the precious fuel that would have to see him through, he hoped, mid-morning. And tomorrow was Saturday, which meant heavy boat traffic. He noticed Fletch chatting with the bartender—the blonde must have had other plans—and gave him the high sign to come join him. There were more than a few things to go over before the night was over.

Jadyn waved goodnight, with Dorris and Lattie in tow. That was good. Gordon would have liked to get Lattie alone and figure out what was eating her, but that could wait. Everyone needed a good night's sleep, not just Fitz. Nevada and Jack stopped him on their way out.

"You must think we're nuts arguing about the Hamboree after a thing like this," Nevada began, but Jack cut her short.

"Now don't start in on that, Nevada. An unfortunate, dirty piece of business, but it could happen anywhere. Man's going to be fine. I hear they're looking for someone on the mainland." Jack looked at Gordon shrewdly for confirmation.

So the island telegraph had already weighed in, Gordon thought, and concluded whatever it was had nothing to do with them or Hogge. He hoped they were right, thinking about the self-appointed victims. But all he said was, "Most likely the case, Jack," to the older man's knowing nod. "Careful in the dark." He waved goodnight.

Gordon looked around the empty restaurant and thought about Renee. Privately, he had to admit, she'd picked a helluva time to throw her wrench in the works. Tensions were already running high. Bringing Hollows into the picture was deliberate, he was quite sure. Renee seldom did anything that wasn't deliberate. It was the real estate agent in her: no action without motive. He had a pretty good idea that she was getting kickback from Hollows—not that it was illegal. Just unethical. And whatever Hollows was cooking up for his next act, Gordon was certain, Renee was in on. But he was equally certain she'd be hedging her bets, playing both sides of the fence. Why else would she have insinuated her way into HICA, seeing to it that she'd have a position on the board? Altruism wasn't her long suit.

He walked among the tables, thoughts scattering, mechanically dousing candles still flickering in their little votive holders. He looked at his watch. The illuminated dial showed just after nine-thirty. And it was still Friday. Christ! It felt like two months had gone by. He wanted another drink, another cigar, another shower, and seven hours sleep. He'd settle for five.

"Nice that the electricity went out on top of everything else." It was Fletch, shutting the door with a bang like a pistol shot.

Gordon looked up sharply, then, seeing his friend, shrugged. "Yeah. Generators should get us by. Palm Electric says they'll be out in the morning. Whatever that means." He sat down heavily in a chair.

Joining him, Fletch laughed and drummed a short riff on the table with his fingers, spoke. "Fitz looked pissed when he tore out of here. More trouble?" he asked, idly.

"Just at home, at the moment."

"Ah, Marly. Jackson Fitz and Marly—could've blowed me down when she showed up married to him."

"He seems to be wondering about that himself. I didn't know you knew her."

"Oh, not well. She was known." Fletch grinned slightly. "Or as they say in more polite circles, her reputation preceded her."

Gordon was puzzled and looked it. "She was a local, you mean? From Palm Point?"

Fletch gave him a funny look. "No. You don't know? She turned up here years ago with Costello. They used to live on a houseboat out there," he waved in the general direction of Gordon's docks. "That was before Costello's 'investments' paid off. I thought you knew."

Gordon was surprised and didn't bother to hide it. "No, I didn't. I've met her before but I had no clue. Ten years on Hogge and you can still shake monkeys out of people's trees." He recalled Marvelita's words about secrets. Prescient, as usual. "Does Fitz know?"

"Dunno," Fletch shrugged. "We're talking over fifteen years ago, before the hurricane. Fitz'd only been on the job a year or two when they met. Once Costello cashed in after the storm, things got ugly pretty quickly. He stayed on Hogge, she left, started doing odd jobs on Palm. Real estate appraisal, bartending. I think she was bartending when Fitz hooked up with her." He paused, then added. "What I heard, Costello had started knocking her around. Drugs were involved, other stuff. Anyhow, he was gone soon enough himself. Place got too hot for him, I guess."

"I'd say Fitz doesn't know," Gordon said slowly. "At least he didn't mention it when Costello's name came up in connection with that house." He sat, silently arranging facts.

"Well, if he doesn't, it's a case of sleeping dogs." Fletch said, breaking in on his thoughts. "If Fitz knows, he doesn't want to talk about it. And if he doesn't, I wouldn't be the one bringing the news to him. No joy there."

"I'm surprised you never mentioned this before," Gordon said.

"Never came up." Fletch said. "Truth is, I'd forgotten about it until you said Fitz was having troubles on the home front. Spend ten more years on this island and there's plenty you'll forget, too." His tone was weary. "Anyhow," he said impatiently, "What does it matter at this point? Ancient history."

"Maybe not so ancient." Gordon said slowly.

Fletch looked at him quickly, interested. A cacophony of voices, crockery and pans banging drifted in from the kitchen.

"Let's go into the office so I can have a smoke. I'll fill you in." They walked over. On second thought," Gordon said, retrieving his jacket and closing the door on the room, "let's go to my place. At least there's a breeze on the deck. It's hot enough to smoke hams in there."

He stopped by the kitchen on the way out to give a few instructions and told Marvelita he'd see her back home. "Take this," he said handing Marvelita a heavy flashlight. "It's black as pitch out there. And be careful."

He collected Fletch, and they left.

"Damn it's dark. Moon was out earlier," Fletch observed once they got into the cart, "clouds must've covered it up. Maybe we'll get rain. We need it bad."

"Maybe not until we get power back," Gordon said, swerving to avoid a low-hanging branch. The cart's headlights weren't much help. The island was shrouded, enveloped in the eerie silence that seems to accompany power outages everywhere. Even the tree frogs, the familiar chorus of the night, were absent.

Just before they turned into Gordon's drive, Fletch pointed toward the Pass. "I see Cross has lights," he said, indicating the big house glowing in the distance.

Gordon turned to look. "Of course. He's got a generator and a propane tank underground that could power half the island. Very proud of it. Probably why he's running it at this hour, just so everyone can see it. Or he's up late composing his latest complaint."

They started up the stairs. Fletch stopped, cocked his head, "Listen," he said to Gordon. "Boat engine. Sounds like it's headed across the Pass." He walked up to the landing and peered out in the direction of the water. "Whoever it is, they're in a hurry. And they're running without lights. Dangerous on a night like this. Probably some drunk tourists out for a joyride. We'll be pulling 'em off the oyster beds in the morning." He shook his head disgustedly.

"Normally I'd agree with you," Gordon said, looking at his watch to make note of the time—ten-fifteen. "But you haven't heard what Fitz told me this afternoon. I'm not a fan of boats in the dark just now."

"Why the sudden concern?" Fletch said, puzzled. "You don't usually have a beef with drunks. That's Cross's department—the protector of Hogge Island morals," he finished up sarcastically. They were upstairs now. The room was dark as pitch.

"Morals have nothing to do with it. Whiskey?" Gordon asked, grabbing the bottle and two glasses off the kitchen counter. "Let's sit outside. At least there's some air."

They made their way to the lanai deck. Gordon switched on a table lantern and the yellow light shone through the table on two bronze mermaid pedestals underneath, making them seem oddly human. "So here's what I know," he proceeded to fill Fletch in.

Fletch didn't comment until he was done. "So," he said, pouring a drink and throwing it back in one go. "You've basically got a guy in the wrong place at the wrong time and three people claiming the attack was meant for them. And," he lit a cigarette and inhaled deeply, "a house with a hoodoo on it. I didn't know Costello still had property here."

"Who is Costello, anyhow. Does he have a first name?"

"I knew him as Two-Finger Louie—no seriously," Fletch said, seeing the expression on Gordon's face. "There were a couple of stories about how he lost the fingers." He held up his left hand with only the thumb and forefinger showing, to illustrate. "He claimed they got blowed off by fireworks when he was a kid. But I've heard different—mob, drugs. He was a rough customer. It wouldn't surprise me."

Initially amused at yet another picturesque island moniker, Gordon gave a grunt and suddenly sat up, alert.

"What? You do know him?" Fletch looked curious.

"I don't know him," Gordon said slowly, "But I think I've met him. In fact, I think I threw him out of my place on Thursday night." He gave Fletch a brief account of the bar fight, describing the man he ushered out.

"That sounds like him," Fletch conceded. "But what the hell was he doing at your place? He's one of Hollows' cronies. He'd be there, if anywhere." He sat puzzling over it. "Any idea who he was meeting?"

"No. I thought he was bullshitting me so he didn't have to leave," Gordon said a little ruefully. "This was Thursday night, remember. Before any of the rest of this crap came down." He slapped angrily at the no-seeums buzzing around his head, annoyed that his usual powers of observation had let him down. Then another thought hit him. "Marvelita said Cross came snooping around that night, too. Showed up just in time for the fight. But he left almost immediately. Looking unhappy, she said. I ran into him the next morning and he was on a rampage." He described the exchange, the threat with the gun. "I assumed he was sniffing around, as usual, for more ammunition. Does he have any connection to Costello?"

Fletch shook his head. "Not that I know of. Cross got here a couple of years after the storm. Costello was gone by then. Pointed a gun at you? That's radical, even for him. Does Fitz know?"

"I mentioned it but didn't make a big deal out of it. Didn't want to complicate the issue with a personal matter. Cross doesn't frighten me. I can take care of him."

"That," Fletch said, leaning forward and stubbing out his cigarette, "is your tragic flaw, Gordon." He was only half joking. "You're so used to taking care of things on your own, you don't open up to people. You're a great friend, but you make a lousy lawman."

"Which," Gordon said with sudden venom, "is why I never went into that particular line of work. And I don't want to be in it now." He filled his glass, downed it, and poured another, stewing.

"Well no use getting hot under the collar," Fletch tried to mollify him. Then, as another thought occurred to him, "Who were the drunks? The two you threw out first?"

"I don't know that either. I run a restaurant, Fletch—lots of guys drift in off the water. I don't get everyone's name." Gordon's irritation was returning. He made an effort to ignore it. "One of them looked familiar." He described the man he had subdued by partial asphyxiation.

Fletch looked interested. "Sounds like some of Sharpe's crew. In which case you have your answer for the fight, anyhow. No love lost there. There are still some of Sharpe's crew around who remember when Costello put the squeeze on. So you probably had the right read on the whole thing."

"I hope so," Gordon said, dubiously. But he was left with the nagging suspicion that he'd missed something.

Fletch, meanwhile, had moved on. "So getting back to the attack," he said, "whoever did it, I wonder if they know?"

"Know what?" Gordon dragged his thoughts back from his plunge into self-doubt.

"That they whacked the wrong guy. That's why you were worried about the boat? You think they'll be back?"

"No," Gordon said, sitting up. "Actually, I never thought about that. Maybe I should have." He wondered if Fitz had considered this angle. It would give more weight to his concern for Doris.

"Well, frankly," Fletch said, "given the people involved, I wouldn't lose sleep over it. I mean," he clarified, "I don't know Max Lopez well. I met him when he first got here a year or so ago. He didn't have much use for me." He laughed, remembering. "But I've heard a little about him. Seen him, actually. He was at the restaurant Thursday. Ate alone and left fairly early, just before I did."

"I know the name but not the guy. What's he look like?" Gordon asked.

"'Bout my height, dark hair, expensive clothes—had on a blue silk shirt."

"Yeah, I know the one." Gordon cut in. "Looked like he might have an attitude."

Fletch nodded in agreement. "Kind of guy who walks into a place looking like he's thinking about buying it. You know him. Or you know about him. He's the one who's breaking Sharpe's heart over that house on the East end. I heard they had a pretty good argument yesterday, in fact. Don't ask me from who—" he put up a hand as Gordon formed the question, "You know how it is. You hear things on the dock."

"You tell Fitz this when he talked to you?"

"It didn't come up. He was more interested in how I spent my morning. Not beating people half to death, I told him." Fletch crushed the cigarette out, lit another one, smoked a bit.

"He seemed to believe me, but he doesn't trust me, I can tell. Trusts you alright. Man has bad instincts," he chuckled.

Gordon ignored the dig. He was considering Fletch's information as a whole. Interesting as it was, the most likely scenario was still the one he suspected initially: a non-islander with a grudge. He said as much to Fletch.

Fletch nodded, sleepily. "The guys from Sharpe's crew are the best candidates," he said finally, yawning. "None of them live here. Should be easy enough for Fitz to chase down where they live on the mainland and see when they got home."

Gordon was inclined to agree. "I'll put Fitz in the picture in the morning. He's headed back to Palm early." He looked out toward the Gulf. The moon was disappearing, reappearing through the clouds. "I said from the beginning this whole investigation belonged on the mainland," he finally said glumly. "I don't know why Fitz roped me into it in the first place."

"Yeah you do," Fletch said with a faint grin. "Can't be helped. You're a fixer, people come to you. Maybe it's because you're a big guy. But I've seen it happen to you a dozen times easy since you got here. Probably why Cross hates you so much." He laughed, then eyed Gordon appraisingly. "Bet it's been that way your whole life. And I'll bet," he wasn't flippant now, "it's gotten you in plenty of trouble."

"Plenty," Gordon said with grim amusement. "But I figured in this godforsaken place I could leave all that behind. All I want to do is run a restaurant, watch the sun rise and set from this deck, smoke my two cigars a day and drink bourbon when I want to. Can't seem to get away from trouble," he sighed, more to himself.

"You know how it is, Gordon." Fletch poured himself another whiskey. "No matter where you go, there y'are." He sounded like he was speaking from experience.

No matter where you go, Gordon thought. And he'd gone plenty of places—Hamburg, Moscow, Paris, London, Rio, Iquitos, New Orleans, Manhattan. And now, Hogge, backwater of backwaters. And everywhere the story was the same.

The time I wasted; always looking for action. Out of nowhere, his father's voice, unbidden, clear as if he was on the lanai deck with him. A voice he hadn't heard in forty years. The last time they'd met, Gordon had taken him for a walk—one of the last the old man was able to make—down an overgrown path through the marshes in a nature preserve in Connecticut. A final outing from the last stop nursing home he'd landed in. The path led to the Long Island Sound. Standing by the water's edge, as the weak tide lapped over polished stones, the old man, still a giant but with the meat hanging off of him now, skipped rock after rock across the brown water, regretting a misspent life. The way old men do when death is around the corner, and they've seen its face. *Always looking for action.* And perhaps, Gordon thought with sudden clarity, that was the reason action was the last thing he sought. But Karma is a funny thing.

The sound of the front door closing brought him back to the lanai deck on his house in Hogge.

Fletch had finished his drink and was looking at him, quizzically, the corner of his mouth once again drawn up in its trademark half-smirk.

"Ruminating?" he said, not expecting, not needing an answer. He got up and arched his back. "Unless I miss my guess that's Marvelita come in. You two have some catching up to do and I'm not her favorite when the bottle's out. Time I got some shut-eye anyhow. Don't bother," in answer to Gordon's offer of a ride, "it's a short walk. I'll be out on the water early but I'll talk to you when I get in."

He left through the outside screen door and padded down the spiral staircase, catlike, into the night.

. You will have some trouble
up. He said, "Go to her. I've seen the picture myself. Look
at him if you want to know. Don't bother me anymore."
And he opened the door and I went outside. To go for another
drink.... She... She... you told me I had...
...him... the people screaming... and... blind. Did I
say too much?

CHAPTER 17

Gordon fixed his last drink of the night, a small one from the bottle on the table. He would have preferred bourbon, but that meant getting up and going inside and just now he didn't want to get up. He often didn't at the end of a day but this one had been particularly long. No let up since dawn. He sat holding the glass idly, letting the tension leave his shoulders. There was a freshening breeze drifting through the screen. The rustling fronds of coconut palms framing the house made a soothing sound— like raindrops.

He could hear Marvelita moving around downstairs in her tidy apartment. After a while, she came up and joined him on the deck, wrapped in a teal blue sarong patterned with hibiscus flowers. She had a mug of Japanese Green tea with toasted rice. It was her favorite beverage next to coffee, which she only drank in the morning. Gordon ordered the stuff online, by the pound. He never developed a taste for it himself but she drank enough for both of them. Her long hair was down, hanging in one black plait over her shoulder. In the dim flickering light, she looked twenty-five years younger. Gordon wondered if he looked as good. He doubted it.

Marvelita sipped some tea. "I brought it in a thermos from the restaurant," she explained, as if she knew he was wondering where hot tea had come from. She looked at him expectantly. "So." It was more a statement than a question. No questions were needed between them. She drank tea in silence, dark eyes steady and watchful, as Gordon filled her in on everything he'd learned, including his last conversation with Fletch.

When he was done she set the mug down and began laying out a game of solitaire from the worn deck she'd brought up with her. An old habit. Cards, she told him long ago, helped her think. Gordon once showed her the game could be played on a computer, but, she told him, that would be betrayal. Her cards spoke to her, she maintained, because she kept them active, warm. The statement would have seemed lunatic coming from someone else but coming from Marvelita it had the ring of simple truth.

Gordon sat patiently, nursing his drink, while she played her game out. Finally, sweeping up the cards and tidying them into a deck, she spoke.

"I said that she would bring trouble and I was right." Characteristically, she fixed on Lattie, the one person Gordon hadn't talked about. For Marvelita, people's emotions were always more interesting than the events surrounding them. "You did not mention her, but I can see. Something is wrong. She was happy enough selling me the fish this morning. Where did she go after?"

Gordon sighed. "I don't know. She hasn't been very talkative since all this happened. I asked her that when I was at their house this afternoon, but she didn't give me a straight answer. But I can't believe she's mixed up in any of this."

"I did not say she was, but she hates that man, Hollows. Many times, I have heard her say she'd like to kill him." Marvelita said in a matter of fact tone, fanning the cards out on the table.

"That's just talk, Lita." Gordon shifted uncomfortably. "I wouldn't repeat it, under the circumstances."

She looked up, reproachful. "When do I repeat? I'm just telling you." She gathered up the cards again and tapped on the table for emphasis. "You listen, but sometimes you do not hear. It's not your fault. You are a man," she said generously. "That Sheriff Fitz who has made you his friend—"

"Deputy—only temporarily."

"You cannot rely on him. He is *cornuta*, that one." She made the universal sign with her index and pinky finger. "What is in front of his face he cannot see. Or won't."

"So you knew about Marly, too?" Gordon said, mystified. Was he the only person on Hogge in the dark?

"No," Marvelita was scornful, "not what you just told me. But I have met her twice. It was enough to see into her heart. She is selfish and full of deceit. And she drinks too much," she added. "He will have plenty of trouble one day, if he does not have it already."

To see into her heart. Another phrase that might have seemed odd coming from someone else. But Marvelita's intuition bordered on second sight. Gordon had reason to know it. It had only failed her once, and Gordon knew all about that, too. As a girl of eighteen she had fallen in love, hard, and all her instincts, her intuitions had been blinded by that mysterious force. The marriage was a brief and brutal one, physically and emotionally, as bit by bit the persona the man had constructed to woo her while in the hunt fell away, revealing his true nature—which, she told Gordon with painful honesty, she had all the warning signs of had she cared to pay attention to them. She was not bitter. She merely knew that where she could rely on her judgement of others to keep her safe, her own heart was a closed book. She could have been speaking from his soul so closely did their experiences match. It was if someone had snatched his heart out of his chest and shaken it like a dustrag on the table before him.

That conversation had taken place more than twenty years ago, when Gordon found her, seemingly a lifetime ago, in a small wooden café north of Iquitos where the road ended in a maze of jungle. They shared a plate of tiny fried shrimp (she told him later, laughing, that they were actually grubs). They were an incongruous pair. Gordon, a young man whose size intimidated everyone he met, and Marvelita, barely five foot two, who would not be intimidated. Whose liquid eyes swallowed up his pain. The bond they forged there was immediate and immutable. Fellow travelers protecting each other from the wastes of love.

"You're probably right about Marly, but I don't think she's involved in our present problem," Gordon said finally, dragging his thoughts back into the present. The wind had picked up considerably and was singing through the screens. There would be rain before the night was out, but maybe that would cool things down.

"Wish I'd found out a little bit more about that fight," Gordon said thoughtfully. "As it was, I just wanted to get them out of the place. Fletch agrees with me. He thinks they're most likely the ones responsible."

"It looks that way, yes," Marvelita said slowly. "But then, why did the others say the attack was meant for them?"

"Guilty conscience?" Gordon said, shrugging. "They all probably have something to hide. You said it yourself. All the same, I'll be interested in hearing what Fitz learns from this Max Lopez. Do you know anything about him?"

"Not really, no."

"I know the name but not much about the man." He paused, then asked, "How about Carmen, the maid? How well did you know her?"

"I spoke with her three, maybe four times. She is a strange one, not like the rest. The other workers don't really like her. They have told me. They say she is secretive, never tells anyone where she is going on her day off. She is friendly but does not have friends here—at least not the other workers." She picked up her tea, which had gone cold, put it down. "They thought she was there to spy on them. For the Jefe—Hollows."

"Interesting." Gordon finished off his drink. "Fitz says he can't find any trace of her on Palm. He says no one recognizes her from the description. She must know someone, or someone must know her." He sat, puzzling over it.

"Maybe. But now, I am tired," she yawned sleepily. "Tomorrow is Saturday. We will be busy, power or not. Should I wake you up when I go? It will be early," she picked up her mug, her cards.

"I'll set my alarm. Lita," Gordon put a hand on her wrist. "Have you told me everything you know?" He had to ask. She was a woman who could keep secrets if she thought information could bring distress to those she loved.

"Yes, everything I know," she smiled and put her small hand over his. "Don't worry, Gordon. Perhaps you are right and by tomorrow, all this will be over. But," she got up and moved gracefully to the door, "you cannot change what has already happened."

"Shakespeare would agree with you," Gordon said dryly, not bothering to explain. He put out the lantern and followed her in.

CHAPTER 18

A crack of thunder like gunshot jarred Gordon awake from his deep dreamless sleep. Flashes of lightning followed jumping from cloud to cloud lighting up the sky in brilliant patches. The rain came, starting slowly in large, fat drops and then, all at once, in a deafening torrent. He glanced at the clock to see the time and its black face reminded him there was still no power. He picked up his watch from the nightstand and saw that it was just after five in the morning. Not much use in trying to go back to sleep. It would be light in another hour and he needed to get to the restaurant to check on the generator. Hopefully, it was still running. The intrigue and speculations of last night were rapidly fading from his mind. His chief concern was how to get through a busy Saturday compounded by a power outage. He pulled on pajama bottoms and opened the door, sure he smelled coffee. Likely a hallucination since there was no way to make it.

It was no hallucination. Marvelita, bless her, had dug out the small Coleman stove tucked in the closet and, sitting back on her heels on the lanai deck, was watching the espresso pot keenly. She'd set out two cups on the table and smiled as he came in. The rain tapered off and stopped as suddenly as it started. The storm was already moving north over the Gulf.

"I knew the storm would wake you. The coffee is ready." She brought the pot over and poured them each a cup, hers half sugar, his plain. It was delicious, possibly the best thing he'd had in twenty-four hours, or at least that's how it felt. Over a second cup, they planned out the day.

"Breakfast will not be a problem. I can cook outside. And perhaps the power will come back before lunch," she was saying. "Otherwise, we will use the grill."

"What about water?" Gordon was dubious. "The generator can't run the kitchen and the water pump at the same time. Maybe we shouldn't open until the power is back."

She shook her head. "People will come for breakfast. Business will be good. The food will stay cold enough until noon so we don't need the generator any more for that. It can run the rest. I'm going to shower outside," she finished her coffee. "There is enough water for both of us," she said pointedly.

Gordon nodded unenthusiastically. A shower of any sort was better than none, he supposed, and at least they had the outdoor cistern to rely on. "You go ahead," he said. "I'll clean up here." She left.

Gordon poured out the last dregs of coffee and lit a cigar. Some sleep, coffee and his cigar. He was beginning to feel almost human again. His watch showed five thirty. In another hour or so the sun would be up. The clouds on the eastern horizon were the color of burnished copper and flame, precursor to a spectacular dawn. Probably a good morning for boaters. When he heard Marvelita leave on the cart, he grabbed a towel and headed outside. At seven, shaved and showered after a fashion, he put on fresh clothes, mulling over what he would say to Fitz, and determined to corner Lattie at some point just to see what was troubling her. Smiling, he recalled Fletch's comment: *You're a fixer.* Well, Fletch had that right.

By the time he got to the restaurant a half hour later, the sun was up, banishing the brief cool down brought by the storm, burning the last whispy clouds out of the sky. It promised to be a blistering day of high August heat. He pulled his broad white hat a little lower over his eyes, parked the cart, and climbed out. His cellphone rang at once, insistently. It was Fitz—no doubt in even a lousier mood than he was last night.

"How was—" Gordon started, but before he could finish the sentence, Fitz barked at him.

"Where are you?"

"Just got to the restaurant."

"Stay there. I'm sending Harris for you. We have real trouble. Palm Electric sent a boat out early to deal with the power—the line comes in on State land apparently."

"Yeah, down at the south end. There's a junction—"

"Never mind that. They found a body on the beach. Hasn't been here long, from the look of it. Medical examiner's team is coming in by boat. Harris'll meet him and I want you to come with them. For identification."

The hairs rose on the back of Gordon's neck. His mind started to race. Fletch said he was going out on the water early. "Who is it?" he demanded curtly.

"That's what I want you for. No ID, no wallet. Just a matchbook from your place." There was a pause. "You won't be able to tell much from his face," Fitz said woodenly.

"Strange—keep it to yourself. I don't want this getting out just yet."

He rang off.

Gordon stood staring at the entrance to the restaurant for a full minute, seeing nothing. Eventually, a trickle of sweat ran down his face and dripped onto his hand, bringing him back with a start to his surroundings.

CHAPTER 19

Jadyn Hayes was a creature of certain habits. Chief among them was her daily island walk at dawn—a three mile circuit from Gulf to bay. It was her favorite time of day, full of promise, with much to reflect on, if you were observant. No two walks on Hogge's beach were ever the same. The escarpment she passed yesterday may have vanished overnight, claimed by the sea. On calm days there would be dolphin and osprey competing for fish. On windy ones, there was the breathtaking spectacle of anhinga and frigate birds, spiraling like kites on the high thermals. And, of course, the shells, heaps of them, seemingly identical unless you stopped and examined the infinite variations even in those no larger than a speck of rice. Minor miracles all, even if you didn't believe in miracles. Which she did.

The clap of thunder that jolted her from sleep on Saturday during the power outage came well before dawn. Within moments, a storm was raging. Her first disappointing thought was "no walk until later." Rain didn't bother her; lightning was another thing. But it was early yet. Likely the storm would move off by dawn. Sure enough, as she rooted around the room of her small one bedroom bungalow in the dark for something to put on, the rain started to taper off. The beach after a storm—even better!

An hour later, in her usual uniform of tattered shirt and shorts, she was on her way, marveling at the glorious crimson color radiating from the sky to sea. The sunrise was lovely this morning—but, "red sky in the morning," she muttered, shaking her head. Along with miracles, she also believed a healthy number of superstitions, not that she would have admitted to them. They had long ago become as much a part of her nature as her own name.

Approaching the Pass, where the confluence of bay and Gulf rippled the water with a strong current, she encountered her first obstacle. The tide was very high this morning, churned by the storm, making it impossible to get around the private docks sprouting like tendrils from the large houses ringing the Pass. She'd either have to swim under them or walk over them to continue. Technically, it was trespassing but generally no one minded, as long as people didn't linger to fish or sunbathe. She clambered over the first one and a few hundred yards down came to the second, snaking out from Van Cross's house. *He* would mind, of course, since he minded everything, but he wasn't out on his deck. Likely he was still asleep, like almost everyone else on Hogge. Besides, what was he going to do? Shoot her for walking over a pier?

Up she went and, as luck would have it, at that moment Cross himself appeared at the edge of the mangroves lining the dock. He was unshaven and uncharacteristically disheveled looking. He was also holding what looked like a shotgun, which he pointed straight at her.

"What the hell are you doing on my property? I could shoot you for trespassing!" The man was known to be difficult, but this was too much.

Stunned, she stood rooted to the spot. "What's wrong with you? Are you crazy?" she blurted out. The minute she said it she had the thought that he likely was—crazy drunk, probably. In any case, reminding him of it wasn't the brightest move.

"How long have you been there spying on me?" he demanded. He was red from the neck up and Jadyn didn't like the wild look in his bleary eyes. What had the man been doing? He looked like he was coming off a week-long bender.

She raised her hands and made "calm down" motions. "I'm just taking a walk, Van, like I do every morning. The tide's really high today, that's all." Despite a rising panic, she kept her voice steady and spoke calmly, like you would to someone who was insane. She didn't look him directly in the eye, but over his shoulder. Years in Manhattan had taught her never to make eye contact with strangers or aggressive looking dogs. At the moment, he could pass for either.

"Bullshit." He jerked the gun. "First Strange, now you. He sent you here, right? I should call the Sheriff on you both." He was getting more agitated by the minute and making no sense whatsoever.

"I wish you would," Jadyn said earnestly. *Why, she thought wildly, didn't I bring my cellphone? Why did I pick up that penny lying wrong side up on the beach yesterday?* Swallowing hard she said, starting to back away, "Why don't you go call the sheriff right now?"

"Don't you move. I'm not through with you."

Shock and the preposterousness of the situation almost brought on a fit of hysterical laughter. *Don't laugh. Don't!* She got her nerves under control. "Van," she said in as even a voice as she could muster, "you've known me for three years. Why would I be spying on you? I mean," seeing the ugly look in his eye, "why would I spy on anybody here?" Better he not think up reasons for her supposed spying. In his present state, he'd probably come up with something outlandish. Maybe he was hearing voices. Or maybe his growing tendency to make trouble for half the island had blossomed into complete paranoia, fueled by alcohol. Instinctively, she looked toward the bay, to see if there was anyone else around.

"Who're you looking for," he demanded harshly. "You waiting for someone? Who put you up to this?" He looked around wildly.

This was no good. There was no one coming to her rescue and any minute now Cross would figure out that if he let her go, *she* would likely call the sheriff, which she fully intended to do the minute she got away from this madman. If she got away. As well be a sheep as hanged for one, she thought shakily, vaguely aware that wasn't how it went. Oh well.

She wanted to scream "you bloody fucking sonofabitch," but with great self-control, merely said, "I'm going on my walk now, Van. I'm terribly sorry I trespassed on your property. It won't happen again." She spoke contritely, still using her mental asylum voice. She started to climb down. Her legs were shaking so badly she had to grab hold of a mangrove branch to steady herself. Meanwhile, her apology seemed to have mollified the man.

"That's right," he shifted the gun to his shoulder, "I had every right to defend my property, so don't think you can go making trouble for me. You just admitted you were trespassing. I have you dead to rights." This circuitous reasoning seemed to calm him. Some of his normal swagger was returning. "You start anything and I'll sue you for slander!"

Cross's lawsuits were legendary. He seemed to have an endless pit of money for hiring lawyers. No case was too frivolous if he felt he had been slighted or maligned in some fashion. Even though he was usually the one doing the maligning.

"Don't worry, I won't make trouble." Jadyn scrambled down and hurried away from him as fast as possible. *The hell I won't,* she thought, choking on her fury.

When she had rounded the corner and was well out of ear, eye or buckshot, she sat down on one of the large, flat rocks at the water's edge until her breathing steadied and her heart stopped pounding in her chest. She stared out on the Gulf. A flock of gulls flew by, chasing each other over the water. A great blue heron alighted on a nearby rock, setting its long neck at an angle, seeking fish. But for once, Jadyn saw neither gulls nor heron. Just the face of Van Cross, livid with rage, behind the barrel of a gun. Beside her, an osprey landed on a tall pine and began its piercing call, ending in a triumphant crescendo—a thing that always brought her joy. But today, her walk spoiled, angry tears filled her eyes.

Damn the man! How could he? Drunk or not, she would report him as soon as she got home and at least have the satisfaction of seeing him hauled off by the Sheriff. Or would she? Van was slippery as an eel. He had a way of twisting any event to his advantage. She could see him now, clean and sober, exhibiting none of the paranoia she witnessed, making her out to be the villain. Worse, he would deny the whole thing. But something had to be done.

She lit a cigarette and smoked, thinking. Cross's words came back to her: *"Strange put you up to this!"* Gordon. Yes, she thought with relief, rolling out the lit end of the cigarette between her thin fingers and carefully pocketing the stub, she would go to Gordon. He would know what to do. Besides, he had Fitz's ear.

She got up and walked briskly down the beach toward home, treading heedlessly over the mounds of shell she normally would have pored over. Cross had gotten away with plenty in his life. He was that sort of man. But this time, she thought angrily, he would pay.

CHAPTER 20

Gordon waited impatiently at the dock with Deputy Harris for the medical examiner and his team to show up. He sent word to Marvelita that he was called away, knowing if he spoke to her in person she would immediately guess something was wrong. Of course she would know anyway. But Fitz was adamant about keeping the discovery of the body quiet as long as he could. And how long was that going to be on an island this size? He tried not to think about why Fitz would want him to come and identify it, because that got him to thinking about Fletch. But surely Fitz would have said something if that was the case, he assured himself. He lit a cigar and smoked, pacing the dock, perspiring, as the sun burned higher in the sky.

A boat was approaching. No, two boats, three. It was a damned flotilla. A chopper appeared like a giant insect, flying low, and veered off toward State land. Within minutes, the dock was swarming with emergency personnel, Sheriff's deputies, the medical examiner and his workers.

Gordon collared the medical examiner and his assistant, introduced himself, and left it to Harris to figure out transport for the rest. It would take about fifteen minutes, he figured, before word spread like a grassfire that something was very wrong on the island, given the scene on the dock.

The road was in worse shape than usual, pitted by the morning downpour with ruts and moguls. Gordon kept his foot on the accelerator. The cart bounced along like an unpleasant roller coaster ride. The medical examiner sat next to him, a thin, balding man of about 55 named Janson. His main concern at the moment seemed to be the roughness of the ride. The assistant riding in the back of the cart was getting the worst of it as the cart rattled over the rough surface, but the examiner was the only one complaining.

"For God's sake, slow down. My back can't take it." Janson clutched at his side and grabbed the windscreen for balance as they took a particularly vicious bump. "The body isn't going anywhere. Trust me."

Gordon cut his speed down a bit to negotiate the deep pools left by the rain. The man had a point. Janson took off his glasses and wiped mud off them on his shirt.

"That's a little better. I've never been out here before. It's really quite beautiful," he said congenially, gesturing at the jungle-like canopy. "Of course, under other circumstances..." He trailed off at the expression on Gordon's face.

He tried again. "How long have you lived here?"

"Ten years." Gordon said abruptly. He wasn't in the mood for small talk. He'd tried to pump Harris for information, but the normally affable deputy was tense, lips shut tighter than an oyster.

"A long time. Normally, they'd just bring the body in," the examiner said conversationally, "but the logistics out here are tricky. Must make it a challenge to live here."

"It's been pleasant enough," Gordon said through his teeth, "until now."

Janson gave up and spoke to his assistant in the back of the cart. "You've got the equipment kit, Rogers? They're bringing the rest by helicopter."

Gordon tuned out the rest of the conversation which turned technical. After what felt to him like an eternity, they reached the gate that led to the preserve. Fitz, hands gloved in latex, was on the phone, waiting for them. Harris and two deputies arrived and cut around Gordon, snaking their cart through the rough path meant for the occasional hiker or bicycler. Fitz pocketed his phone, squeezed onto the back of Gordon's cart and they followed.

"Chopper's landing," Fitz said. "Don't want to take the guy out of here on a trailer for everyone to see."

"Gordon? You hearing me?" Fitz poked him in the back.

"Who d'you think it is?" Gordon said, concentrating on getting through the brush.

"If I knew that, I wouldn't have gotten you out here."

"Why me? I'm not the mayor of this place. I just run a restaurant." His nerves were frayed. The result of allowing himself to think things were getting back to normal only to get Fitz's phone call, which went right to his solar plexus.

"Because the only thing the guy had on him was a pack of matches from your place." Fitz was saying. "Figures he's been there at some point. You might recognize him. Or at least know when you last saw him."

"Oh." Gordon considered this. "Maybe. A lot of people come through my place. This one could have come in weeks or months ago. I don't keep a record, you know? How do you know it isn't someone who lives here?"

"I don't know. But," he prodded Gordon again, "if it is someone who lives here, you'll know him, too."

"I'm assuming the body hasn't been moved?" Janson spoke up before Gordon could react to this statement. "I'm also assuming you don't think this is accidental, or you wouldn't have called me out here. There was quite a contingent at the dock, by the way." He seemed to find this amusing.

"Nothing's been moved, Doc. We got the call from Palm Electric just about oh seven hundred. Harris and I were already out here so we were able to secure the scene almost immediately." There was a considerable pause, Gordon suspected, for his benefit. "Body hasn't been moved, but— Palm Electric spotted it by the turkey vultures." He let this pleasant image sink in. "It's just up around that bend ahead." He pointed toward a large stand of seagrapes. "Where it comes out on the beach."

They passed the seagrapes and the path opened up onto the Gulf. Harris and the two deputies were on shore, standing by a lump covered by a blue tarp, surrounded by yellow crime scene tape fluttering in the breeze. The water lapped about ten yards away.

"Water was almost up to his shoes when we found him," Fitz was leading the way, speaking to Janson. "Real high tide last night, they tell me. Going back out now."

They reached the sorry bundle. Janson and his assistant pulled back the tarp.

The vultures had done a pretty good job on the face, starting with the eyeballs. From what was left, it was likely his own mother wouldn't have recognized him. They'd started on the stomach and entrails, as the tattered cloth attested to, but the rest of him was intact, marinating in the heat.

Janson brushed at the flies buzzing on the head. They seemed to have materialized by the hundreds out of nowhere. "There's signs of blunt force trauma here," he ran fingers over a depression in the left temple. A police photographer was snapping away. Janson sat back on his heels. "You told me the body wasn't disturbed but it's been moved. Look there," he said sternly, pointing to the impressions in the sand, faintly visible despite the earlier rain.

"This is how he was found, Doc," Fitz said, "Utility guys swear they didn't touch a thing. Just got the birds off him and covered him up. Maybe the tide shifted him?"

"No," Janson looked around, pointed. "There's the high water mark. Tide never got up this far. Luckily for us." He proceeded with his examination, giving curt notes to Rogers, who tapped away on his iPad.

The chopper whirred noisily about a hundred yards away. Personnel approached with a stretcher and other medical paraphernalia.

Janson got up, brushing off his pants. "No ID. Hasn't been here that long—couple of days from the look of it. We don't need any of that," he yelled over to the chopper personnel. "Just the body bag and stretcher." He looked at the body again, then at Fitz. "He may have come off a boat. Coast Guard report anything?

"No." Fitz said.

"He have anything else on him? His left wrist," he indicated the left arm, lying at a grotesque angle in the sand, "has a tan line. Watch, most likely."

Fitz shook his head. "Nothing." He held out the matchbook. "Only this, like I said. In his left pocket." He dropped the matchbook into a plastic bag and sealed it, then swung around and looked at Gordon, who was staring keenly at the body. "Well? What about it? Recognize him?"

"Not his face. That's past praying for. But from the hair, build, clothes," he looked at Fitz with a curious expression on his face. "I'd say you've found Mr. Max Lopez. Or what's left of him. And what the hell he's doing out here I couldn't tell you. Last time anyone saw him was Thursday night, eating dinner at the restaurant. Alone."

CHAPTER 21

"Max Lopez," Fitz said thoughtfully. "You're sure?"

"I'm mainly going by the clothes," Gordon said. "Fletch reminded me he ate dinner in *Gordon's* on Thursday, actually. I never spoke to him." He hesitated. "Fletch also told me he heard that Lopez and Sharpe—the builder handling his house—had a pretty good argument Thursday afternoon. For what that's worth."

Fitz grunted and made note of this. "There was a phone number written inside the matchbook," he said. He handed Gordon a piece of paper with the number on it. "Recognize it?"

It was a local exchange, but Gordon didn't know it and said so. "Have you tried calling?"

"Yeah. Disconnected." Fitz turned as Janson came over to them, perspiring heavily, pulling off his gloves. The stretcher was being loaded on the helicopter.

"I'll call you with the results as soon as I've finished the autopsy," Janson was saying. "Can't be definite but it doesn't look like he drowned. If I had to guess, he was dead or close to it when he went in the water." He waved over to the men gesturing from the helicopter which had started up with a roar.

"Rogers and I will ride back on the chopper. Done about all we can here." He gave a nod and, ducking low, ran through the storm of dust to board.

"I'll go back with you," Fitz said to Gordon. "Harris and the others can wind things up here."

They climbed into Gordon's cart and started back toward the road. They drove in silence, heat rising in waves around them, until they were about halfway to the restaurant.

"Keep the name to yourself until we ID him formally," Fitz finally said. "Word is already out we have a body on the beach. Press has been badgering the office all morning. I'll deal with them when I get back to the mainland."

"Don't think you'll have that long," Gordon said, recalling the activity on the dock earlier. "I'd say it's a fair bet they're already on the island. And, unless they were in a coma, anyone who lives here knows there's been trouble. Had everything but a ten piece band on the dock this morning. By the way, did Palm Electric get the power back on? I didn't see them out there."

"Yeah. Harris got statements from them and they finished up pretty quickly. They were in a hurry to get the hell out of here. Not that I can blame them." He sighed. "I'd like to believe this some sort of accident, Strange, but from the look of that temple, I don't think so. Don't think you do, either. No," he wiped his face with a cloth, "looks to me like Hogge is in for a nasty dose of the real world." A bright red cardinal darted past them as they drove, coming to rest in a thicket of Brazilian pepper. "A pity. Pretty place, peaceful. But people

are people everywhere. Once you set things in motion... ." He
let the rest of the sentence hang.

Gordon nodded glumly. "*You cannot change what has
happened*," Marvelita had said last night. And where you
might be able to rationalize someone taking a beating, albeit
mistakenly, there was no getting around a corpse. Fitz hadn't
actually said "murder," but he would soon enough. There was
also no getting around the fact that every sign pointed back to
Hogge, to someone who lived among them. And, if the two
incidents were connected, someone growing more dangerous
by the day.

They were near the restaurant now. The Gulf sparkled
blue between the trees on their left. A few fishing boats dotted
the water. For them, it was just another Saturday, Gordon
thought. He stopped the cart under the shade of a giant
Strangler Fig anchored to the earth by a maze of aerial roots.
Boats. That reminded him. "Last night about ten when Fletch
and I got back to my house we heard a boat. Fletch spotted it,
said it was running fast, without lights across the Pass. Fletch
thought it might be drunk tourists." He eyed Fitz, who nodded.

"Could be connected to this here," the sheriff said. He was
making notes again. "I'll know more once Janson confirms the
manner and time of death. And when I have a better idea of
just who this Max Lopez was." He leaned back, balancing one
foot on the dash. "What can you tell me about him?"

"Almost nothing," Gordon said frankly. "First I heard of
him was about a year ago, when he bought that property and
started building a house. Heard he was from Miami, heard he
was in banking. How true that is I couldn't tell you." He
hesitated, then said, "From what I heard of his behavior at the

restaurant, he's not someone I would have particularly cared for. Arrogant, smug. You said he was in the habit of renting that house, the one where the attack happened, to stay in when he came out here to check on his construction job. So he must know Hollows. Which makes me wonder why he'd come to my place for dinner—didn't mix with any of my regulars."

"Maybe he liked the food better at your place," Fitz said sardonically, flicking a bug off the windshield. "Or maybe he was looking for someone. Or avoiding someone. There's a mess of questions he could answer if he wasn't in a body bag. Starting with why he left me that message." He was frustrated. "This is going to be a bitch of a case to run down. Not a popular guy but hasn't been here long, from what you've told me, which leaves anyone and no one with a motive, and opportunity by the bucket thanks to a blackout." He shook his head. "Maybe I should've gone to Naples after all," he muttered.

"Naples?" Gordon looked at him, mystified. "What's that got to do with anything?"

Fitz explained his conversation with Marly the morning the original call came in. "Which reminds me," he said, "I'd need to get home, get a change of clothes. Deal with Marly. I've had a dozen messages from her. Keeps asking me where it happened. Like that would do her any good. She's only been here a time or two. Guess I can't blame her for being curious, though."

Gordon said nothing. If he needed confirmation that Fitz was ignorant of Marly's history on the island, this was it. He looked at Fitz. Slouched against the seat, wide damp patches on his two-day old shirt where the material strained against his paunchy front, he cut anything but a dashing figure. With sudden sympathy for the sheriff, he thought about Costello. Well, he didn't have to go into Marly's history—that was her story to tell. But the rest of it could be important. He cleared his throat and plunged in.

"Speaking of curious, there was a fight at the bar on Thursday night. I'd forgotten about it until Marvelita reminded me. Didn't seem important at the time since I didn't know the guys involved. But last night Fletch told me he did, at least from my description. Fletch left my place early Thursday," Gordon explained. "He says it was Costello, the one who used to own that house where the attack was." He left it there.

"Costello?" Fitz turned to him, alert. "You sure?"

"Fletch was sure. Unless there's another guy running around that matches his description, missing fingers off his left hand. Fletch knew him as Two-Finger Louie. Tough customer. He might not be using that name now," he added drily.

"Was he with anyone?"

"No, unless you count the two guys he had the fight with. One threw a drink in his face. I tossed him and his buddy out, and then told Costello he had to leave, too. Rules are rules, I told him. Wasn't happy about it—they never are, and it's never their fault. Insisted he was meeting someone. I figured he was just saying that so I'd let him stay. But now I'm not so sure. Anyhow," he shrugged, "Like I said, I didn't exactly know who he was at the time and didn't pay much attention. He looked like trouble and I just wanted him gone." He looked at Fitz who was chewing on his lower lip, thinking. "From their description Fletch thinks the other two might have been from Sharpe's crew. But again, he wasn't there, so he couldn't say for sure," he finished up.

"What time was this," Fitz had his pad out again.

"Nine-ish. Dinner was winding up. The German guy had come in not long before that and he was the last customer."

"You see how he left? Was it by boat? Or did he have a cart?"

Gordon sighed, "I really couldn't tell you. I just wanted him gone. Once he left, I didn't think about him again. Bar fights out here can get ugly. I had one get out of control ten years ago when I first opened. Then I wised up." He started the cart and drove slowly to the restaurant. Fitz was silent for the rest of the ride, deep in thought.

By the time they got back to the dock the emergency vehicles were gone. Only the green and white Sheriff's boat remained. Fletch's boat wasn't back yet, so he was still out on the water. A charter, most likely. The one addition was a camera crew with a tripod set up on the dock pointing toward the restaurant. They were taping a gangly youth of about twenty, dressed in a hot looking suit and lurid tie, talking animatedly into a microphone. As he'd suspected, Gordon thought with irritation, the press had arrived.

He said as much to Fitz, who groaned in resignation and said, "It's private property. Can't you get rid of them?"

"I could," Gordon said slowly, "but they'll just move down to the beach. That's public. Plus, they'll be pissed at having to do it. Why don't I park and we'll go in the back way," he suggested, "that way you can use my office, clean up, get a statement together."

Fitz agreed readily. They parked in the back and ducked into the restaurant through the kitchen. Fitz went straight to the office. Gordon peeked into the dining room. There were a handful of tables occupied, but the place was pretty empty. Not surprising. It was the mid-morning lull. He walked over to

Marvelita, who was cooking a few *sandwiches cubanos* on the grill, old school, weighed down by bricks covered in tinfoil.

"For take out," she said briskly. From her tone he could tell that she was miffed that he'd left without speaking to her first. Likely she was bursting with curiosity, but she'd die before admitting it. Knowing her silent treatment could last for weeks if he pretended not to notice, Gordon put his hands on her shoulders and said, without preamble, "I'm sorry, Marvelita. Fitz insisted I not speak to anyone before I left." It was half true, anyway. He felt guilty, realizing he had left her alone to deal with no power and the breakfast trade. "I should have been here to help you."

She flipped the cubanos, pressing them down with the wide spatula with perhaps a little more force than was necessary, then turned around and looked at him scornfully. "That was no big problem. There were not many for breakfast. Mostly they just came for gossip, to see all that," she waved the spatula toward the dock. "They were, of course, all asking for you, but I told them you were with the sheriff and that was all I knew." Her tone was reproachful. "You didn't trust me to hold my tongue, knowing I would find out anyway. Why? Who would I tell, besides you?" She was hurt.

Gordon opened his mouth to answer and closed it again. Why indeed? He realized, sheepishly, that it had less to do with Fitz's instructions than his own misguided chauvinism. The instinct to protect the womenfolk from trouble. Come to think of it, the protection instinct was what Marvelita constantly exercised on him. The realization made him laugh. "Of course it wasn't a question of trust, Lita. I didn't want to upset you. How many times have you kept things from me for the same reason?"

Her eyes flickered for an instant, and she turned back to the grill. "That is another thing entirely," she said maddeningly. "The things I don't tell you come to me here," she said, pointing to her forehead and her heart. "They are *not* about dead bodies on a beach." There was still some sarcasm in her tone but the hurt was gone. "So," she said pointedly, "who was it?"

"The banker from Miami. Max Lopez. He's building a house here, or was," he said promptly, ignoring his promise to Fitz. "And we're supposed to keep that quiet for now."

"Of course." She tilted her head to one side, thinking. "You asked me about him yesterday. I don't know him, but you recognized him, yes?"

"From his clothes, mainly. The buzzards had gotten to him," he waved a hand, not wanting to go into it. "He was in the restaurant Thursday night, according to Fletch. Blue silk shirt, dark hair—built a little like Fletch, actually."

"Oh yes, I remember. A big noise, he thought himself. He was very rude." Her eyes darkened, as they did when she was excited. "But his name isn't Max. It is Jaime."

"No," Gordon was puzzled, "Fletch was certain—he knows him."

"Perhaps he does," she said, eyes flashing, "but I heard him make a phone call while he was here. He complained about his dinner and I came to see what the trouble was," she explained, "*estupido*, telling me it was trout and not tripletail—and he was on his phone, calling someone. He said "*Hola, soy Jaime—nos vemos en la casa, nueve y media—* Hello, it's Jaime—" she started to translate.

"We'll see each other at the house at nine thirty," Gordon finished up. "Did he say anything else?"

"No," her annoyance returned, "he hung up and sent me away, said the fish was okay, it was fresh enough. A man like him just likes to complain. It makes him feel important." She shrugged. "And now he is dead," she said matter-of-factly, "so all that does not matter." She turned back to the grill.

Presumably, death forgave all insults, Gordon thought, momentarily amused. Then the faint smile that had come to his lips faded as he watched Marvelita competently transfer the cubanos into aluminum take out containers. All very well, but who was Max talking to? Which house did he mean? And why the hell had he called himself Jaime?

CHAPTER 22

Fitz emerged from Gordon's office looking clean-shaven and a bit less rumpled. "I borrowed your electric razor," he said apologetically, "and some Bay Rum. Nice stuff," he rubbed his chin and grinned. "Guess I'm ready to go talk to them now. Oh," he stopped in his progress toward the door and came over to Gordon, "almost forgot. Got an email about you this morning," he peered at his iPad, scrolling through it. "Anonymous. Not the first one I've had, by the way," he eyed Gordon for a reaction.

"There have been a few of those going around the island," Gordon said, amused. "Signed 'A Concerned Citizen'? Lots of capital letters? What am I supposed to have done this time?" He gave a short laugh.

Fitz cocked his head. "That's right. Then you know who's sending 'em?"

"I couldn't prove it, but I have a pretty good idea."

Fitz looked down at his iPad. "This one demands to know why someone with your background has been taken into the confidence of the police. Doesn't say what your background is supposed to be, incidentally. Also suggests your liquor license should be investigated, and asks why, quote, 'that boat jockey, Fletcher James does so many after-hours runs for you into town.' "Also," he looked a little embarrassed, "makes a few suggestive remarks about Marvelita. Basically implies a lot but stops just short of accusation. Sound familiar?"

"Very," Gordon said with grim humor. "Whoever it is specializes in innuendo and has a nasty talent for cherry-picking facts and half-truths and making the whole canard seem almost convincing. This is a new tack, though. Guess whoever it is doesn't like your choice of deputy."

"So who do you think it is?" Fitz persisted.

Gordon hesitated. He was fairly certain it was Van Cross, but without proof he was reluctant to level the accusation. He had enough trouble with Cross as it was and likely more to come. Finally he said, "I thought it might be Alan Hollows at first. He wasn't happy about the competition when I got here. Even less so when I refused to do business with him. His idea of business," Gordon added, cynically. "But he doesn't fit the profile. He's mean-natured and dangerous, but he gets what he wants by steamrolling, flexing muscle. You know, 'nothing personal, just business.' These are personal. Vindictive." He paused. "I've had a heap of trouble from Van Cross the last few years. Complaints about the restaurant, that sort of thing. I have a drawer full of correspondence with local and state officials following up on his trumped up charges. I'm guessing he's behind it. An anonymous smear campaign to bolster his cause—whatever the hell that is. Damned if I know." He shrugged again. "Email makes it easy. Anyone can hide behind that."

Gordon scratched the side of his face, making up his mind. Finally, he added, "Cross came snooping around here Thursday night—has a habit of doing that from time to time—Marvelita told me he saw the fight and left looking mighty unhappy." He pointed to Fitz's iPad. "Your email is probably a result of that."

Fitz made a face. "I know the type," he said, "We get a lot of crap like that. Most of it is nonsense. Sounds like you have your hands full with the guy. You ever confront him about it?" He waited.

Gordon half smiled. "I can deal with Cross," he said. "He's a type. Eventually he'll dry up or find some other issue to get twisted over."

Fitz nodded, satisfied.

Gordon glanced out the door. The young man with the microphone was walking up the path with determination, camera crew in tow. "I think your fan club has arrived," he said, pointing. "When you're through with them, let's talk. We've got bigger fish to fry at this point than 'Concerned Citizen.'" He didn't want to drop Marvelita's bombshell on Fitz just before the sheriff spoke to the press. Once they were squared away, he'd fill Fitz in and they could put their heads together over this latest complication.

Fitz nodded, tucked his shirt in and went out to face the music.

Gordon went back and poked his head in the kitchen. The cubanos smelled awfully good and he was starving.

Marvelita anticipated him, as usual, and came over with a large, freshly made sandwich, still hot from the grill. "I will be busy with lunch soon. Many more boats today, probably because of that." She gestured toward the reporter who was busily interviewing the sheriff.

Gordon sat down with the plate and dug in. Cuban sandwiches could be heavy and greasy, but Marvelita's were light, crisp. In a moment she returned and without a word put a bottle of bourbon, glasses, and a pitcher of ice water on the table.

"Good woman," Gordon smiled up at her through a mouthful of sandwich. "You might make one for Fitz. He hasn't eaten anything, either. He's coming back once he's through out there."

"I might," she agreed, giving a hint of smile before vanishing back into the kitchen. So all was forgiven.

Between bites of sandwich, Gordon pondered the information that had come to light since Thursday—all the secrets that had awakened, as Marvelita put it—sorting out what was relevant from what really just came under the heading of gossip. That was the trouble with too much information. After a while, you could connect the dots to form any picture. Which was worse than no picture at all.

CHAPTER 23

Gordon finished his sandwich, pushed back his chair and stretched his legs out, a bourbon on ice in hand. He was deep in thought when the kitchen door squeaked open. He looked up expecting Fitz, but it was Jadyn Hayes. She came over, pulled out a chair and without so much as a hello, sank into it, eyes burning in her face.

"I need your advice, Gordon." Tension was evident in every word. She bent her head to light a cigarette. Her hands weren't too steady.

"Van Cross threatened to shoot me this morning," she said evenly, brushing her hair off her face.

Whatever Gordon was expecting, this wasn't it. If it had been anyone else sitting in front of him he would have suspected gross exaggeration. But Jadyn was a pretty straight arrow. She was one of the few residents who had Marvelita's approval, chiefly, Gordon suspected, because she was strong-willed and spoke her mind, as anyone who got her goat readily found out. And Jadyn, like Marvelita, possessed intuition bordering on second sight, was able to read people with remarkable accuracy. Gordon put his glass down and cleared his throat. "Why don't you tell me what happened?" His tone betrayed nothing. He offered the bottle but she shook her head.

"I went for my walk this morning, after the storm passed over. The tide was very high around the pass, you know, where the docks come out?"

He nodded. The medical examiner had mentioned the tide. That brought up a picture of the burden under the tarp. He shook it off.

"Well, I had to go over the docks or swim under them. Nobody minds if you're not using them for fishing or hanging out there. When I got to Cross's place, he came out of the bushes pointing a shotgun at me. Accused me of trespassing. He threatened to shoot me."

Gordon made a wry face and hastened to reassure her. "He behaves like a jackass sometimes, Jadyn, but I really think he's just throwing his weight around. Did the same thing to me yesterday morning because my cart was a foot or so in his driveway." He thought, but didn't add, and he's going to get his ass kicked pretty soon if he keeps this up. He looked at Jadyn sympathetically. "I'll have Fitz speak to him." he said. "He can't threaten people with a gun every time he gets a gas pain."

Jadyn's lips were drawn tight. She shook her head slowly. "It's more than that. You know me well enough. Would I run to you if it wasn't serious? He looked like a maniac. Hair and clothes a mess, bloodshot eyes. I figured he was really drunk. He was making all kinds of wild statements." She looked at him to see if he was taking her seriously. "He accused me of spying on him. Asked me if you sent me to spy on him. Gordon," she leaned forward and rested her thin arms on the table. "Something's very wrong. He was way paranoid." She hesitated. "It reminded me of someone having a psychotic episode, or at least becoming delusional. He wouldn't let me leave. He kept that gun pointed at me." She looked down at the table, clearly shaken at the memory.

"Wouldn't let you leave?" Gordon sat up, frowning.

"No," she said quietly. "He kept saying he wasn't done with me yet, demanding to know who sent me and why I was spying on him." She paused and took a deep breath. "I finally got away by apologizing and promising not to make any trouble." Tears of frustration filled her eyes. "I don't know if I'll be able to even walk past that property again," she said, furious. "I can't let him get away with that. And I just don't know what to do about it." She wiped a hand across her face and looked at him intently.

"Fitz is due back in here any minute," Gordon said slowly. "I think you should tell him everything. Let him decide how to handle it."

"You know Van," Jadyn said angrily. "He'll have sobered up and claim I'm exaggerating or making it up. But I swear to you, I don't scare easy. That man is a menace and he's going to hurt someone." She looked outside and saw Fitz and the camera crew just beyond the door.

"They're here about that tourist that got attacked?"

Gordon stared at her. "Don't you know?" He'd assumed she like everyone else had heard about the discovery on State land and, rattled by that, attached more significance to Van's outburst than necessary.

"Know what?"

"Didn't you wonder what all the commotion was about on the dock this morning?"

"I didn't see any commotion. I didn't see anyone. After that walk I went straight home. This is first I've been out." The statement seemed to depress her. "You know me, Gordon. I'm not in the loop—last to know anything around here. What's going on?"

"A body was discovered on State land this morning by the Palm Electric crew." He hesitated. "A man. They're trying to identify him."

"Oh God," Jadyn's eyebrows shot up. "He wasn't...Was he shot?" She looked ill as she said it.

"No, no," Gordon put his hand over hers. "Looks like he might have drowned, or—" He cut himself off just in time. "They'll know after the autopsy."

"Jesus, Gordon," Jadyn wrapped her arms around herself, shivering. "What's going on on this island? It's like we're in some sort of weird vortex. Maybe that's why Van has gone off the deep end." She glanced up at him and away, quickly. "I told Marvelita about Van when I came in. She needs to know."

As Gordon started to respond to this, Fitz came in, slamming the front door behind him. He was beginning to look rumpled again after his stint in the sun. "They ask the same question fifty different ways, like I'm going to tell them something I haven't told them," he fumed. "How long can you beat a dead horse?" He mopped his brow and looked from Gordon to Jadyn. "I'm interrupting something," he said.

"Why don't you eat the sandwich Marvelita's bringing over," Gordon suggested, as she materialized with a plate and a coke, having heard Fitz's entrance. "Jadyn has a pretty odd story to tell. I think you should hear it. And I think you're going to have to do something about it."

Fitz didn't look too pleased but brightened at the sight of food and drink. "Awright," he said, resigned, "I'm listening. Shoot."

Jadyn rolled her eyes at his unfortunate choice of words— the first glimmer of amusement she'd shown—and launched into her story.

CHAPTER 24

"Upsetting as it is," Fitz said, wiping a few crumbs from his mouth when Jadyn had finished speaking, "all I can really do at this point is give him a warning." He had his pad out and was making notes. "Unless—you're filing a formal complaint? Pressing charges?" He asked, skewing a glance up at her.

"Ye—es. Yes. I think I should," Jadyn said, looking at Gordon, who was silent, frowning. "If I don't, won't he just get worse and think he can get away with anything?"

Fitz was noncommittal. "I'll make a report on it and pay him a visit. There were no witnesses?"

She shook her head, looking glum, as if she knew where this was heading.

"Gonna be a case of his word, your word. Unfortunately, he didn't actually fire the weapon, so…"

"Yes," Jadyn cut in, exasperated, "if he'd actually shot me, or better, killed me, then you'd have something to sink your teeth into!"

"Not exactly what I meant," Fitz said, uncomfortably, but the look on his face betrayed that he was likely thinking along those very lines. "Just that I don't guess he's going to admit to all this." He turned to Gordon. "You want to press charges, too? I'll have a better case if there were two of you." He looked down at his pad, thinking. "He make a habit of this sort of thing?" He directed the question at Gordon.

Gordon hesitated, weighing his words. Finally, he said, "Van's a crank, but he's never threatened anyone with a gun before. He shot at a wild pig once that got on his property and was eating his landscaping, but he missed. I've never really considered him dangerous, just a nuisance. But now," he shook his head at looked at Fitz, "I'm not sure I can say that, especially given the item on the beach this morning. Maybe there's no connection," he picked up his glass, "and maybe there is. I want to know what's making him paranoid, why he thinks we're spying on him. Not sure we're going to find that out if we press charges." He put up a hand as Jadyn started to protest, furious. "On the other hand, if we *threaten* to press charges, you might have a little leverage in getting him to talk to you."

He eyed Fitz speculatively. "Maybe you can ask him what he was doing here the other night, too. He's a slippery customer. By now he'll be expecting you, so he'll have his game face on and try to make us both look like fools. You'll have to press him." Gordon looked as if he wondered if Fitz could do that. "What if I go with you. In my official capacity," he offered, only half kidding. "That'll would really piss him off. Poke him enough with a stick, he might just lose his temper and let something slip." He sat back. "Besides, I'd enjoy doing that," he admitted. "Just a suggestion."

Fitz mulled it over. "Not a bad idea. We both go. Better to have a witness if nothing else." There was a pause, then he said, "If you're right about those emails, and given this here, this is a guy who likes to hide. Behind regulations, threats, letters. Direct action seems out of character. But something's gotten him going." He frowned. "Besides, I don't need another loose cannon roaming around this island right now, especially in the middle of a—" He remembered Jadyn just in time. "An unexplained death," he finished up.

"You were going to say 'murder' weren't you?" Jadyn demanded, lighting a cigarette. "You don't have to sugar coat it for me."

Fitz was impassive. "Haven't had the autopsy results yet. Nothing's definite." He looked at Gordon, accusingly, obviously wondering how many cats he'd let out of the bag.

"I told Jadyn that a body was discovered on the beach and you're trying to identify him. Everyone on the island knows that much by now," Gordon said mildly. He turned to Jadyn. "I don't think you'll have any more trouble with Cross once Fitz and I have spoken to him. Why don't you go home and try to put this morning behind you? I'll give you a call later today and see how you're doing, let you know how things went."

"Okay. I knew there wasn't much you could do but maybe a visit from the law will be enough." Jadyn stood up. She didn't look happy, but some of her normal fight had returned. Looking from one to the other of them, a hand on her hip, she said, "I can promise you this, though. If I catch that man when he's not carrying, he's going to be singing soprano. And if he tries to sue me, I'll slap him with a sexual assault charge. His word, my word," she said sweetly to Fitz. "Time Mr. Cross got a little of his own back!" She stubbed her cigarette out in the tray in emphasis and left, the door swinging shut behind her.

Fitz stared at Gordon once she was out of earshot. "Think she'd do it? Or is it that just anger talking?"

Gordon raised his eyebrows. "Oh, she'd do it—she may be rattled right now, but I told you, Jadyn knows how to handle herself. She's not going to knock on his door but if I were Van Cross I'd think twice about running my mouth in her company." He swallowed the rest of his drink. "He's picked the wrong time for these antics. Everyone's on edge here as it is. Likely to be more so now."

Fitz agreed, looking grim. "Community like this," he waved a hand, "you have your tensions, disagreements, but everyone gets by. Violence upsets the balance, makes everyone jumpy. Add murder—which is what we're dealing with, I'm pretty sure—and unless it's cleared up soon, everything comes apart, fast. That's why I need you here." He stopped, rubbed the back of his neck. "Look Strange, I think you might be willing to look the other way if someone who had something coming to him got it—say a kick to the balls. But I don't think you'd condone murder. Am I right about that?" He spoke casually, but his look was serious.

"Of course," Gordon said without hesitation. "Why even ask?"

"Because you live with these people. They're your neighbors. A lot of them are your friends. Now, it may turn out that whoever did this is someone you don't care about. That's fine. What happens if it turns out to be a friend. Say, like Mr. James?" He said it half joking, but he was serious.

"I see what you're saying," Gordon said slowly, but he wasn't thinking about Fletch. He was thinking about Marly.

How certain would Fitz be of his own actions if she turned out to be involved somehow? How certain was he if it came to it? Fairly certain.

Thirty years ago he had faced that very issue and in the end, there was no question of what he had to do. Sadness, grief, disbelief, anger—all those things, yes. They came back to him now remembering the woman he thought he knew, the woman he loved—his wife, standing in their apartment, mind addled by drugs and alcohol and a worsening mental illness he refused to see, telling him she'd killed their only child, Cassandra, a beautiful girl of seven, for "talking back to her one time too many," as she put it. He could have given in to her pleas to blame it on someone else, like she begged him to, but he didn't. He knew that she would never be safe again, to herself or anyone else around her. The only thing that saved him, saved him still, he could only describe as a numbing cold that cauterized his nerve endings and sent its icy fingers deep into his heart. He'd already faced the worst life had to offer. Whatever Hogge served up would be pale by comparison. But Fitz didn't need to know all this, sitting there watching him intently, waiting for an answer. Gordon cleared his throat and shifted forward in the chair.

"Look," he spread out his hands, "we really don't know what we're dealing with yet. But I can tell you that if it turns out he was murdered, and not, say, some sort of accident, then whoever is responsible needs to be caught. Whoever it is. This is a good place, with good people. If someone's gone rotten...." He shook his head. "They're unsafe. That's unacceptable."

"You seem to know something about it." Fitz looked at him, questioning.

"I do. It's in the past. Another life. And that's all you need to know."

Fitz looked as if he'd like to know a good deal more, but he let it go. "Well, I had to ask. Once the autopsy is in, likely the Sheriff's office will send a detective out here to handle the investigation," his tone was dubious. He grimaced, rubbed his neck again. "But without any local knowledge, no connections—not sure how far that's going to get us. Besides, whoever they send isn't going to stay out here too long. I need you in the picture. Someone who speaks the lingo. I wanted to make sure you're willing to help, wherever it leads."

"Wherever it leads," Gordon repeated gravely. "Speaking of help, there's something you don't know, pretty important." He went through what Marvelita had overheard in the restaurant Thursday night, with Fitz writing it all down.

"And she has no idea who he was talking to or what house he meant?"

"No, just that he called himself 'Jaime' and made an appointment for 9:30 at a house. Can't even tell if he meant that night, the next morning. Or whether it was even here, on the island."

Fitz frowned and bit his thumbnail, considering it all. "He had no phone on him so no help there. We'll see what turns up on his background. Gotta be someone to notify, maybe in Miami. I'll know more tomorrow. By the way," he asked casually, hunched over his notes, "where's your pal? Fletcher? Harris said his boat wasn't at the dock this morning."

Gordon wasn't taken in by Fitz's conversational tone. But, to be fair, the man had to do his job and until a few things got sorted out, everyone was under the gun. "He had an early charter—he told me last night," Gordon offered. "He usually gets back to the dock about 4." He looked up as three parties came through the door and checked his watch. Just before noon. The Saturday lunch rush was starting. "This place is going to fill up fast in the next 20 minutes," he said. "Why don't we pay Cross a visit? That way we can get back in time for you to talk to Fletch before you have to head back to the mainland." He was hoping Fitz still planned to go back. The past two days he felt like he'd been attached to the sheriff at the hip and it was wearing on him. Besides, he wanted to have a private word with Lattie without benefit of law enforcement, see what was troubling her.

Fitz looked like he'd like nothing less but agreed to the plan. "May as well get it out of the way. Don't expect anything useful will come of it, from what you've told me," he grumbled as the two men walked toward the door. "Guys like that aren't happy unless they're making trouble for somebody."

"Look on the bright side," Gordon said, as they pushed through the door into the searing noonday heat. "At least he's not one of *your* neighbors."

CHAPTER 25

Saturdays were turnover days for renters on Hogge. Carts hauling trailer loads of tourists arriving or departing competed for space on the narrow paths, along with cleaning carts studded with brooms, mops and sacks of clean or dirty linens.

"Does this go on every weekend?" Fitz asked, ducking to avoid having an eye put out by a broom handle hanging out of a passing cart.

"Pretty much," Gordon said as they rounded the north end of the island near Okum Pass. In the bay, a pod of dolphin surfaced and dipped in graceful arcs, to the delight of a dozen or so tourists who'd lined up on the sandy beach to video and photograph them with their cellphones. "It's low season now so it's not too bad. Try March or April if you really want to see busy."

Ahead lay Van Cross's pile, backlit by the sun in turreted splendor. They drove up to the property, manicured within an inch of its life, red mulch laid down in vast tracts. Fitz climbed out of the cart, pulled back the gate and started walking up the long, cobbled drive. Gordon followed in the cart, half expecting to see Van jump out from behind a tree, Hatfield-and-McCoy like. He parked, and they walked up three hot flights of stairs to the front door. Fitz rang the bell to signal their arrival. Unnecessary, Gordon guessed, as he was pretty sure he saw Van watching them from an upper window.

After a minute or so, Van opened the door. Clean shaven, dressed in pink Bermuda shorts, white polo shirt and sandals, hair neatly combed back, he looked almost boyish, the picture of affable respectability. Inside, behind him, they could hear the yowling of what sounded like a dozen cats.

"Sheriff Fitz, Mr. Strange?"

Gordon's eyebrows went up at the "Mister" but he said nothing.

"What can I do for you?" He'd stepped outside, closing the door behind him. "Have to keep the door shut. Can't let the kitties get out."

"Actually, we'd like a word with you, Mr. Cross. Mind if we come inside? It's hot out here." Fitz had already started to perspire, sweat beading on his wide forehead.

"Both of you?" Cross sounded surprised, but he kept his tone cordial. "I assumed Mr. Strange merely gave you a ride over."

"He's here in official capacity," Fitz said.

Cross's eyes flickered at this, but he opened the door. "Certainly. Just—if you wouldn't mind leaving your shoes in the hall?" He looked down pointedly at Gordon's bare feet.

They followed him in, and while Fitz bent down to unlace his shoes, Gordon looked past him with interest at the interior of the house. He'd never been in it before, although he'd heard about it.

The house was built in the typical upside-down style, living space on the top floor, which they were on, to give full advantage of the magnificent views of water and sky. Presumably so as not to compete with that, the entire interior was white: white walls, plush white carpeting, white tile, white sectional couches. Tables, counters—everything white. The only adornment was an enormous abstract painting hung over the white mantle at the far end of the room: three Siamese cats, the originals of which prowled about the place meowing loudly. The kitties, Gordon thought, bemused. At least the man had a soft spot for something.

"Can I offer you something?" Cross asked congenially, when they'd situated themselves in the living room. "White wine? Sprite? Seltzer? Water? I'm sorry," he said to Gordon condescendingly, "no Bourbon. Stains—but I can offer you Vodka if you need a drink."

Fitz waved off refreshment. "I'm sorry, Mr. Cross, but this isn't a social call. We've had a serious complaint—two in fact—and I'm here to follow up with you." He pulled out his pad, flipped it open.

"I saw the activity on his dock," Van indicated Gordon, "but I really can't tell you anything about that. Haven't been out this morning. More trouble with drunks?" He looked smug as he said it, shaking his head sadly at Fitz as if to say, 'this is the sort of thing we have to put up with.'

"Actually, no," Gordon interjected leaning back, one arm lounging on the back of the couch. "We're here, Van, because you, my friend, crossed a line." He waited, brought out his pack of cigars. "Mind if I smoke?" Knowing he would, of course.

"Yes, I mind. You can't smoke in here. It's bad for the kitties. You can go outside if you want to smoke." He was sounding less gracious now. He addressed himself to Fitz. "What's he talking about? You said you had complaints. Well, what are they?" He crossed his arms and stared at Fitz. One of the cats jumped on the mantle and was toying with a white porcelain figurine of a dolphin, trying, apparently, to smash it on the tile below. "Crackle, get down," Cross said sharply, half rising. The cat jumped down on an end table and lay down, kneading a doily with its paws.

Fitz was done with pleasantries. "This morning, just after sunrise," he read from his notes, "an island resident reports that you threatened to shoot her for walking over your dock. Furthermore, you held her there at gunpoint while you made accusations." He flipped back a few pages. "Friday morning, Mr. Strange here reports, you pointed a gun at him, threatening to shoot him if he didn't leave your property. You seem fond of both guns and threats, Mr. Cross. That's an unhealthy combination."

Two bright spots of color appeared on Van's cheeks. Otherwise, his face was as pale as the room itself. "That's a lie," he said angrily. "Furthermore, it's libelous."

"Slander," Gordon said lazily, "you never seem to be able to keep them straight."

Cross glared at him, continued. "I asked Ms. Hayes to cease and desist from trespassing on my dock, which she has done numerous times, as she well knows. I did have my shotgun out because I was cleaning it, but I never threatened her with it and certainly didn't hold her at gunpoint." He stopped to disentangle the cat's claws from the doily, which the animal appeared to be in the process of shredding. "And you, Strange—"

No "Mister" this time Gordon noted, amused.

"You know very well you were trespassing as well. You were halfway up my driveway. Knowing your habits, I assumed you were drunk," he added, nastily. "I did point a gun at you but only after you got off your cart and threatened my person." He was affronted, his face a masterpiece of righteous indignation. "In fact," he addressed Fitz again, "I intended to contact your office and lodge my own complaint. Only reason I didn't was because it wouldn't have been neighborly. Now, I wish I had. I'd like to do so now." Another cat had joined Crackle, and the pair of them began to claw at the sides of a white leather ottoman.

Before Fitz could respond, Gordon broke in, watching the cats wreak havoc on the furniture. "What were you doing at my restaurant on Thursday night, Cross? Marvelita said you came snooping in through the back. You weren't there for dinner."

Cross hesitated a split second before firing back. "It's a public restaurant. I have a right to come in if I want to."

"Through the front door, like everyone else, yes," conceded Gordon, "but you snuck in the back." He was deliberately offensive. "And the next morning you were extraordinarily belligerent, even for you. See something you didn't like?" He waited.

Cross was angry, struggling to keep his temper in check. "I certainly did!" His voice went shrill. "A bunch of drunks fighting at the bar and you in the middle of it. You allow Sharpe's crew to drink at your bar, you get what you deserve!" He was red from the neck up now.

"So you recognized the combatants, Mr. Cross," Fitz put in coolly, taking out his pen. "I'd like to get confirmation of that," he said as an aside to Gordon, "And did you see who they had the fight with?"

Cross opened his mouth, shut it. Then said, "No. I mean, I saw him but didn't know him. Some lout with a thick neck. Someone should pull your liquor license," he spat at Gordon, "and maybe the Sheriff's office should think twice before taking someone with your past into its confidence."

Fitz looked up quickly, interested. "You think so?" he said, taking out his cellphone, scrolling. "I had an anonymous email suggesting those very things. Same wording, too. Might that have come from you?" He gave Cross a hard stare.

Instantly, Cross's demeanor changed. He was admitting nothing. "I've heard that comment from plenty of people on this island. And a lot of decent folks are fed up with his establishment." His tone was smug again, but there was a wary look in his eye.

"Why do you think I'm spying on you, Van?" Gordon lobbed the question in, hoping to wipe the look off his face. He succeeded, partially.

"What do you mean?"

"Spying on you. You accused me and Jadyn of spying on you. Said, in fact, that I sent her there to spy on you. Why would I do that?" He looked at Van innocently.

A third cat entered the room and curled around Cross's feet, complaining loudly.

Cross looked momentarily disoriented, collecting his thoughts. Taking advantage of the silence, Fitz spoke up.

"Mr. Cross, charges have been made. You deny them. I have to tell you both parties are preparing to press ahead.

Given what's happened on this island in the past two days, I have to take all this pretty seriously." Without missing a beat, he said, "Where were you on Friday morning from sunrise until 8a.m.?"

"Here. Asleep." Van said. He looked startled by the question.

"And Friday night? The night of the power outage?"

"At home. Taking care of the kitties."

"Any witnesses?" Fitz was busy writing.

"No," Van's tone was becoming shrill again. "And I don't appreciate what you are implying!"

"Now why would you say that?" Fitz's voice was deceptively bland.

"Just—it's that…" Cross was beginning to sputter. "Everyone knows what happened at that house on Friday morning. And all the emergency vehicles this morning… Word is you found a body."

"A few minutes ago you asked Mr. Strange here if all the commotion was more drunks. Seems like you knew what it was about all along." Fitz got up and looked out the large bay window. "Can't see his dock from here. You weren't at the restaurant this morning," he eyed Gordon, who shook his head in confirmation. "So how did you find out?"

"It's a small island. Everyone knew about it by mid-morning. Someone told me."

"Who?" Fitz shot the question at him.

Cross looked at him. It was apparent that he was doing a rapid mental calculation.

"I don't remember." He finally said.

"Someone call you?" Fitz persisted. Gordon wondered where he was going with this line of questioning but didn't interfere.

"Yes. That is—no. No it wasn't a phone call. Someone passing by mentioned it."

"Would that be before or after you encountered Ms. Hayes?" Fitz asked.

Cross was getting a cornered look.

"We need to check on all these things," Fitz said idly, "The detective coming out will likely be asking everyone the same thing." He waited.

"I heard it on the police band radio if you must know. I monitor it."

"So why all the subterfuge? It's not illegal. Lots of people do it. Were you monitoring the radio on Friday morning, too? When the call came in about the attack?"

"Yes." Now Cross just looked relieved. "I heard that call come in. That's why I was worried when you suddenly showed up on my property," he said to Gordon.

Fitz was thumbing through his notes, head down. Without looking up, he said, "But Mr. Strange here was on your property before that call came in." Now he looked up, frowning. "You want to get your facts straight, Mr. Cross?" His voice was like steel. "You've changed them about four times while I've been sitting here. I told you these charges are going to be investigated. You'll have to answer them. Better you tell me whatever it is you're holding back. Don't bother to deny it. You know something or you're hiding something. Either way, it could be dangerous."

The cats were on the sofa now, three pairs of piercing blue eyes fixed on their master. Cross pulled himself together.

"Sorry, there's nothing more I can tell you." Jaw set, he was staring past Fitz and Gordon, out the window. Finally, he turned to Gordon. "If you press charges, I'll take you to court," he said. But the fight had gone out of his voice.

"I have no more questions for now," Fitz said in official tones, getting up, ready to leave. "But I don't want any more trouble with guns being pointed at people," he said warningly, "or you're going to have to find someone to take care of them for a while." He pointed to the cats. "Don't bother," he waved Cross down, "we'll see ourselves out."

The two men left, shutting the door carefully behind them. Inside, the cat chorus had started up again.

CHAPTER 26

"Nice place he's got," Fitz said, surveying Cross's house and grounds as they backed out of the driveway. "Where did he get the money, do you know?"

Gordon explained Van's job as a fish spotter for Protiex. "They pay pretty well, from what I understand, and he's good at what he does. One of the best, apparently."

"Pay well, yes—but not that well," Fitz's gesture took in the entire compound. "How long's he been here?"

"He came right after the storm. Bought the place cheap— a lot of houses had considerable damage. That one took a bad hit being right on the water. Lots of folks bailed after Hurricane Charley. They didn't have the money or the stomach for repairs. It was like the wild west out here trying to get anything done. Not enough contractors, at least decent ones. All sorts of characters showed up for a while. Rumor was Hollows made a deal with a local prison for cheap labor. He claimed not, but you had to wonder. Some pretty rough crews. Head of one, a painter, had a young girl with him. Looked like a runaway." Gordon paused, remembering. "I heard they arrested him eventually in Cape Coral on a rape charge." He stopped the cart in the shade of some seagrapes. "Why were you so interested in who Cross talked to?"

Fitz didn't answer right away; he leaned back against the seat. "You know the saying 'the best defense is a good offense'?"

"Of course."

"Well, that's Mr. Cross's M.O. He's very good at it. I get the wind up with a guy like that. Usually they have something to hide. But no one ever gets around to what it is because they're so busy dodging all the random bullets— the accusations, insinuations. He's your anonymous emailer, by the way, no doubt about that. Used the exact same words objecting to your involvement."

"That hadn't escaped my attention," Gordon said sardonically. "Not much surprise there. I figured it was him."

"Anyhow," Fitz continued, "I asked him who he talked to precisely because it was an innocuous question—to most people. But he was evasive. Tells me he doesn't like to deal in specifics, especially when they pertain to him. So I pressed him on the times, too. Again, evasive."

"You think he's involved in the attack? Or Lopez's death?"

"He could be," Fitz conceded, "but all I know for certain is that he couldn't give a straight answer to a simple question. Was afraid to. Man does that, he's hiding something. What, I don't know—but I'll find out." He sighed. "What time is it?"

"Just about 1:30," Gordon said, glancing at his watch. "Fletch won't be back yet, if that's what you're thinking."

"I can talk to Mr. James over the phone. I'm inclined to take your word for his whereabouts at this point. Tell him to call me as soon as he gets in and we can cross him off the list. I need to get back to the mainland, see what they've found out about Mr. Lopez. Until we know that, we'll just be chasing shadows out here."

Gordon agreed and pointed the cart back to the dock. "Leaving anyone out here? Harris? One of the other deputies?"

"Not at this point. Detective will come out Tuesday morning, I figure. Think you can hold the fort for a few nights?" He half smiled at Gordon, but his tone was serious. "I don't expect any more trouble, but..." He waited for an answer.

"If you're talking about Cross, I can handle him," Gordon said, "with or without his shotgun. The contractors and their work crews aren't out here on weekends. They'll be back Monday morning. Hollows and Sharpe live on the mainland. You can catch up with them there." There was a long pause. "There are a few people I want to follow up with myself," he said, thinking of Lattie. "But none you'd be interested in. Just a few loose ends I'd like to tie up."

"Anything I should know?" The watchful look in Fitz's eye belied his casual tone.

"No. Not even speculation at this point." Gordon was firm. His concerns about Lattie were personal. They had no bearing on Fitz or his investigation. As for the rest, he needed to have a few hours to himself, to think, sort through the blizzard of information and gossip and figure out what, if anything, was important. Something he'd heard or seen in the past two days was nagging at him. At the moment, it was lost in all the noise. But it would come.

They'd reached the dock. It was a busy Saturday, as he'd suspected. Boats jammed every available slip and the lot was full of carts. He let Fitz out by the Sheriff's boat. "You'll call me when you have anything on Lopez?"

"Won't have the autopsy results," Fitz warned him. He climbed aboard his boat, started the engine.

"I'm less interested in that than I am in just who this Jaime, or Max, or whatever he's calling himself is. What he does in Miami. How he got here. You can dig deeper into all that than I can. Maybe Sharpe can give you something. He works for the guy. Or did. Also," he leaned forward on the steering wheel, "I think the reason Mr. Hollows gave you for thinking that attack was meant for him was awfully thin. Be curious to see what he comes up with when you question him further."

Fitz's eyes narrowed. He paused in undoing his docklines. "You want to tell me what you're thinking?"

"Nothing," Gordon said, exasperated. "Nothing and everything. That's the trouble." He started the cart and waved, heading back to the restaurant.

CHAPTER 27

With the sheriff on his way back to Palm, Gordon's plan was to pay Lattie a visit. First, he stopped to have a few words with Marvelita and to look in on this restaurant of his while he had the chance. He went in through the kitchen, which was bustling. Marvelita came over to him, replacing a few strands of hair that had come loose from the neat coil on her head.

"Jadyn told me about Mr. Loco," she said at once. "You left with the sheriff—to speak to him, yes? What did he say?"

"Denied everything, of course, or tried to." Gordon frowned. "He's holding back on something, though. Fitz was sure of it. When we left him, he was pretty subdued. I don't think he'll make any more trouble."

"For now," Marvelita said darkly. "I don't trust him. He lives alone. With cats." Marvelita was deeply, unreasonably, suspicious of cats, a feeling rooted in centuries of superstition and local custom, rather than any personal experience. Gordon didn't know she knew about Van's cats. Then, there wasn't much she didn't know.

"Three of them. Siamese," he said. "Noisy, interfering little beggars. Surprised they haven't taken his house apart. He seems to like them, though." The kitties. He smiled again at the term.

"Of course he does," she said with contempt. "They are troublemakers, like him." It was a pretty fair assessment, under the circumstances.

He waved off Van, shifted to the matter at hand. "The sheriff's gone back to the mainland. There's a detective coming out Tuesday morning, but until then…" He hesitated, looking at her.

"He left you with the babies," she said, eyes snapping.

"Holding the baby, yes, sort of," Gordon said. "We don't expect more trouble, though. I think the attack and this—death—are connected. But not to anyone here. At least," he corrected himself, "not to anyone who's here right now. Doesn't figure." This last he said more to himself.

Marvelita shrugged impatiently. "Who expects trouble? That's what trouble is, what you don't expect." She looked up at him, a hint of anxiety in her dark eyes. "Is there still danger?" She kept her voice low.

"I don't think so, no." Gordon said. But he wasn't entirely convinced himself. "There is no danger to us," he said reassuringly. That much he was fairly sure of, unless Van Cross surprised them all and went off his rocker.

Marvelita didn't look happy, but she didn't press him, turning the conversation to business. "There is a full house this afternoon. Many, many boats. Some people from the island but mostly tourists. The generators kept everything fresh and the power is back, so we are okay. *Gracias a dios*," she lifted her eyes.

"Good," Gordon nodded, moving to the door to take a look in the dining room. "I'll put in an appearance. Then I'm going to Doris and Lattie's house. Need to talk to them."

"The turtle lady is having lunch here, with a friend. I don't know her." Marvelita offered. "The other one is not here. When will you be back?"

"By four, anyway," Gordon said with a quick look at his watch. "I need to talk to Fletch."

Marvelita nodded and turned back to the stove.

Gordon stepped out into the dining room. He spotted Doris at a table by the mermaid mural with a pleasant looking woman he didn't recognize, about her age. Not far from them Jack and Nevada Campbell were having lunch, wide-eyed and attentive, listening to Jadyn Hayes. Well, he knew what that was about. The rest of the patrons looked like tourists or boaters, come in from the heat. He walked over to Doris.

"Hey, Doris," he put a hand on her shoulder. "Good to see you. How did you make out with the power outage?"

"We sweat some," Doris said, munching her burger, "but we survived. I see *Gordon's* came through it okay. Alice, this is Gordon," she introduced him to her friend. "He owns the place. Alice is an old college chum from Ohio. We all played softball together eons ago."

He greeted the friend briefly, then asked, "Where's Lattie? I haven't seen her around?" Gordon spoke casually but was watching her closely.

"She's home. With a headache. I think the heat got to her," Doris said, not meeting his eyes. "But she'll be okay." She paused, glanced at her friend. "We saw all the activity on your dock this morning. Chopper looked like it was headed to the

South end. Heard they found someone. I told Alice it was probably a drowning." She looked at him, questioning.

"Something like that," he said vaguely, and changed the subject. "Tell Lattie I hope she feels better. Heat gets to everyone this time of year and no power is no fun. Enjoy lunch," he left the two women and went over to the Campbell's table. Jack's face wore a look of measured concern. Nevada was sitting upright in her chair, indignant.

"Jadyn told us what happened to her this morning," Nevada said, her fine eyes angry. "She told us you and the sheriff were paying Cross a visit. Well," she demanded, "did Fitz arrest him?"

Jack sighed and covered her hand. "I told you I didn't think that was likely, Nevada, but," he looked at Gordon, "surely some measures have been taken? Emails are one thing—"

"So you've had them, too?" Gordon cut in.

"The 'concerned citizen'? Yeah—it's him. Has to be him. Most of us who've been here long enough know he's full of shit," Jack said gruffly, "but the newer people... ." He grimaced. "He's very—plausible—when you first meet him. Charming, even. But this," he shook his head in disgust. "He can't be allowed to terrorize people with a weapon. What's Fitz going to do about it? Jadyn tells me she's filed a formal complaint. You have, too." The attorney in him was fully roused.

Gordon briefly described the interview with Cross. "We'll go ahead with the charges," he assured Jack, finishing up, "but in the meantime, I think he's been warned off any more shenanigans."

Jack gestured with his fork, his face stern. "He bears watching."

"Oh, he will be watched. I guarantee it," Gordon said grimly. He still hadn't ruled out pasting the smug look off Van's face, regardless of what Fitz had to say about it. "And don't you worry about your walks," he said seriously to Jadyn. "If necessary, I'll go with you."

At that, Jadyn laughed outright, the nervous tension leaving her shoulders. "It would have to be really serious for you to offer that, Gordon! When's the last time you walked?"

Gordon smiled a little ruefully. "Physical exercise isn't my strong suit," he conceded. "But I'll go with you if you're worried. Nothing I'd like better than to meet Mr. Cross in the mangroves with no one around to watch but the gulls."

He looked at Jack, speculatively. *Those of us who've been here a long time,'* the man had said. That gave him a thought. "Jack, when you're finished up here I wonder if you'd have a few minutes for me? I have a question or two for you."

"I'm done now," Jack said, rising from the chair, looking interested. "Shouldn't be too long, Nevada," he said to his wife. "If you need to get back, I can always get a ride."

She waved him off. "Go on," she said, "Jadyn and I have plenty to catch up on."

Gordon led the way to his office. The temperature inside was actually pleasant. Beni must have worked his magic on the air conditioner, he thought, sitting comfortably behind his own desk for the first time in two days. Jack sat opposite him, folded his hands on the desk and looked at him as if he were taking a deposition. "What happened down on State land?" he demanded. "There's a rumor going around someone drowned."

Gordon debated how to answer this, took out his cigars. "Mind if I smoke?"

"It's your office," Jack shrugged.

"Palm Electric guys found a body early this morning." He eyed Jack seriously. "This is in confidence. He doesn't look like a drowning victim from the look of it. Won't know anything definite until they've finished the autopsy."

"Who is it?" Jack spoke evenly, but his face was drawn, etched with lines of concern. "Does this have anything to do with that attack?" Before Gordon could answer, he went on. "If the residents of this island are in danger, we should be notified." He was all business now, his civic instincts fully roused.

Gordon lit up his cigar, exhaled. "They haven't officially identified him yet. And until we know more, there's no reason to think the two things are connected. Although," he was aware the man opposite was watching him closely, "it's a little hard to believe they aren't. But," Gordon spoke with confidence. "Even if they are, I still think—"

"People from the mainland are involved. This isn't a Hogge Island problem. That's what you were going to say?" Jack finished for him, nodding in agreement. He looked somewhat relieved.

"Well, it's a problem in that it landed in our laps, so to speak. But otherwise, no. I don't think anyone from our community is involved."

"This is what you wanted to discuss with me?" Jack said. "I appreciate your taking me into your confidence." He looked like he was about to get up.

Gordon put up a hand. "Partially," he said. "I also have a few questions. You've been here a long time," he said.

"Almost three decades."

"I need a little background on some of the names that have been floating around. What can you tell me about a guy named Costello?"

Jack gave a sharp laugh. "Two-Finger Louie?" He held up his left hand, thumb and forefinger waving, pincerlike. Gordon nodded with a slight smile, indicating he was familiar with the moniker.

"Well," Jack continued, "I can tell you everyone was relieved when he sold his place. One of the more colorful characters on this island, but a nasty bit of goods." He settled back in the chair. "Got out here some years after we did. Don't remember when exactly. He lived on a houseboat out there," he waved to the harbor beyond Gordon's docks, "with a little blonde—can't remember her name now. She worked part-time for one of the real estate people—Jerry Munson. Before your time. Died just before the storm. Pancreatic." he said, shaking his head sadly.

"Costello have money?" Gordon asked.

"Didn't have a pot to piss in when he got here, so far as I know. Hence, the houseboat. But about five years in, he was suddenly flush. Investments, he *said*."

"But you don't believe that?"

"I do not," Jack said emphatically. "Pretty sure he was running drugs. Pot, cocaine, I even heard heroin. Hogge was pretty isolated then. Off the radar, even more than now. He had a clear field. No one could ever pin anything on him and since he wasn't dealing on the island..." He shrugged. "It's always been live and let live out here. Sheriff's office had even less interest on what went on then than they do now."

"They're taking this death pretty seriously," Gordon objected.

"Really? I don't see any law enforcement out here. They deputized you and left us to it. Not," he put up a hand, "that I object to your status. But it gives you a pretty good idea of their priorities. Anyhow," he continued, pointing out the window toward the grass airstrip, "back then there were a lot of small planes that landed here. Never seemed to bring passengers or stay for more than an hour or two. Costello managed to be on hand to meet most of them."

"Anyone ever report him?" Gordon asked. "Did you?"

"I had a word with the authorities," Jack conceded. "You understand, we weren't on the island full time then. We only came for six months at a stretch. Anyway, they came out and searched his houseboat, found nothing. That was that. At some point he must have gotten out of the business and went legitimate. Had enough money to buy a place here. That was almost worse." Jack's brow was furrowed, bushy eyebrows drawn low. "The man was a lout. Abusive. The woman left him after a while—just got out with her skin, most likely." He gave Gordon a shrewd glance. "You know something about it." It was a statement, not a question.

"A bit. Rather hear what you have to say."

Jack nodded, continued. "Well, none of us had much to do with him after that. At some point, I guess he got tired of the cold shoulder or found other interests on the mainland. In any event, he sold the place. Interesting that the attack on the tourist should be in his house," he added, waiting for a response.

"Fitz certainly thought so," Gordon said, and left it at that.

Jack grunted. There was an appreciable pause. Then he leaned forward, pointed a finger. "I could never prove it but I'm pretty sure he bankrolled Hollows at some point—before the storm."

"How do you figure?" Gordon was intrigued.

"Hollows was going belly up, practically bankrupt. He'd overextended himself—sort of like he's doing now, except this time he seems to have drummed up deeper pockets, deeper than his own, anyway. Back then, we all figured he would be gone in a matter of months and then, suddenly, he was back in business. With a vengeance. Money came from somewhere. No one who lived here could stand him." He sat back, done with his story.

Gordon smoked, mulled it over for a few moments. When he looked up, Jack was watching him with a curious expression on his face.

"Is Costello mixed up in all this?" Jack asked, bluntly. "If he is, doesn't surprise me you have a body on the beach."

"No indication that he is, Jack. I'm just trying to get some background." He took another tack. "Do you know a Max Lopez?" Fitz would have a fit if he heard him bring out that name, Gordon reflected, but Jack was trustworthy. He might connect the dots but he'd keep it to himself. If asked.

Jack thought about it, made a wry face. "I think that's the guy building the house on the east end. From Miami, I think. He your body?" The lawyer in him was on full alert now.

"Could be," Gordon said evasively. "In any event, keep it to yourself. What do you know about him?"

"Not much," Jack said. "He has no history here, if that's what you're asking. Showed up about a year or two ago. One of Hollows' deep pockets." He cocked his head. "Hollows started a construction business after the storm, remember? Most of the newer places were his jobs, most of them done on spec." He waved a hand at the expression on Gordon's face. "Oh, I looked into it. Had to. All sorts of things were going on here after the storm. Island's interests had to be protected." He suddenly looked tired. "I was sure Hollows was up to something, but I couldn't find anything solid to hang my hat on. Just a run of luck for the son of a bitch, I guess." He sighed.

There was a knock at the door. Nevada popped her head in. "I'm ready to go. Need more time?"

"We're about done, Nevada. Thanks, Jack," Gordon got up, offered his hand. "I appreciate your insights."

Jack smiled and shook his hand. "Anytime. Happy to help," he said, getting up slowly, walking to the door.

He turned on his way out. "Hogge is deceptive, Gordon." His tone was serious. "Sort of like the water it's surrounded by. Without local knowledge, you cruise along thinking everything's fine. Next thing you know, you're aground on an oyster bar, praying for the tide to come in."

CHAPTER 28

Gordon suspected Jack could tell him a lot more about Hogge's colorful history, but for the time being, he'd filled in a few important gaps. The new information gave him an ugly little tickle in the back of his mind, but nothing definite. At this point, he decided wearily, it would be best to visit Lattie while she was alone. He'd have more success discovering whatever was bothering her without Doris present. He slipped out through the kitchen and headed for the modest bungalow the two women shared on the west end.

Their tidy one-bedroom cottage was a holdover from the old Florida style, built low to the ground, nestled in mature vegetation. A gaily painted mobile of shells tinkled gently on the front porch. He knocked at the door, called out.

"Lattie? It's Gordon. Are you up?"

There was no answer. He knocked again, a little louder. After a bit, he heard sounds of movement within.

"Gordon?" Lattie opened the door to him. She looked fuzzy, like she'd been asleep.

"Sorry if I woke you," Gordon said, stepping inside, not waiting for an invitation. "I need to talk to you." He looked at the woman's face with concern. Deep purplish patches under her eyes spoke of little sleep. Her mouth was drawn, lined, far more than he remembered. "You don't look well," he said.

"I've had a headache." Lattie moved toward the kitchen. "Can I get you something?"

"No." Gordon walked over to her, put her hands on her shoulders, and turned her around, towering over her. "What's wrong with you?" he asked bluntly. "You haven't been yourself since Friday morning."

Alarm flickered in her eyes, died, replaced by a dull look. "I haven't been well, that's all." She went into the living room and sat down on the couch, gesturing for him to sit on the matching loveseat.

Gordon ignored her and sat down next to her on the couch. "Lattie," he said gently, "whatever it is that's bothering you, you can tell me. There's been a lot of trouble in the past two days." Trouble. He was beginning to hate that word. "I'm worried about you." He looked at her gravely. "You have to tell me what's up. Because something is. Any fool can see that."

To his surprise, he saw tears forming in the corner of her eyes. Her mouth was working. Finally, she wiped a hand over her eyes and said in a choked voice, "I've done something awful."

Wherever it leads. Fitz's words came back to him with a jolt. But no, he thought looking at the seventy something woman sitting next to him, whom he'd known for ten years, it wasn't possible.

"What have you done?" His voice was harsher than he intended. "Tell me what's happened," he said, more gently.

Lattie swallowed and put her hand over his. "The other morning, after I came to see you…"

"After you sold the fish to Marvelita," Gordon said, remembering. "You said you were going out to check on things."

"Yes," she put her hands in her lap, looked down at them. "Well, I did. I went to see what Hollows was up to." She looked up, some of the old fire back in her eyes. "All his heavy equipment was lined up on the canal. They'd already pulled out tons of mangroves. You know he doesn't have a permit. Paying someone off." Jaw set, she continued. "I—I put sugar in all the gas tanks." She sat back on the couch, defiant.

Gordon was caught between shock and amusement. Lattie? Sugaring Hollows' equipment. He suppressed a grin. It was serious enough, with hundreds in damage, likely. He shook his head. Never underestimate someone with fierce convictions.

"Are you going to tell Fitz? Report me?" she demanded.

"No." Gordon made up his mind swiftly. Lattie had committed vandalism, not murder. Let Hollows do his own dirty work. Fitz, too, if it came to that. No children had died here, as the expression went. "Does anyone else know?"

Lattie looked ill. "I had to tell Doris. She knew something was wrong. I was glad when I did it, but then—" She broke off, tears starting up again.

"You felt bad about it. I can understand it. Well, I don't think Doris is going to turn you in," Gordon said mildly. "And I won't either—only," he cupped her face with one hand, turning it toward him, "promise me you won't do anything like this again? It solves nothing."

In answer, she twisted away from him, covered her face with her hands and burst into sobs.

Gordon was a little taken aback. Remorse, he could understand. But the woman was inconsolable.

"Lattie," he pulled at her hands. "We all make mistakes. It'll be okay."

"No. No it isn't going to be okay." Presently, she stopped crying, sat staring at him, struggling to find words. When she spoke, her tone was dull. Her eyes had a glassy, hunted look that Gordon didn't like. "I said no one else knew but that wasn't true. Someone saw me on Hollows' property that morning. I don't know if he knew what I was doing, but he saw me there." Hysteria was creeping back into her voice.

"Who saw you?" Gordon said urgently, staving off a fresh storm. "Who?"

"Jervis Potts."

"Potts?" Gordon was stunned. "Are you sure he recognized you?"

"Oh yes. I saw that skiff of his but he wasn't around. No one was. But I know he saw me because he came here and told me so. He's crafty, Gordon. He scares me sometimes. Everyone knows he's a loon but…." She took a deep breath and went on. "He said he saw me walking around the equipment and heard about what happened, so…." She trailed off, despairing.

"So being Potts he'll keep his mouth shut if you make it worth his while," Gordon shook his head grimly. Poor Lattie. She was paying a heavy price for her first foray into environmental activism. "What does he want?"

"He *said* he wanted to sell me a watch," she said. "Jervis said he saw me at Hollow's place, and if I bought the watch from him he'd keep his mouth shut." She shook her head in exasperation. "He doesn't see it as blackmail, of course, because he's Potts. In his world, it all makes perfect sense."

"What was he doing at Hollows' in the first place?" Gordon demanded. "This was what—not even eight in the morning? Early for him to be out. He's a night person, from what I know."

"He does odd jobs for Hollows. God knows what."

"Where did he get the watch?" Gordon asked, feeling a qualm.

"He wouldn't say. I asked him if he stole it and he said no. I," she swallowed hard, "I gave him money. I just wanted him to leave but he insisted on my taking the watch. I didn't want the damned thing." She shuddered, then added, "It looks expensive."

"You have it? Let me see it."

Lattie got up meekly and went into the bedroom, returned holding the thing out to him. "I wish you'd take it. I never want to see it again."

Gordon heard her, but he wasn't listening. He was looking at the solid gold Rolex she held out to him, wondering how closely it might match the tan line on the wrist of the body found on the beach. Reluctantly, he turned it over and looked at the ornate letters engraved on the back of the faceplate: *J.M.L.*

The look on his face gave him away.

"What is it? What's wrong?" Lattie said, her voice panicky.

Wherever it leads. Fitz's voice echoed again dully in his brain. And now what.

Gordon didn't answer her right away, turning ideas over. None of them terribly ethical. No matter how he sliced it, though, he didn't see any way out. The watch led to Potts, and Potts wasn't likely to hold his tongue if it meant getting in trouble. That much he was sure of. Lattie would have to take her chances with Fitz. Maybe he, Gordon, could run interference with Hollows and persuade him not to press charges. Money should do it. That and the satisfaction Hollows would get over having something over him. The thought was distasteful but looking at the distraught woman sitting in front of him, he had to try. She was watching him now, with a terrified look on her face, hands working in her lap.

He cleared his throat and plunged in. "I can't say for sure but I think this watch belonged to the man found on the beach this morning," he said, watching her. "I assume you've heard about that?"

She looked at him, lips white. "We saw all the emergency vehicles. Doris thought maybe someone drowned. There have been a few incidents—like that tourist that tried to swim out to the sand bar last month." Her voice trailed off. She suddenly looked sick. "You mean Jervis took this watch off—from—" She shuddered, unable to complete the sentence.

Gordon nodded but didn't elaborate. He looked at the watch in his hand. This was a hell of a complication. He made up his mind. "Under the circumstances, I have to turn it over to Fitz. I'm sorry, Lattie."

"Potts will tell them he saw me there if you do that," her voice was frantic. "You can't, Gordon. Hollows will sue me.

We'll lose this house. We'll have nothing." The tears were starting again.

"Hollows will likely press charges—you damaged expensive equipment." There was no point in soft-soaping it. "But maybe I can head him off, offer to pay the damages. I don't know if Fitz can let it go, but he might if Hollows doesn't kick. Island being what it is," he finished up, vaguely. "I don't see any choice, Lattie. This was stolen from a dead man. Besides, Potts is unreliable. He could be back demanding more money. You want to live under that shadow?"

Lattie looked miserable, but she nodded her head. "No. That's what I'm afraid of. I should have kicked Potts out from the first, but he scared me when he said he saw me there and besides…" She looked down at her hands.

"You had a guilty conscience." Gordon said.

She still looked stricken, but calmer. "Yes. Guess so. I lost my head." She looked at him anxiously. "You're sure you can…can fix it with Hollows?"

"I can't promise anything. I'll do my best. At this point," he waved a hand in exasperation, "you'll just have to face whatever is coming. Get through it."

"I'll never forgive myself if he ends up driving us off this island. He'd love to do it, too. Just for spite. I'm a thorn in his side, you know," she said with a hint of pride. "But now…" She broke off, staring beyond him, imagining what he could only guess.

"Don't jump to conclusions," Gordon said roughly. "Let's just take it one step at a time. I'll speak to Fitz Monday when he gets back here, although—" He was thinking. "I'd like to know where Potts got this watch. Think I'll pay Potts a visit tomorrow. See what I can shake out of him. I suggest you," he tried to lighten her mood, "stick to fishing. You make a lousy criminal."

Lattie still looked ill, but nodded gamely, seeing him to the door. "I'm sorry for all this trouble, Gordon. I never meant to get anyone else involved."

So that, Gordon thought, driving back to the restaurant, explained Lattie's odd behavior. His curiosity was satisfied all right, but he'd gotten more than he bargained for. Some fixer. Maybe for once he should have let well enough alone. Now, he thought bitterly, he had an unpleasant conversation to look forward to with Fitz, who was likely to take a dim view of Lattie's activities, and an even more unpleasant session with Hollows, who'd lord it over him while Gordon ate crow on Lattie's behalf. It didn't help that the backdrop to all this was Marvelita's voice saying, "*I told you those vieja's would bring trouble!*"

She didn't know the half of it.

CHAPTER 29

Saturday afternoon Hogge returned to some semblance of normalcy, at least on the surface. The news crew left, trailing Fitz back to the mainland in the hope of gleaning more information. New renters, eager to explore the island, roamed the island in carts, half of them with children behind the wheel gleefully violating the "must have a driver's license policy" they signed in their rental contracts. A fresh crop of umbrellas, mini-tents and shell seekers littered the beach, blissfully ignorant of the corpse so nearly in their midst.

Gordon's was slammed with customers throughout the day. Around four, the heat that had been building all day reached the breaking point. Towering white clouds stacked up on the horizon and moved in from the east, heralding a late day thunderstorm in the typical rainy season pattern. With an eye on the weather, boaters hurried to finish their meals and get back to safe harbor before the blow came in.

Around 4:30, Gordon spotted Fletch tying up on the dock, back from his charter. After his party had left—two men and three boys somewhere between ten and thirteen—Gordon walked over to tell him the latest developments. Fletch looked hot and aggravated.

"Successful day?" Gordon asked, as Fletch stowed his gear and started to spray down the boat.

"From their point of view." Fletch said. "They caught enough fish to make it worth their while, anyhow. Also managed to break two reels and foul up my best line. Two grown men—you'd think they'd help out with the kids a little. But they just sat back and watched the little buggers climb all over everything." He shook his head. "Tipped well enough, though, so it wasn't a total loss. How's everything here? Power back?"

"Great," Gordon said without preamble. "They found a body on the beach, down at the South end."

"Who found a body?" Fletch looked up startled, tripped over a cleat.

"Palm Electric guys, early. Fitz dragged me out there to see if I could identify him. For a minute, I thought it might be you."

"Thanks," Fletch said, sourly. "So did you recognize him?"

"Barely. Max Lopez." He let this sink in.

Fletch was looking at him bug-eyed. "Accident?"

"Not much," Gordon said. "They're doing the autopsy now. Looked like he had some help. That's all between us. Officially, it's a possible drowning, victim not yet identified." He reached down and tightened a dockline. "Fitz wants you to give him a call. I said you were out with an early charter but I think he'd like to hear it from you."

A look of annoyance came and went from Fletch's eyes. "It's getting unhealthy to be up before dawn around here," he said sarcastically. Then, more seriously, "The renter yesterday, now this. Does Fitz have any idea what's going on?"

Gordon shook his head. "He's hoping to find out more once he talks to Hollows and Sharpe. And once they know for certain how the guy died. And when."

"This keeps up everyone's going to be at each other's throats." Fletch said. "Who do you like for it all?"

"A couple of people are frontrunners," Gordon said, "but there's no clear picture."

"Wonder if there'll ever be. They never got to the bottom of that arson." He coiled up the hose, slowly, thinking. "This is a funny place."

"Absolutely hilarious at the moment." Gordon said grimly. "Anyhow, once you've cleaned up, give Fitz a call. I have to get back. There's weather coming in and the place has been jammed." He decided not to say anything about his conversation with Lattie. Fletch looked like he'd had a long enough day as it was.

"I will," Fletch said. He looked preoccupied as they walked back down the dock.

By five-thirty, Gordon's was practically empty. Marvelita and Gordon took a welcome break and shared some refreshment in his office—his, a bourbon, hers, tea—watching the local news on his tiny black and white TV. The Death on Hogge was the lead story, but aside from showing some repetitive images of the Gulf—which Gordon suspected was stock footage—and a brief, uninformative interview with a grumpy looking Fitz, there wasn't much that could be made of it. There was a mention of a tourist hurt the day before, but since the sheriff's office hadn't released any details, it didn't merit more than a sentence. Coverage moved on to a troubling home invasion in Estero, a piece about a drunk motorist who was pulled over, apparently with a squirrel in his shirt, and the latest black bear sighting, with home-grown footage of the creature curled up peaceably near a sofa on the family's lanai deck. This was accompanied by a breathless, "What did you think when you saw it?" interview with the housewife who took the video with her cellphone. The largest segment was given over to the weather—always a serious concern in summer—but the latest disturbance was apparently swirling away to the north, the announcer noted with a touch of chagrin.

Deep rumbles sounded from the storm moving in. Gordon reached over and switched off the set, finished up his drink. Marvelita looked sleepy. It had been a long day for her, starting with no power at dawn and nonstop customers since breakfast. There was the faint flash of lightening and a crack of thunder, closer now, as the wind picked up. Within minutes, it was raining hard.

Marvelita roused herself. "We won't have many for dinner if it rains all night," she observed.

"It won't," Gordon said, although he almost wished it would. He'd spent a tedious afternoon making small talk with diners once he'd gotten back from his visit with Lattie. In normal circumstances, he didn't mind engaging with the customers. It was a form of theater for him and made for good repeat business. But circumstances were anything but normal at this point and he was having a hard time focusing on being the affable host, his head crowded with questions and concerns. He glanced at Marvelita, head back, resting in the chair. Her eyes were closed. With uncanny instinct she hadn't asked him about his visit with Lattie, waiting for him to broach the subject when he was ready, certain that he would. He looked at her uncomfortably, not really wanting to go into it.

"So it did not go well with her," Marvelita spoke as if reading his mind, her eyes still closed. "You have not been yourself since you came back."

Gordon exhaled loudly and felt for one of his cigars. "No," he lit up, "Lattie's got herself in a real mess."

Marvelita nodded. He expected her to launch into an "I told you so" tirade but she didn't. Eyes still closed, she said, "Tell me."

He put the whole picture before her, including his own plan to talk to Fitz and deal with Hollows. "So tomorrow morning," he finished, "I'm going to take a boat ride over to Potts' place and see what I can find out."

Throughout it all she hadn't interrupted. When he was done, she didn't speak right away, mulling it all over. Finally, she opened her eyes, sat upright in her chair, and asked, "So you think she is telling the truth?"

Gordon was taken aback by this. "Yes," he said, frowning. "Why would she make it up?"

Marvelita shrugged. "I do not doubt she put sugar in the gas—stupid woman. But you say this watch was the dead man's—"

"I *think* it is," Gordon said.

"Very well. How can you know it came from Potts? Perhaps she took it herself."

"What? When?" Gordon demanded. "How would she have gotten it."

Marvelita shrugged. "The man was found dead on the beach. She is out alone always and has a boat. Who knows what reason she may have had? She is always interfering where she has no business. Her story is a good one, yes, and she has put it in your lap, knowing you would help. She could have found him, taken the watch—and is using you to make…" She waved her hand in frustration, searching for the right word.

"An alibi?" Gordon just looked at her. "For what?"

"Who knows?" Marvelita's eyes were wide open now. "She is already in trouble because of the equipment. Maybe she's afraid of getting into more trouble."

It never occurred to Gordon to question Lattie's tale. Her distress was genuine, he was sure of it. Of course, it would be in any case. "Anything's possible, Marvelita," he said dubiously, "but there's Potts. If she didn't get the watch from him, he'll say so. He may be loony but his number one concern is his own skin."

"And if she paid him to say so?"

"Again, even if that were the case, the minute he figures out what's involved, he'd turn on her."

"And who would believe him?" Marvelita asked innocently. "Take the word of a crazy man over someone who has been here so many years, everybody's friend. Would you, Gordon?" She was watching him very carefully now. "If she is lying, she has picked the right person to hang. Maybe not so stupid a woman," she said, thoughtfully.

"Lattie couldn't kill anyone, Marvelita, if that's what you're implying," Gordon objected. That much he was certain of.

"I did not say that," Marvelita retorted. "But she could be involved in some other way that you cannot see. And so," she said simply, "she could by lying."

However unpleasant, it was possible, Gordon had to admit. Three days ago it would have been inconceivable, much less possible, but that island, that reality, was gone, replaced by a shifting landscape in which friend questioned friend. There was, however, the issue of motive and Lattie didn't even know Lopez was the dead man, much less have a reason to steal a watch or cover up his death. He pointed this out to Marvelita.

"As far as you know," she reminded him. "But how well do you know anyone here? How well do they know you? Just what they tell you, what you tell them. They have not lived your life and you have not lived theirs. I warned you about secrets, Gordon. You did not take me seriously, I could tell. You should now." She paused, deep in thought. "You say you will go to Potts. You should not go alone. I will come with you."

"No," Gordon objected immediately, "I need you here. Besides," he hesitated.

She arched an eyebrow at him, mouth drawn up slightly. "You are afraid there will be trouble?"

"I don't know that," he said a little testily, "but if there is, I'm not letting you in for it." She did have a point, however. "I'll get Fletch to come with me. You're right. Better if there are two of us. He can be a witness to whatever Potts says. Fitz knows I trust him. He'll do." He was firm.

She sighed but accepted his decision. "Very well then, take your friend." The storm had been a brief, violent one and now the rain had stopped. Marvelita got up, preparing to go back to the kitchen. "But go early, before he climbs into his bottle," she admonished. "Even a small woman would be more use to you than a drunk man."

As usual, Gordon was forced to agree.

CHAPTER 30

Fletch returned Gordon's call late Saturday night and agreed to take him out to Jervis Potts' house on Okum's End early the next morning. "Why Potts?" He was curious. "You think he had something to do with the dead guy?"

Gordon hesitated, not wanting to go over the whole thing over the phone. "Only indirectly," he said. "I'll tell you all about it on the ride over. How did your call go with Fitz?"

"Pretty routine. I told Fitz where I was and gave him the name of the people I took out. Seemed satisfied. He was in a hurry to get off the phone. I could hear Marly yapping in the background." There was a pause. "He seems to have a pretty full plate at the moment."

They agreed to meet at seven at Fletch's boat. Early enough, Gordon figured, to catch Potts at home before he left to do whatever it was he did on that deserted strip of land.

Sunday morning they took off in a slick calm, horizon indistinguishable from sky, in stark contrast to the raging surf the night before. Hogge might not have seasons, Gordon thought, but it had the sea—ever-changing, inscrutable. Half a dozen boats already dotted the Pass. It was a good day for fishing. On the brief ride over he told Fletch about his visit to Lattie.

Fletch gave a soft whistle. "I saw her out that day," he admitted, steering the boat toward the tiny harbor and patch of sand in front of Potts' place. He threw out the anchor, jumped down and secured it in the sand. Gordon joined him, using the rickety ladder.

"When did you see her?" Gordon was curious.

"In the morning, after I brought the tripletail to Marvelita. I went out to get bait for a half-day charter. Saw her taking her boat into the canal, by Hollows place." He cocked his head. "Didn't think anything of it at the time. You know how she's always keeping an eye on him. But later…" He hesitated. "Hollows was screaming like a stuck pig all over the island about his damaged equipment. I did wonder." He left it there.

"You didn't mention any of this to me," Gordon said pointedly, looking at his friend.

"Didn't see the need," Fletch gave him his lopsided smile. "Fitz had you in tow by then and—well, I'm not a meddler. I like Lattie. I don't like Hollows. I figured things would sort themselves out eventually. Besides, I didn't actually see her messing with anything, so there was no point in starting trouble." He shook his head, "Dumb ass thing to do, you ask me."

"That's putting it mildly," Gordon said.

Fletch gave the line a tug to make sure it was secure, and the two men walked up the beach. "How are you going to tackle Potts about the watch? Just ask him outright?"

"Pretty much. Fitz has kept the identity and murder under wraps so Potts shouldn't be spooked by that," Gordon said. "I have the watch with me." He took it out of his pocket. It glinted in the sun.

"Nice. Worth a packet. Wonder if Potts knows just how much?"

"I doubt it," Gordon said. They reached the door. The weatherworn shack looked held together by crazy glue. One good blow, Gordon thought, and it would fall where it stood. He knocked on the door and it swung open slightly at his touch, the ancient, rusted handle lying askew. Not surprising, Gordon thought. Why would Potts lock his door?

He poked his head inside. It was dark. Potts had no electricity. The windows were covered with what looked like scraps of sheet—Potts's rudimentary heating and air conditioning system. The pungent odor of rotting fish and general disrepair nearly gagged him. "Potts?" Gordon called out. "It's Gordon Strange. I need to talk to you."

There was silence. He tried again, louder. "Potts? You in there?"

"His boat's tied up over there," Fletch observed, pointing to a rusted dingy tied to a clump of mangroves in a small cove. "He must be here somewhere. People say he's obsessed with finding buried treasure, digs holes all over the beach. Let's hope we don't have to search the entire island for him. It's bigger than it looks—especially in 90 degree weather." He swatted a few mosquitoes buzzing around his head. "I'll have a look around back."

"Go ahead. I'm going in, maybe leave him a note to come see me," Gordon said, pushing open the door. It took a minute for his eyes to adjust to the gloom. The one room living space was meagerly furnished with whatever leftovers Potts had managed to salvage over the years. Paperback books and yellowed magazines were strewn haphazardly near the door. A small campstove and a few cans were stacked next to a table with three legs, the fourth supplied by the chair it was resting on. Three plates were set out, as if company was coming. Shells were heaped everywhere, accounting, no doubt, for the strong smell of rotting fish. It was evident the place hadn't seen a broom, much less a mop or a vacuum, in years. The pathetic furnishings of a pitiful existence. Gordon's throat constricted.

It took a few moments for his eyes to adjust fully to the darkness. At the far end, he could make out a cot—some sort of army cast-off, with bedding scrunched up at the foot. On the floor, looking not much different from the pile of bedding was a slight figure lying at an awkward angle.

Gordon walked over slowly, scalp prickling. Maybe the man had passed out, was drunk or ill. He was a frail man. Potts lay crumpled on his side, eyes open.

Gordon knelt down beside him, put a hand on his wrist. The body was cool to the touch, but not cold. He felt for a pulse, not really expecting to find one. He didn't. Jervis Potts was dead.

"He's not out back," Fletch came in the front door, "Jesus, it stinks in here!"

"Stay there!" Gordon yelled harshly. "Don't touch anything. He's here all right. Dead." He swiveled around, still crouching. "Lift up one of those sheets on the window so I can see," he said roughly.

"Dead? Are you sure?" Fletch demanded, but did as asked.

The ramshackle hovel looked even meaner with sunlight streaming in through the window. Gordon saw a patch of blood on the base of the man's skull, a slight depression that brought to mind the body on the beach. He stood up heavily, walked back toward the door, grabbed Fletch's arm, and propelled him outside. The sunlight was dizzying after the gloom of the cottage. Gordon leaned against the doorjamb and fished his cellphone out of his pocket.

"What d'you think? Heart attack?" Fletch was asking, a sharp edge to his voice.

Gordon shook his head, dialing Fitz's number. "No. And not an accident," he said thickly. "Hit from behind, I'd say. And not long ago—" He broke off as Fitz answered groggily, as if he'd been sleeping.

"Sorry to wake you. It's Gordon. I'm over at Jervis Potts place on Okum's End. Fletch is with me. Fitz—the man's dead. No," he said, "from the look of his skull I'd say it was no accident." Staccato barks could be heard from Fitz on the other end of the phone.

"I'll get into all that when you get out here. It's—" he held his breath for a moment, blew it out, "sort of a long story. Yeah, we'll wait." He rang off, turned to Fletch who was smoking, staring out at the water thoughtfully.

"Wants us to wait for him. He's calling the chopper." Gordon looked around for somewhere to sit down, opted for the rickety plank that did for a front step. He felt for his cigars and his hand touched the Rolex he'd planned to confront Potts with.

It felt like a ten pound brick in his pocket.

Fletch came over and sat down next to him. He looked uncharacteristically serious. "Poor bastard. How long's he been dead?"

"I'm no coroner but he's still—cooling off." Gordon said, abruptly. "You see any other boats when you had a look around?"

Fletch shook his head no. "So he hasn't been dead long." He was silent for a minute or two, thinking. Then, "You realize how this is going to look to Fitz? Once he hears the whole story? Not to mention we look pretty suspicious right now, I don't care how much Fitz likes you." He didn't look happy. "How're you going to explain that watch in your pocket?"

Gordon hurled his half-smoked cigar toward the sand. "Tell him the whole damned story. What else? You think we look suspicious? How do you think it looks for Lattie?" He brought out his cellphone. "I'm going to call her," he said, bringing up the number.

Fletch looked at him with a strange expression. "Really think you should do that? You're in deep enough at this point. Let Fitz handle it from here."

"What do you mean?" Gordon's voice was harsh.

"You know damned well what I mean. Ever think she might have been playing you? I know—seems impossible," he said as Gordon started to speak. "But at this point, I'm beginning to think anything is possible." He looked down, grinding a few shells into the sand with his heel.

"I was only going to say that Marvelita had the same idea." Gordon said. "That's why I asked you to come with me."

"She thought Potts would be killed?" Fletch was incredulous.

"No, of course not. But she was afraid Lattie might be giving me a cock and bull story to cover for something else." His face hardened. "I still don't believe it. But I'd like to know where she is right now." He ignored Fletch's advice and called Doris and Lattie's house, letting the phone ring and ring. No answer. He hung up without leaving a message, put the phone away.

"They go out early," Fletch offered.

"Yeah. We know that already. Like you said, it's getting unhealthy to be up around here before dawn." He got up and walked toward the cove, punting shells toward the water, hard. The web was growing good and thick now and he was right in the middle of it. Of course, Fitz might have turned up something useful talking to Hollows and Sharpe. He hoped so. But, he thought cynically, guys like that were very good at covering their tracks. That's the way they lived. Examples abounded—breaking laws, getting convicted, doing time, none of it seemed to matter. They always seemed to land on their feet, reinvent themselves, and go right on doing what they had been doing. Honest citizens didn't stand a chance. For a woman like Lattie, one foot down the wrong path wasn't just a slip-up, it was a fall into the abyss. He looked at the water, calm and placid, not a ripple breaking the surface. But who the hell knew what was going on underneath?

He was so lost in thought that the roar of the chopper landing took him by surprise. Fletch had walked down the beach toward it. Fitz and a police photographer, by the look of her, jumped out and ducked under the blades, coming toward him at a fast clip. Fitz looked grim, almost angry. He came straight over to Gordon.

"Where is he?" He demanded.

"Inside, next to the bed."

"You disturb anything?"

"No. Just the sheet on the far window, so I could see."

"Don't go anywhere," Fitz warned him, heading inside. "I want to know just what the hell you two are doing here." He seemed to have forgotten Gordon's so-called deputy status. Trust was definitely in short supply this morning.

After they were done inside, Fitz came out and made a phone call. He walked down the beach a bit, out of earshot. In a while he came back over to Gordon and Fletch who were standing by the porch. His face was expressionless, the mask of officialdom.

"Take it from when you got here—time, what you saw. You know the drill." He had his pad out, ready.

Gordon did the speaking. "We got here about 7:20. I needed to speak to Potts because—"

Fitz stopped him. "We'll get into all that. Right now I need the details on this here." He waited.

"Okay. Got out here like I said about 7:20. I didn't check the time but we left Hogge just after seven. Didn't see Potts around and he didn't answer so I went in to leave him a note. The door was ajar; not locked anyway. Found him just as you see him. I checked for a pulse, came out. Called you."

"Fletch go in with you?"

"He came in a minute after. He had a look around first to see if Potts was out somewhere."

"You see anyone? Anything?" Fitz turned to Fletch.

"Nothing—except for his dingy tied up over there." Fletch indicated the mangroves. "No other boats on the shore, just ours. And the ones out there on the Pass, fishing."

Fitz wrote busily, slapped at the mosquitos which were becoming a problem. He looked around but aside from the shack, which was unappetizing in the best of circumstances, there was no place else to go except the chopper.

"All right. I want the rest of it but not here. We'll wait for Deputy Phalen to get here and then," he pointed to Fletch, "you'll take us back to Hogge." He looked from Gordon to Fletch. "Technically, I should bring you both back to headquarters." He glared at them.

"I have no problem with that, Fitz." Gordon's voice was like steel. "It was your idea to get me involved in all this from the beginning. I told you at the time, you knew nothing about me. You're the one who claimed you trusted me. A little late for remorse, isn't it?"

"All right, all right. Don't get touchy." Fitz sounded more conciliatory. "I don't suspect you of killing the man. But," he pointed at Gordon, "I knew you weren't telling me everything when I left yesterday. And now, unless the guy was practicing ballet steps and cracked his own skull, we've got a second murder."

"Sheriff's boat's coming in," Fletch interjected, gesturing toward the cove. "Why don't you deal with them and then—let's get the hell out of here." He watched Fitz jog down to the water with a wry expression on his face.

"And if you think he's twisted now," he said to Gordon as they walked to the boat, "just wait until he hears that story of yours. Might just be the end of a beautiful friendship."

CHAPTER 31

Fletch made the trip back to Gordon's dock in record time, skimming over the glassy water. It was a grim little party. No one had much to say. Fletch tied up while Gordon and Fitz walked to the restaurant. There were a few people having breakfast inside but Gordon hardly noticed them. Fitz led the way to Gordon's office and installed himself behind the desk. Gordon sat opposite him and presently Fletch came in and sat lazily in a chair, legs stretched out in front of him.

"So what were you doing out there?" Fitz wasted no time on preliminaries.

Gordon gave him a full accounting of his conversation with Lattie, explained his plan to confront Potts and see where he had gotten the watch. Fitz was busy scribbling. He looked up once or twice and shook his head but said nothing.

"Let's see it," he said when Gordon was done.

Gordon took the watch out of his pocket and handed it over.

"Rolex. Probably gold. You mean to tell me Potts didn't know it was worth more than a couple of hundred bucks? He'd have to live under a rock."

"He practically does," Gordon said. "If you knew him, you wouldn't be surprised. Potts lives—lived—in his own reality. Ever since I can remember he's been half in, half out." He hesitated. "I know it looks bad but I believe Lattie's story."

"So where does that leave us?" Fitz demanded. "Blackmail—whether he used the word or not—is a pretty powerful motive." He tapped his pad. "Let's get her in here. You have her number?"

"She wasn't in earlier," Gordon said, uncomfortably. "Maybe she got back in."

"When earlier?" Fitz said.

"I called her from Potts' place." Gordon dialed. Still no answer. "They must be out. Doris had a friend visiting. Maybe they went somewhere."

"Maybe," Fletch piped up from his chair, "but Lattie's coming in now—she's tying up on the dock." He pointed out the window. "She's alone."

Fitz could move quickly for a bulky man. He was out the door heading to the dock in an instant, with Gordon at his heels. They got there just as Lattie was stepping out of her skiff. She was dressed in her usual fishing uniform, loose shirt and shorts, holding a string of trout in one hand, looking pleased with herself. She held them up as the men came over. "Had a good morning." Her voice was cheerful but there was a wary look in her eye.

Gordon noted with dismay that there were bloodstains on her shirt. Before Fitz had a chance to speak, he said casually, "That blood on your shirt, Lattie?"

She looked down. "Nicked myself getting a hook out," she said sheepishly. Then, taking a breath, she faced the Sheriff squarely. "Well. I guess you want to see me about the equipment." She looked at Gordon. "Did you speak to Hollows? Is it going to be okay?"

Fitz put up a warning hand to Gordon. To Lattie he said, "Ma'am, you'll have to come with me. I have a few questions."

Lattie nodded glumly. "Can I put these in your fridge, Gordon?" She handed over the trout. "We have a friend staying with us and I thought I'd do a fry-up for brunch." She sounded forlorn, and Gordon felt a surge of anger at her, Fitz, and the whole situation. Did Fitz really believe this woman, talking wistfully about breakfast, had dashed out and killed a man before doing a spot of fishing? Or was he, Gordon, the world's prize sap and she the world's greatest actor. But he just took the string and said, "I'll put them on ice for you."

Fitz led Lattie back inside. Gordon joined them there a few minutes later, dragging another chair into what was becoming a very cramped office.

Fitz looked warningly at Fletch and Gordon and asked pleasantly. "Ms. Mainstay, Lattie, where were you this morning, from six to eight a.m.?"

Lattie looked at him in surprise. "I just told you. Fishing. I'm planning—"

"Yes, a fish fry. Nice string of trout you had there." He smiled. "Did anyone see you while you were fishing? Did you see anyone?" His tone was still conversational.

Lattie thought about it. "I went out early at first light. I was mostly on the bay. That's where the trout are," she explained for Fitz's benefit. "I saw two kayakers going around the pass. The water taxi came in around seven so they might have seen me." She shrugged, shook her head. "Guess that's all I can remember. Why?"

Fitz ignored the question. "Did you happen to go by Okum's End? Maybe stop in there to have a word with Jervis Potts?"

"No," she said with distaste. "I don't want to have anything to do with Potts." She looked uncertainly at Gordon. "Did you have a chance to speak to Hollows?"

"You can talk to him later," Fitz cut in quickly before Gordon could answer. "Gordon told me all about your visit to Hollows' property. Potts must have really upset you." His tone was sympathetic. "Not a very nice thing for a woman like you to have to deal with." He looked at her, questioning.

"It was horrible. And then when Gordon told me who the watch belonged to—that Jervis stole it off a, a—dead man." She threw her hands up. "It was like a nightmare."

"Now let me get all this straight," Fitz said, thumbing through his notes. He still sounded like a benevolent uncle, but Gordon wasn't deceived. "According to Gordon here you said you were responsible for vandalizing Alan Hollows equipment early Friday morning. Put sugar in the gas tanks, it seems. Next thing, Jervis Potts paid you a visit—when was that, by the way?"

Lattie frowned. "Saturday morning; yesterday. I—I can't remember exactly when."

Fitz nodded. "Tell me how that went."

Lattie took a deep breath. "I was surprised to see him. I don't have much to do with Potts."

"By the way, were you alone or was your friend Doris there?" Fitz interrupted her.

"Doris was out. I was alone. Anyhow, he said he'd seen me hanging around the equipment at Hollows' place. He took me completely by surprise. I hadn't seen anyone around. I checked." She looked at Fitz shyly, who nodded, encouragingly. "He'd heard about the equipment, I guess from Hollows. I didn't ask him. And then," she swallowed, "he said he'd keep his mouth shut if I'd buy the watch from him."

"That must have been a shock," Fitz said.

"It was. First, I told him I wasn't going to be blackmailed into buying his stolen goods. He kept insisting it wasn't stolen. Also that it wasn't blackmail, it was a business transaction." She snorted. "That's Potts for you. He only sees what he wants to see. He argued with me. He was very persuasive in his own lunatic way. Said Hollows was offering a reward to find out who damaged the trucks. I didn't know that. He said I could pay him to stay quiet or he could turn me in and collect from Hollows." Her face was very white. "I had no choice."

"I can see that," Fitz said reasonably. "This the watch, by the way?" He held it out to her. She looked at it without touching it. She was still very pale.

"Yes." She looked away.

Fitz put the watch back in its plastic bag. "And then Saturday afternoon Gordon came to see you. Tell me about that."

Lattie looked at Gordon again. He felt sorry for her but kept his face impassive. He could only make things worse by interfering at this point.

"He said he knew something was wrong. I told him the whole story. It was a relief in a way, to tell someone about it."

Fitz nodded. "I'm sure it must have been."

"Gordon said he'd speak to Hollows. And to—to you." Another shy glance at Fitz. "And somehow we'd work it out. It was the best way, he said, because otherwise Potts might come back again. Want more money. I was afraid of that, too. And that sort of thing never ends," she said.

Gordon experienced a deep qualm. He saw where this was going and Lattie was headed there like a sheep. He glared at Fitz, who flashed him a warning look to keep silent.

"So you were pretty certain Gordon could straighten it all out, were you?" Fitz said.

"Well, he said he couldn't promise anything and I understood that," Lattie said, fairly. "But I know you'll do your best." She addressed this to Gordon, who nodded. Her eyes were watery, he noticed. She was hanging on, but by a thread.

"Well, I can't speak for Hollows, but I can assure you, you won't have any more trouble with Jervis Potts." Fitz sounded almost flippant. "He was killed this morning." He watched Lattie closely as he brought this out.

"Killed!" She gasped and looked wide-eyed from Gordon to Fletch, then back at Fitz. "Oh my God. What's happening on this island?" She worked and worked her hands in her lap, tears dripping down.

She doesn't see it, Gordon thought. If she had anything to do with it, she would have seen it coming. He looked at Fletch who was sitting up in his chair now, watching Lattie with concern.

"Who would want to kill Jervis Potts," she said softly to no one in particular, her voice shaking.

"Aside from you, you mean?" Fitz said blandly, eyes hard on her.

"ME?" She looked at him first in disbelief, then with growing alarm. "You don't think I killed him? I can't stand the man and never should have let him blackmail me. But kill him?"

"I'd say you have a pretty good motive," Fitz sounded more official now. "And opportunity—you were out on the water alone, no one saw you. It's what? Twenty minutes maybe to Okum's End. Plenty of time to pay Potts a visit and still bring in a good stringer of trout." He looked down, frowning, thinking.

Gordon felt another qualm. In a minute Fitz's going to go there, he thought. He did.

"Where were you on Friday night, the night the power went out, Ms. Mainstay?" Fitz's voice was silky.

Lattie was getting a hunted look in her eye. "I was here. For Paella Night."

"And after that?"

"We went home, Doris and I. You remember, Gordon. Jadyn drove us home."

Gordon nodded at Fitz to confirm this.

"And then—well, there was no power. We just went to bed."

"Just went to bed." Fitz said slowly, fell silent for a minute. Then, he looked up and said abruptly, "How well do you know Max Lopez?"

The question took Lattie by surprise. "I don't know him. I mean, I know his name. Everyone does. He's building that big house out on the East end." She gestured vaguely.

"Yes, that's right." Fitz said evenly. He looked at her appraisingly. "You've lived here a long time, haven't you?

"Twenty-eight years," Lattie said, with a little smile.

"Mmm. You've seen lots of changes and now—people like Hollows, Lopez—they're changing Hogge even more, aren't they?"

"Ruining it, you mean," Lattie said, sounding depressed.

Fitz was nodding his head, thinking. "Would it surprise you to know that the man found on the beach was Max Lopez?" He asked the question sharply, watching her very closely as he brought this out.

Lattie looked stunned. Her surprise had to be genuine. Gordon was convinced of it.

Fitz didn't wait for her to respond, but continued. "And he didn't drown, Ms. Mainstay. He was killed. In much the same manner as Mr. Potts."

"Oh dear God," Lattie, stricken, looked at Gordon, who started to speak, thoroughly alarmed.

Fitz silenced him and continued. "Now, unfortunately we only have your word for it that Potts sold you this watch. And Potts is also dead." He looked her over. "You're a strong woman. Have your own boat. You know these waters like the back of your hand." His voice had hardened. "There's been nothing but trouble on this island the past few days, Ms. Mainstay. Starting with your visit to Hollows property. Is it possible, I ask myself, that you're at the bottom of it?"

The web was good and tight now. Lattie was no idiot. She pulled herself together. When she spoke, her voice shook, but there was anger in it. "Do you actually think—are you accusing me, ME, of..." She stopped, mouth drawn in a hard line. "Do I need a lawyer, Sheriff Fitz?"

"I think that would be advisable," Gordon interjected, ignoring Fitz's furious look. "In fact, I'm going to call Jack Campbell right now and see if he can arrange for someone.

This," he said to Fitz, "has gone far enough. It's all circumstantial. No!" he held up a hand to Lattie, who started to speak, "Not another word. I don't care if you're innocent as a newborn. Plenty of innocent people behind bars as he," Gordon jabbed a finger at Fitz, "can tell you."

"I have enough to charge her," Fitz said stubbornly. "If nothing else, I'm taking her into custody for questioning until some of this is cleared up."

"Arresting her, you mean?" Gordon's voice was hard.

"Technically, yes."

"Gordon!" Lattie's voice rose in a wail. "You can't let him do this. It's insane. Please tell me there's something you can do?"

"I'm doing the best thing I can do right now," Gordon said tersely, dialing Jack's number. "I can't stop him from taking you in. You can sue him later," he added, ignoring Fitz's sour look.

Fletch had been silent throughout the interview. Now, he rose to his feet and stretched. "You need me here anymore," he said lazily to Fitz, "because I've had about as much as I can stomach. Been up since dawn. I need my beauty sleep."

Fitz had his phone out, was dialing. "You can go for now," he said gruffly.

"I must say, you've strung all your little dots together pretty neatly, Sheriff. Problem is, I think you're missing a few." His tone was dangerously off-hand.

"What do you mean by that?" Fitz snapped, in no mood for riddles.

"Try asking your wife." Fletch shot back. He patted Lattie's shoulder comfortingly on his way out the door, slamming it behind him.

CHAPTER 32

"Just what the hell did he mean by that?" Fitz demanded angrily as soon as he and Gordon were alone in the office. "What does Marly have to do with anything?" A tearful but still game Lattie had been collected by Jack and Nevada who drove her home to get a few things, with a promise to come right back. Jack, furious, had delivered a few choice words to Fitz. He wasn't well pleased with Gordon either, it was clear.

"I don't know," Gordon said, determined to let Fitz sort this one out himself. "Why don't you do as he says and ask her?"

"Ask her what?"

Gordon shrugged. "Obviously Fletch thinks Marly might know something about what's been going on out here. Just my guess," he added.

"That's ridiculous! She's been here a handful a times. Doesn't even know anyone." Fitz paused. "I think he's just showing his ass. I don't appreciate it." There was a shade of doubt in his tone. He looked at Gordon, pointed a finger at him. "You're holding something back from me. Again. What is it?"

Gordon's eyes narrowed. "It's for Marly to say, not me. Don't ask me again. That's all I have to say about it."

The two men glared at each other, at an impasse.

Gordon broke the tense silence first, changing the subject. "You've got the wrong angle on this, Fitz. You really intend to take Lattie into custody? None of it will hold up, you know."

"Yes. If nothing else, she's a material witness." Fitz was truculent.

"Witness to what?" Gordon demanded. "You know as well as I do, once you get some solid information she's going to be cleared. Meanwhile, you're dragging a seventy something woman, who's lived on this island for over twenty-five years, to the hoosegow based on nothing but conjecture. Once a lawyer gets involved you won't be able to hold her for twenty minutes."

"Then I'll charge her with vandalism and hold her on that. She did plenty of damage, over a grand I'd say, and admitted it. That's a third degree felony in these parts." He looked unhappy but he was sticking to his guns.

"Has Hollows pressed charges?"

"No, but you can bet your ass he will tomorrow."

Not if I get to him first, Gordon thought. Aloud, he tried another tack. "Be reasonable, Fitz. Lattie's not a young woman. I'm worried about her health. This is taking a helluva toll on her. Can't you see that?"

"I'm worried about her health, too," Fitz shot back. "Did it ever occur to you that maybe she's safer on the mainland where I can keep an eye on her than she is here? Bodies are piling up at an impressive rate on this little island of yours."

Gordon stared at him. "Is that why you're taking her in? You could have said that from the beginning."

"I'm not convinced she isn't involved," Fitz was noncommittal. "But if it turns out she isn't..." He leaned forward and slapped his palm on the desk. "Then whoever it is, let'em think they're off the hook. You may have noticed that it's not real easy to pin anyone down around here. Did they ever solve that arson we were talking about?"

"No."

"Yeah, well I don't want this to go the same way. There are a lot of leads to chase down. Let's say I'm buying time." He looked at Gordon to see if he was getting through.

"Not much," Gordon said. "Besides, you could at least tell *her* what you're doing."

"I tell her it's all over the island in ten minutes. And we're right back where we started. No. We do this my way." He was firm. "But don't make any mistake. I'm not convinced she's as innocent as you seem to believe," he warned. "And, like we agreed the other day. Wherever it leads, it leads." He looked at Gordon, jaw set.

"Yes." Gordon said. He gave Fitz an appraising look. "Just remember, that goes for both of us." With that, he walked out the door leaving a startled looking Fitz to make his phone calls.

CHAPTER 33

By eight o'clock Sunday night, word of Lattie's arrest in connection with the death on Okum's End had traveled from one end of Hogge to the other, the story becoming more colorful and outlandish in each retelling. As he prowled the restaurant, perfunctorily greeting patrons, Gordon overheard snatches of conversation at virtually every table.

"They say the man was a recluse, a millionaire, who had jilted her years ago," one woman, shoulders and neck beet red from the sun, was saying, sipping wine. "Now she lives with a woman. You know what *that* means. I guess she finally snapped."

A man with a horrible comb-over, spilling vodka on his loud pink-and-green patterned shirt, told the rapt listeners at his table, "They suspect her of killing two men in a different state, but I was told that confidentially, so keep it under your hat."

"Can you imagine, in a place like this?

"It's not surprising," a young mother paused from spooning orange mush into the mouth of a baby with chubby pink cheeks. "I heard that half the people who live here are felons, escaping from the law. They come here to disappear."

"No, Rita, you're thinking of Bimini," her tired-looking husband said, pushing food around on his plate.

"Well, I know what I heard," she replied stubbornly, wiping the baby's mouth as the mush oozed back out.

Between bites of grouper a large woman with dark bangs and dangling gold earrings confided to her friend, "She had an accomplice, an old guy. I saw them when they tried to put her in the helicopter."

"I thought they took her off on a boat," her companion said doubtfully.

"Well, she tried to make a break for it anyway."

Gordon slumped into a chair at his table by the door with an audible groan. Poor Lattie. By morning she'd be a cross between Jack the Ripper and Lizzie Borden.

Marvelita came over to him with his bourbon and a glass. For once, he declined. "I have the mother of all headaches already," he said, weary. He'd already told her the whole story after he left Fitz in the office.

She wasn't a fan of Lattie's but now she said, "She may be hiding something but she did not kill those men, Gordon. The sheriff is an idiot for thinking so."

Gordon didn't bring up Fitz's other reason for taking Lattie into custody. Fitz was going to have to wear the "idiot" label for a while.

"Blaming Potts, yes, she would do, but if she took that watch it was because she was where she had no business. She is nosey, not a murderer." Marvelita looked at him intently. "I think you should go home. We will finish up dinner and close. You need to sleep." She patted his arm.

Gordon sighed, looked around. "Have you noticed there are no islanders here? They're closing ranks. Think I sold her down the river. Jack was pretty pissed this afternoon. Haven't heard from him since. Only person that called was Doris." With a twinge, he remembered the string of trout still on ice in his refrigerator. Lattie so looking forward to her fish fry.

He banished the thought and leaned back, twisted his neck from side to side, getting a few cracks out of it. "Tomorrow I have to go deal with Hollows." His face darkened at the thought.

"What sense is there in doing that?" Marvelita frowned. "She is under arrest. Damaging his machines cannot matter now."

Gordon decided to trust her. "I'm pretty certain," he said quietly, "that the murder charge won't hold up. You're not to tell anyone that," he warned. "But if I don't convince Hollows not to, he'll press charges for vandalism. Then Fitz will have to charge her."

Marvelita's eyes widened. She understood the significance of what he was saying perfectly. But all she said was, "So. Fitz is not the complete idiot." She seemed satisfied.

Gordon was conscious of more than a few looks thrown their way. "God knows what story they're cooking up for us," he grumbled. "I think you're right. I should go home. Have to clear my head. Think." He sighed again and covered Marvelita's small hand with his own—damn the looks. "Thank you, Lita. Be careful on the way home." He got up, kissed her gently on the forehead, and went out.

Behind him, the tongues clacked on.

CHAPTER 34

Monday morning Gordon woke up at six, an hour before the alarm. Given the headache and relentless stream of thoughts that climbed into bed with him, he figured he'd have a fitful sleep, at best. He was wrong. He slept like the dead. Now, somewhat refreshed—the headache was not so much gone as lurking behind his temples—showered, and dressed, he geared up for his conversation with Hollows. He wasn't sure what time Hollows got in, but he figured eight was early enough. He might be able to head the man off before Fitz got to him. If he hadn't already.

Marvelita was already gone. She left a note saying coffee was on the stove and could be heated up and that she'd have a late breakfast ready for him later at the restaurant. At the word "breakfast," his stomach growled. But this morning, time was of the essence. He gulped down an espresso and headed over to the Hogge Island Club. The air was thick with humidity, oppressive, courtesy of a stalled low front that had set up over the entire peninsula and showed no signs of leaving. By the time he got to the club, his head was throbbing again.

Two maintenance people were puttering around the heavily landscaped entranceway and a few maids were readying a cart for take-off. Hollows' boat wasn't in its slip. The twenty-foot skiff with two 115hp Yamahas was a recent acquisition, a replacement for the cruiser he'd parked on an oyster bar a few months back.

Gordon sank gratefully into one of the comfortable wicker armchairs under the Coconut Palms framing the office and waited. He surveyed the freshly painted buildings, many of them new, the neatly manicured shrubs. The large construction site beyond the docks was just visible behind a stand of recently planted Arecas. He hadn't actually seen the club since shortly after the storm. Hollows was doing pretty well for himself, he had to admit. A roar of engines heralded Hollow's arrival. Hollows tied his boat off and came up the gangway holding a parcel under his arm. If he was surprised to see Gordon sitting in front of his office, he didn't show it.

"Morning, Strange, what brings you here," he said, unlocking the door. "As if I didn't know," he couldn't resist adding.

Gordon followed him into the cool, spacious office, tastefully appointed with blonde furniture, chairs plump with leaf patterned cushions. Hollows sat down behind a massive desk, adorned only by a phone and one of those miniature basketball games advertised in catalogs aimed at executives with time on their hands. There were no papers or files in evidence anywhere. Presumably, the real work was done somewhere else. Behind him, stretching the length of the wall was a gallery of photographs. Six-inch high bold letters announced "The Hogge Island Club Rental Homes and Residences."

Hollows sat with his arms folded, looking at him with a mixture of amusement and derision.

"Mind if I smoke?" Gordon brought out his cigars just to irritate him.

"I can tolerate your bare feet, Strange," Hollows said, "but not your cigars. No smoking in here. What do you want?"

"You can probably guess." Gordon said, lounging, one arm resting on the back of the chair. "I'm here about Lattie."

"I heard about the arrest," Hollows was dismissive. "Can't say I'm surprised. She's obviously unbalanced. What do you expect me to do about it?"

"Spoken to Fitz already then?" Gordon said casually.

"I have a voicemail from him. He wants me to call. I'll do that as soon as you clear out and let me get to my work."

Gordon ignored the remark. "I'm not here about the arrest. You know as well as I do she didn't kill anyone. She may get worked up over issues, but she's no murderer."

"First time for everything." Hollows eyed him. "I heard she snapped. Like I said, doesn't surprise me. She's been here a long time, maybe too long. Maybe you should think about that. It's been, what? Ten years for you?"

Gordon was fully aware that the man was baiting him, but he didn't rise to it. "All that will sort itself out," he said with a vague wave. "I'm here about something else. I hear you had some equipment damage a few days ago."

"What do you know about that?" Hollows said sharply, sitting forward, interested.

"Fitz is going to tell you Lattie was responsible for it," Gordon said, pointing to the phone. "He's going to ask you to press charges. I'm here to ask you not to."

Hollows looked at him, expressionless, but it was clear his mind was working. He got a calculating look in his eye. "Why shouldn't I press charges? She did thousands in damage. Unbalanced, like I said. We don't need that sort out here." He sat back, the picture of respectability, marred only by the scar that ran from his left ear to his jawbone. The scar was like a litmus strip. It colored when he was angry or excited.

"Lattie doesn't need any more trouble right now. I thought maybe you and I could come to some private arrangement," Gordon said, in a matter of fact tone. "I take care of the damages, and you let the whole thing drop." He sat back, waited.

Hollows looked at him intently. "You seem awfully eager to have this go away. Considering the woman's being held on a murder charge, I find that interesting. What gives?"

Gordon considered his words carefully. "Fitz can't hold her for long. I'd like Lattie to be able to come back here without charges from you hanging over her head. She's been through enough as it is."

"She should have thought of that before she trespassed on my property and fucked up my trucks. Besides," Hollows said unpleasantly, "she's your friend, not mine. I don't give a shit what happens to her."

"I'm not appealing to your sense of decency," Gordon said with considerable effort, "you said you're a businessman. This is a business proposition. I pay for the damages—in exchange for your dropping the matter—your equipment gets fixed, Lattie avoids an ordeal, and you look magnanimous. Better for everybody. Might even improve your stellar reputation," he couldn't resist the jab.

"I don't give a crap about my reputation," Hollows spat back. But his mind was still squirming. "I might be willing to come to some arrangement," he finally said, pressing the lever on the basketball toy, making the tiny ball bounce toward the miniature basket. "It would have to be legal, papers drawn up. I'm not doing anything with you on a handshake."

Gordon bit back the numerous snide retorts that sprang to his lips. "What do you have in mind?"

"You pay for the damages—"

"From an invoice," Gordon cut in.

"Fine. *And*, that piss-ant Hogge Island Civic Association stops objecting to my expansion." He waved in the general direction of the construction. "That has to be in writing, too." He sat back, arms folded, smug.

Gordon stared at him. "You're asking a lot."

"So are you," Hollows shot back. He resumed trying to tap the ball into the net.

"I could talk to the folks at HICA." Gordon had a mental image of Jack having apoplexy at this suggestion. "But people can do what they want as private citizens. There are laws governing that sort of thing," he said pointedly.

"I don't care about individuals. I want that association off my back. They have funds and besides, the County recognizes them as some sort of island authority, God knows why. They agree to it or no deal," he said, satisfaction oozing from every pore.

"Money I can give you right away," Gordon said. "The other thing will take time. I can't promise that."

"Then," Hollows said with a smirk, "I pick up that phone and return Fitz's call. And your girlfriend goes to jail. Where she belongs."

No one on Hogge could exploit an advantage quite like Alan Hollows. Gordon wanted to pull him out of his chair by the collar and throw him off the dock. Instead, he said, "You sure you're the best judge of who belongs in jail?" He leaned forward and roughly shoved the toy Hollows was still playing with aside. "Don't overplay your hand, Hollows," he warned. "I have my limits." Hoping to wipe the smug look off Hollows' face, he pointed out the window. "Where's all the money coming from? Just curious."

"None of your fucking business."

"Maybe I'll make it my business."

"You threatening me, Strange? You came here asking me for a favor. I don't like your attitude. Not one bit. Maybe I just make that phone call and you get the hell out of here." His fleshy face was white with rage, the scar screaming red from his pale, rapidly blinking eyes to the tight, drawn mouth.

"And maybe Lattie takes her chances in court. There were no witnesses. It's all hearsay."

Hollows pounced on this. "You said she admitted it to Fitz. That's all I need."

"Without benefit of counsel. I don't think it will hold up." Gordon looked around, bored, as if he was preparing to leave.

"If you're so sure, why the hell did you come sniveling to me in the first place? And who says I don't have witnesses? Maybe I do?"

"Who?" Gordon asked sharply.

Hollows got a guarded look. "That's none of your business either," he said, clearly annoyed that he'd been provoked into offering information.

"Have it your way," Gordon shrugged indifferently. "I was just trying to save everyone a lot of trouble. I thought maybe, just once, there was a chance you'd be reasonable. Guess I overestimated you. Again." He gave Hollows a lazy smile, stood up, towering over the desk. "So go ahead. Make your phone call. We'll see how far you get."

Hollows looked disconcerted. With that scar, Gordon thought, he'd make a hell of a poker player.

"Hold on," Hollows said, chasing the tatters of his disappearing leverage. "No need to get heated. You talk to HICA and see if they'll play ball. I don't want trouble any more than you do." His tone was wheedling. "I'll give you time. Say, to the end of the week."

He doesn't want to make that phone call, Gordon thought, enlightened. What provoked the sudden change of heart? He decided to ask. "Why the about-face?" He played a hunch. "Afraid your sordid past will catch up with you?"

Hollows flared up. "Don't give me that bullshit, Strange. How about your past? You're no choirboy, the way I hear it."

"No," Gordon said mildly, hand on the door. "Then again, I don't *pretend* to be one."

"I'll give you until Friday," Hollows repeated loudly as Gordon opened the door. "I'll be expecting your call."

Don't hold your breath, Gordon thought, walking to his cart.

All very well, he thought, driving out of the grounds, but he was fairly certain that without intervention Hollows would eventually make that call, if nothing else, out of spite. Lattie might actually beat the charges, but she'd be put through several hells in the meantime. He had to at least talk to HICA, to Jack, and see if there was a chance they'd go along. Meanwhile, Hollows had let one or two things slip that bore thinking about.

Gordon sped toward the restaurant, bouncing heedlessly over the ruts, eager to distance himself from the Hogge Island Club as quickly as possible. Negotiating with Hollows left him feeling like he'd rolled around in mud—and no amount of showering was going to help.

CHAPTER 35

The restaurant was quiet when Gordon returned, not surprising for a Monday morning. Marvelita appeared shortly after he came in with his breakfast—a fluffy omelet flecked with chorizo, with a helping of fresh fruit salad on the side.

"Am I on a diet?" Gordon asked, out of sorts.

Marvelita raised her eyebrows at this. "It is not good to eat heavily in this heat. You know that." She searched his face. "The meeting did not go well?" It was a question. Sort of.

"I detest that man," Gordon said emphatically, reaching for his fork. He looked up at her. "Sorry, Lita. I'm frustrated because I can't punch him in the face, which is what I'd like to do. Don't mean to take it out on you. I could use some coffee."

"Making a deal with the devil is not pleasant, no," Marvelita agreed, shaking her head. "I don't like it. Now he has something to hold over you."

"That was made fairly obvious," Gordon said in disgust. "Got to be done, though." Was he convincing her or himself? He resumed eating his breakfast. "Anyone in looking for me?"

"No. Only the workers for breakfast, early. It will be a slow day. I can do the menus for tomorrow when you are ready."

"I'll take coffee in the office," Gordon said. "Got a few things I have to sort out. And a few calls to make," he said, without enthusiasm.

She nodded sympathetically and left him to his troubles.

Anything could be faced with a small pot of espresso, Gordon thought shortly afterward, sitting in front of his computer in the office. He picked up his phone and called Jack. Might as well get that over with first thing. There was no answer, so he left a voicemail asking him to get in touch as soon as possible. While he was leaving that message, he got an incoming call: Fitz.

"You were my next call," Gordon said, not bothering with 'hellos.' "How's Lattie holding up?"

"She's not here." Fitz sounded annoyed. "Jack Campbell showed up this morning with a high-powered attorney out of Ft. Myers who started yelling about false arrest and a half a dozen other things I won't go into. She's staying in a hotel on the mainland for now, with Doris. I got them to agree to that much." He paused. "I haven't heard back from Hollows and I left him a message. Odd, isn't it?" His tone was dry.

"I spoke to Hollows this morning," Gordon said frankly. "Persuaded him not to press charges right away."

"And just what did that cost you?" Fitz was clearly irritated.

"That's my problem," Gordon said. He refused to be drawn. The sheriff didn't need the details of that conversation at this point. "Where are you with Max Lopez? I thought by now you'd have something. It's been two days."

"I have some information. More coming. It's hard to get hold of people over the weekend, Strange. This isn't TV." Fitz still sounded put out. "You're supposed to be on that island keeping an eye on things for me, not gumming up an investigation. What happened with Hollows?"

Gordon hesitated but finally gave in. "Short version is I left him hoping I'd convince the people opposing his building to back off in exchange for not pressing charges against Lattie. That and money, of course, for the damages." He paused and drank some coffee. "We got into it toward the end. Can't be helped with a guy like him. In the process, he let a few things slip."

"Like what?"

"He claimed to have a witness to the vandalism. I asked him who, and he suddenly clammed up. Then, as I was leaving, he pissed me off good, so I told him to call you back, press charges, and be damned. All of a sudden, he wasn't so eager to do it. He's hiding something. Don't know if it's connected to recent events or something in the past. I imagine his isn't pretty."

"Nothing on record, at least since I've been here," Fitz said. "I could dig deeper," he offered.

"Not worth wasting time on now," Gordon said. "We've got two men dead and another in the hospital. How's the German making out, by the way?"

"They're releasing him in a few days. Fractures to the head and jaw, but he's stable. On the other two," Fitz could be heard rustling papers, "they're still working on Potts, but the autopsy on Lopez came in. Here it is: Hispanic male, 48, five foot nine. He didn't drown—no water in the lungs. Blunt force trauma to the head. Coroner says time of death was around 10 or 11p.m. Friday night, but he can't pin it down better than that--took a while to die. Internal bleeding."

"So someone left him on that beach to die?"

"No. He was dead by then. Whoever killed him did it somewhere else and dumped the body."

Gordon was silent, thinking. Friday night. The night the power went out.

"You still there?" Fitz demanded.

"Yeah. That was the night the electricity went down. You were on the island. Pretty ballsy move."

"Or pretty desperate," Fitz said.

"What did you find out about him?" Gordon asked.

"Standard stuff. He's from Miami, like you thought. Owns a nice waterfront condo on Miami Beach, worth a bundle, I would guess. Was a Senior Vice President at Bilboa Bank, Mortgage Division in Miami—they're based in Spain. Got most of this from their HR department this morning," Fitz continued. "They were pretty upset. Seemed to be well-liked there."

"More than he was here, at any rate," Gordon said.

"Yeah, well. Worked there since 2004. Before that, he lived in Gainesville, Ocala—worked for Citibank, then Wells Fargo, as a teller for a few years. Then made loan officer, transferred to the mortgage division, and finally landed the SVP job at Bilboa. Worked his way up the food chain, I guess. Started out as a part-time public adjustor in '95, but there's nothing before that. All this stuff's off his resume," he explained, which Gordon had gathered by now. "Still have to check it all out. Anyhow, he's been with Bilboa the longest."

"Seems to have done pretty well in a relatively short period of time. Any school?"

"Yeah—degree in business from University of Florida, doesn't give a year. Not too shabby. The HR department told me there was a life insurance policy on him. Part of their package of perks, I figure. The beneficiary is a sister, or maybe step-sister. She has a different name. The address for her is the same as his in Miami. She's also the emergency contact. There was a cellphone number for her but it's been disconnected. We're still trying to reach her."

"What's her name?" Gordon was curious.

"Carmella Duarte."

Gordon lit a cigar, poured some cold coffee. "That's interesting," he said, thinking.

"What is?"

"Carmella isn't that far from Carmen. Remember the maid that vanished? Think there's any connection?"

"That's a stretch," Fitz said. "Carmen's a pretty common name." He paused. "But I'll check it out once we find her. Bank's trying to get hold of her, as well. Financial information hasn't come through completely yet, but there's a will—filed in Miami-Dade. We're getting a copy from his lawyer."

"Interesting career path, from part-time public adjustor to Senior VP, don't you think?" Gordon asked dryly.

"Maybe he worked hard." Fitz's tone was hard to read.

"Or maybe he got in with the right people. Or person," Gordon countered. "Waterfront condos in Miami don't come cheap. And from what he was building here, money seemed to be no object."

"I wondered about the money myself," Fitz admitted. "We'll have a better idea once I get hold of his finances, but it's going to take time. Meanwhile, I'll see what more I can find out about Mr. Lopez's life in Miami, talk to some of his neighbors, friends—he must have had some. There's no wife."

The mention of a wife brought Fitz's to mind. "How's Marly, by the way?" Gordon asked casually.

There was an appreciable pause. "Fine," Fitz said gruffly. "She's out of town for a few days. Visiting friends in Ft. Lauderdale." He sounded like he didn't want to discuss it. Gordon let it drop, moved on to another subject.

"You haven't mentioned Richard Sharpe. Did you ever get hold of him?"

"Yeah," Fitz said. "I went by his place Sunday morning and woke him up. Seems he left the island on the work boat Friday afternoon before five. Ten guys rode the boat with him. And then," Gordon could hear Fitz rifling through his notepad, "he spent the rest of the night getting hammered in the Rat Snake—biker bar on Palm," Fitz explained. "Bartender says he closed the place. One of his pals had to drive him home. We're still keeping the Lopez murder under wraps until we reach his next of kin, but I can tell you, Sharpe has nothing good to say about him. All he can talk about is how much money the guy owes him—thousands, he says. He was still obsessing about it when I left him." Fitz sighed. "Unfortunately, he doesn't own a boat and was apparently blind drunk Friday at midnight. Plus he's got more to lose with Lopez dead than alive. I'm pretty sure that lets him out as a suspect."

"Too bad," Gordon said reflectively. "Maybe he sobered up or got a ride out with one of his buddies?"

"Not likely," Fitz said. "When I got to him Sunday morning he was still drinking. For a builder, he lives in a helluva dump," he added as an aside. "He has a record. I checked. Eight years for cocaine trafficking and an assault charge. That was twenty years ago. He's been clean since, or so he claims. I'll keep an eye on him, but I don't think he's our man," Fitz said with regret. "Which leaves nowhere." There was a pause. "Lattie's still looking pretty good," he said tentatively.

"Which tells me just how desperate you are to hang this on someone," Gordon said. "Instead of figuring out how to make yourself look ridiculous arresting a seventy-five year old woman for something you know she didn't do, why don't you concentrate on Lopez—and finding this half sister of his. I'm going to follow up on something here."

"What?" Fitz demanded suspiciously, "You have a lead I don't know about?"

"Not so much a lead as a feeling," Gordon said slowly. "Since eight o'clock this morning I've found myself asking the same question twice. I think I'm going to take my own favorite advice," he said.

"What question? What advice?" Fitz sounded mystified.

"Follow the money," Gordon said with a sharp laugh. Only he wasn't joking.

CHAPTER 36

Gordon hung up with Fitz and brought out his laptop. Outside, thick, bilious-looking clouds obscured the horizon, enveloping the island in a rainy, overcast gloom that matched his own. A low pressure system like this could set up for days. In twenty-four hours every path would be under water. At least, he thought, firing up his computer, the bad weather might keep any further incidents at bay.

He wasn't sure exactly where to start, or even what he was looking for. Might as well begin with Max Lopez. Fitz had his official sources, but a surprising amount of information could be gleaned these days from a person's electronic footprint.

An hour later, he was still at it. He had narrowed down the seventy thousand or so hits to about six hundred. There wasn't much personal information about the man online—he didn't seem to have any sort of social media profile. There were numerous business references that at least let him know he had the right Max Lopez—mostly from his position at Bilboa Bank. These were chiefly press releases put out by the bank, drumming up business. The man didn't seem to exist before that.

Maybe, the thought came to him, because he wasn't always Max Lopez. He started over, adding "Jaime" to his search, briefly cursing Google for eliminating its "search within" feature—no doubt because that brought users to useful information too quickly. After what seemed like hours later, he was staring at a reference to J. Maximo Lopez on a court document pulled up from the Florida public records database. It was a mortgage in the amount of $1.3 million for a home on Hogge Island, signed in October 2004. The date in particular caught his eye. After Hurricane Charley hit in August 2004, he wasn't aware of any home that didn't have hundreds of thousands in damage. Certainly none that could be worth $1.3 million at that point. He printed out the entire thing to take a closer look.

The mortgage was granted by Bilboa Bank, signed by Mr. J. Maximo Lopez for the bank. He didn't recognize the name of the grantee, Braxton Rufford, from Nebraska. The property in question was on Brown Pelican Drive, on Hogge Island. He knew the road. It hugged the water on the Gulf side, leading to the South end. He copied down the address and followed up with another search, this time on Braxton Rufford. In a few minutes he was looking at two documents. One was a balloon mortgage in the amount of $350,000, taken out by Mr. Rufford a few days after the first one, payable in 60 days—to Ocean Homes LLC. The second was a contract of sale, also dated in October 2004, indicating Mr. Rufford had sold the home to Ocean Homes LLC for $1.8 million.

He turned over the information in his mind while the printer spit out the pages. He didn't have the full picture of what he had uncovered, but there was certainly a lot of money changing hands in a short period of time. At least on paper. And Mr. Lopez was apparently right in the middle of it.

Ocean Homes LLC was his next target. There were hundreds, if not thousands, of LLC's in Florida. If he was lucky, this one was formed in the state and not on some Bahamian island. He was just about to pursue this avenue when there was a knock at his door.

"Who is it?" He couldn't keep the annoyance out of his voice.

"Me," the door opened and Jack Campbell walked in, looking stern. "I just got back from Palm Point. Gordon, we have to talk." He lowered himself into the chair opposite Gordon's desk, pulling if forward.

"I left Lattie and Doris in the Holiday Inn in town— they're beside themselves over all this." His face was drawn. He looked every one of his 85 years. "How could you have let Lattie incriminate herself that way with Fitz," he demanded. "I know you're not a lawyer, but common sense, man, common sense! I'm very disappointed." A Bassett Hound couldn't have looked more mournful.

Gordon sighed and spread his hands. "Look, Jack— everything snowballed yesterday morning. I admit I was slow on the uptake, but once I realized where Fitz was headed, I did stop it. You have to understand—I went out to Okum's End to have a conversation, not to find a dead man. Things got pretty complicated at that point. If you've talked to Lattie, you know what I mean."

"I realize she put herself in a compromising position," Jack was mincing his words, "but even if you have sworn loyalty to Fitz, you should have realized—"

Gordon cut him off. "Not for a minute," he said firmly. "I never thought she was involved in Jervis's death or Lopez's. That was Fitz's bright idea. The minute I saw where Fitz was going, I stopped him—called you."

"Damage was already done." Jack shook his head.

"That may be but—" Gordon hesitated, unsure of how much Fitz had taken Jack into his confidence. "Fitz had his reasons. Maybe he explained that to you?"

"Fitz shared nothing with me except his harebrained notion that he could hold Lattie on a murder charge. The lawyer I arranged for relieved him of that idea pretty quickly. She has good grounds for a lawsuit," he added.

Gordon decided to take Jack into his confidence. The man had been reliable so far and, besides, he needed Jack's help—which he wasn't going to get as long as the man sat there glowering at him.

"I'm going to share something with you Jack, but I need your word that you tell no one, not even Nevada. People's safety may be at stake."

Jack sat up and looked at him, eagle-eyed. "You have my word," he said seriously. "Go on."

"Part of the reason Fitz took Lattie in was to get her off this island…for her own safety." While Jack digested this, Gordon went on. "That, and he's not entirely convinced that she isn't hiding something. She didn't help matters with that stunt she pulled at the Hogge Island Club. You know about that, right?"

Jack nodded his head yes, unhappily. "That was a mistake on her part. I told her that."

"To put it mildly," Gordon said with emphasis. "I spoke to Hollows this morning, asked him not to press charges. I told him I'd pay the damages if he let it go."

The expression on Jack's face, which had been dour up until now, changed. "That was very generous of you. Considering your relationship with him, it must have been a difficult thing to do." The warmth was back in his tone.

"Yeah, well, Hollows wasn't willing to let it go that easily." Gordon grimaced, and plunged into the next part. "He's demanding a pledge, in writing, from HICA, that it will drop its opposition to his expansion project. Otherwise, he says he'll go ahead and press charges for vandalism. Claims it runs in the thousands. Exaggeration, of course, but we'll have a hard time proving it."

"That's outrageous," Jack was instantly furious. "It's...why it's blackmail, that's what it is!" He was halfway out of his chair, agitated.

"Blackmail of a sort," Gordon agreed. "Problem is, Lattie let herself and everyone else in for it when she did what she did. At one point I told him he could press his charges and be damned. She could take her chances in court. But given everything else that's transpired..." He gestured helplessly. "At the very least, she'd be put through the wringer. Which leaves all of you in about as difficult a position as I've found myself in these past twenty-four hours," he said pointedly.

Jack was pacing the floor in the small office while Gordon spoke. He didn't speak at once. "This is a terrible" he finally said, sitting back down. "And I'm sorry I misjudged you. As you say, a difficult position. More than that. Insidious. But we have to consider it." He looked about as unhappy as Gordon had ever seen him. "I'll have to speak to the Board. She's a good friend, and an old one. But this—" He broke off, stared out the window, brooding. "This sort of thing could tear this island apart," he finally said.

"*Could* tear it apart?" Gordon said sharply. "I'd say that process started three days ago. Unless we make some headway with these murders, no one is going to trust his friend, much less his neighbor. Lattie's escapade couldn't have come at a worse time. Makes you wonder if we haven't all wandered into some sort of vortex."

"Please, Gordon. Now you sound like Jadyn Hayes!"

It was an attempt at humor and, however small, Gordon was glad for it. The man had been badly shaken and he was no youngster. "Anyhow, Hollows says he'll wait until the end of the week," Gordon continued, "to give HICA time to decide. He made a lot of noise about going through his lawyers, all on the up and up." He made a face. "That posturing of his makes me want to grab him by the throat. He sits there feigning respectability and expects you to buy it. I'd love to know more about his background. I don't think he got that scar playing lacrosse," he said caustically.

"There have been plenty of rumors about an unsavory past," Jack conceded. "But the family had money. They either had the records sealed or bought someone off. Either way," he said impatiently, "no one has ever been able to pin anything on him. And believe me," he skewed Gordon a look, "it's been tried."

Gordon grunted, then pulled over the pages he'd printed out. "Speaking of records, did you know Braxton Rufford? Had a house on Brown Pelican? Sold it in 2004, I think."

"Know the name, but not the man really. He didn't spend much time here. I think he rented the place out. It was a wreck after the storm. He never bothered to repair it, just sold it and left the island. House has been done over since then." Jack looked at him, curious. "Why do you ask?"

Gordon didn't want to share all his thinking just yet. "I'm looking at a few things," he said vaguely. "And it came up. You remember the house? What do you figure it went for?"

Jack shrugged. "The house was a total loss. It was across from the beach, not on it." He did some mental calculating. "I'd say the land was worth maybe $350,000, $400,000 at best, if someone really wanted it." He looked at Gordon keenly. "That tally with what you're looking at?"

"In its way," Gordon said cryptically. He looked at Jack for a few seconds. "I'd like to go into it, but I can't say anymore right now, Jack. And I'm going to have to ask you to keep everything we've discussed to yourself. I wouldn't have brought you into the picture if I didn't think you could do that."

Jack looked disappointed, but he was a man of his word. He stood up, preparing to leave. "You can rely on me," he said. "So far as I'm concerned, everything that has transpired in this office comes under the heading of attorney client privilege." His grave dignity and somber expression left no doubt that he took Gordon's request seriously and Gordon was grateful for it.

Without another word, the two men shook hands and Jack left. Through the window, Gordon watched Jack walk slowly toward his golf cart, one hand shielding his face from the rain.

CHAPTER 37

Gordon wasted no time getting back to his computer as soon as Jack left. He spared a few minutes to stick his head out the door and flag down Beni to request another pot of espresso and no interruptions, from anyone, for the next few hours. He picked up with Ocean Homes LLC. His luck was in. It was a Florida outfit incorporated in Miami-Dade in 2004 by a Benito Salazar, at an address that he had seen before. Thumbing back through the pages in front of him, he found it. It was the same as that given for Max Lopez.

There was a light tap at the door and Marvelita slipped in, bringing the espresso. She was curiously excited.

"Beni said you did not want to be interrupted, but this is important, Gordon. The maid, Carmen—she called me just now on the restaurant phone. She wants to speak to me, to us—but she is afraid to come to the island and will not talk on the phone. What should I tell her?"

"Tell her to call Fitz. I can't leave right now to go chase her down."

"I told her to do that. She says she cannot trust him."
Marvelita gave an expressive shrug.

"Goddammit." Gordon slammed the desk in frustration.
Then he calmed down. "Maybe she'll talk to Fletch. Get him
on the phone and see if he'll go. Where does she want to
meet?"

"At the Palm Point marina. She said she would be there
for one hour only, then she is leaving. She sounds—*histerico*.
She will not talk to Fletch, Gordon, but I can go with him. She
will talk to me." She nodded confidently.

It was a thought. Marvelita was the one the woman would
talk to in any event and it shouldn't take *too* long. Maybe they
could just close for lunch. It was a Monday and things were
slow anyhow.

"Okay," Gordon said, "Tell the staff to take the afternoon
off and come back in time for dinner service. I'll pay the off
time, if they ask."

"It is not necessary," Marvelita objected. "Beni is here
and he can run the kitchen. It is a very slow day. It is bad for
business to be closed."

"Okay, fine—you're in charge. Get hold of Fletch and
make sure he has his cellphone." Marvelita hated cellphones
and refused to own one, calling them a "devil's invention."
There were times Gordon agreed with her. "Call me as soon as
you're headed back here. I'm going to let Fitz know what
you're up to. Don't worry, I'll tell him to lay low until you've
spoken to her." He looked at her doubtfully. "Lita, be careful.
If the weather gets worse stay on Palm until it clears. Fletch is
a good captain, the best—but let's not take any chances."

"Good." She came over and patted his hand. "Do not worry about me. Finish your work." She smiled and hurried out to make her arrangements.

Gordon experienced a twinge of doubt as he watched her leave his office, but he suppressed it. They'd been all over that before. Marvelita didn't appreciate coddling any more than he did. Nevertheless, it wouldn't hurt to let Fitz know what she was planning. He made the call and had a brief conversation with Fitz. The man sounded agitated when he answered the phone and from her strident tones in the background, Gordon was pretty sure he'd interrupted some flap with Marly. He gave Fitz a concise update and extracted a promise from him not to put in an appearance. That wasn't too hard. Fitz sounded like he had his hands full.

That taken care of, Gordon turned back to the computer eagerly and began digging in earnest. Now that he knew what to look for, the data was easy to mine. For the next several hours he pulled documents from every database he could get his hands on from building permits to old real estate records. The pile of printed pages was growing on his desk. When he finally emerged from the depths of the internet, the stack was three inches thick and his vision was blurry. But he had a fairly clear picture about what he had uncovered, and it was pretty telling.

It was a complicated maze of financial trickery involving inflated insurance payments, fraudulent construction permits, spurious mortgages based on overinflated housing values, and kickback, in the form of balloon mortgages that he couldn't quite believe were legal. Maybe they weren't any more, but back in 2004 no agency seems to have cared. Vultures, one vulture in particular, had descended after the storm and found willing partners in the owners involved, desperate to cash out, and small cadre of dishonest cohorts on the island, eager to cash in. It was a tidy scheme. All it needed was a dishonest bank executive, a shady broker, an easily manipulated builder, shell investors, and a crooked appraiser willing to put whatever price was asked on a particular property.

He had names for all the players except the appraiser. The last document he got his hands on revealed that, too: Marlene Flaherty. With feeling of foreboding, Gordon did an image search on her, already suspecting what he was going to find. The photo was from an old HICA newsletter, grainy, but clear enough. Pictured with the late Jerry Munson, of Munson Realty, was his newest island staff member: hair longer, a few pounds lighter and looking surprisingly carefree was an earlier edition of Marly Fitz. Sheriff Fitz's wife.

Phone in hand, a dozen questions piled up in his head. How much did Fitz know? He hadn't seemed aware of Marly's earlier connection with Costello. Maybe he had found out? Maybe that explained the sheriff' eagerness to fasten on Lattie as a suspect? Or, if he was clueless, how would he react? The man was only human after all. He'd had integrity up to this point. Maybe. But would he still, with it hitting this close to home? Did anyone know how they really would react when their principles were tested directly, when the shit finally downloaded on them?

Gordon put the phone down. The only thing he knew for certain, other than the body of evidence sitting on his desk, was that this was going to require careful thinking and even more careful action. He didn't relish going over Fitz's head— wasn't even sure who that meant going to. He needed to sort this out with someone he could trust. On that thought, realization hit him like a hammer. He hadn't heard anything from Fletch or Marvelita. He looked at the time—two hours he'd been buried in his computer. No calls. Where were they? He called Fletch, who answered on the first ring.

"What's going on? Where are you?" Gordon said. He couldn't keep the tension out of his voice.

"I was going to call you in a few minutes." Fletch sounded defensive. "I'm docked at the marina. It took us a while to get here. Weather. Carmen met us at the dock but she insisted on talking to Marvelita alone. They went to the chiki hut on the other side of the dock. I'm cooling my heels here. Been here close to an hour and the weather's not improving. We may be stuck here overnight." He spoke in his usual flippant manner, but Gordon detected anxiety in his voice.

"Why don't you go see what they're up to," Gordon said forcing a calm he wasn't feeling. Far from it. "If that spooks Carmen, too bad. Call me when you find them." He paused, then added. "I've had a pretty interesting afternoon here. Dug up a ton of information."

"Hot stuff?" Fletch asked.

"Explosive," Gordon said grimly. "Go. I'm getting concerned. Been too long."

He hung up, feeling uneasy. The revelation about Marly was still dogging him. *Marly*. Gordon closed his eyes, replaying his phone call to Fitz hours ago. Telling him Marvelita was going to speak to Carmen, telling him when, where. Fitz and Marly arguing. Over what?

His phone rang. He snatched it up. Fletch. The connection couldn't have been worse. Every other word was lost in the crackling on the line.

"Marvelita hurt.....*garble*...EMS is on its way. Airlifting...*garble*....Lee Memorial. They think she's going to be okay. Gordon? Did you hear me?" Suddenly the line was bell clear. "I'm going with her. Fitz is meeting me there. Gordon?" Again, frantically, "Are you hearing me?"

Gordon made some reply, he couldn't remember what. He pocketed the phone and gathered up the papers, stuffing them into a briefcase. From the back of the file cabinet he took out his 9mm Luger, loaded the clip with deliberation, placed it on top of the papers and snapped the case shut. On his way out of the restaurant, he grabbed Beni, told him what he knew, told him he was going to Marvelita in the hospital.

"Close up," he said tersely, "Hang a sign on the door. Say whatever you want."

"How long?"

"I don't know. I don't give a damn if I ever see the place again." He swallowed, put a hand over his eyes, collected himself. "A week, tell them," he waved toward the staff, "with pay."

Beni was nodding, urging him to the door. "You go now. Find who hurt Marvelita," he said, voice thick with anger. "You kill him. Or give him to me." The glint in his eye matched Gordon's own.

Gordon nodded, put his briefcase under his arm and walked out into the rain, oblivious of it and the low heavy clouds coloring the whole world gray. His had gone red. Red and very black. He climbed into his boat and started the engine. The actions of an automaton.

The last thing he remembered before putting off was Beni, wet from the rain, running down the dock to hand him his shoes.

CHAPTER 38

As if Gordon's frame of mind wasn't bad enough, the trip across the bay to Palm became an exercise in slow torture. The rain had tapered to a light drizzle but heavy fog had set in making visibility treacherous. It forced him to a crawl. The trip dragged on interminably, a slog through a watery hell with no familiar landmarks or shoreline to judge distance by. The marina, appearing suddenly not thirty feet in front of him, took him utterly by surprise. He bumped the boat roughly into a dock and tied if off. Clutching the briefcase like a football, he ran, legs like stumps of lead, to the car he and Fletch shared. The engine sounded rough, but it started.

An hour later he was in the hospital elevator, going up to ICU. Winded, like he'd run a marathon, he walked the halls and found the room Marvelita was in, tubes and wires snaking from her small body to monitors that beeped and clicked with ominous efficiency. Her eyes were closed but she was breathing, aided by an oxygen tube running under her nose. Fletch was sitting in a chair by the bed, rigid, tense, paler than Gordon ever remembered seeing. He made a move to get up, but Gordon waved him down, went over to Marvelita and touched her face. It was warm. Ugly reddish marks, already purpling into bruises, ringed her delicate throat. He drew back, his hand over hers, and saw with surprise that his fingers were shaking.

Marvelita's eyes fluttered at his touch. She opened them briefly, and her hand haltingly crept over his arm. Squeezed. Then she drifted off again. Gordon picked her hand up very gently, kissed it once before laying it down on the bed.

Fletch looked at him with a wretched expression. "The doctor was in just before you got here. She's going to be okay. They've given her a sedative for—" he swallowed, "for the pain." He looked away. "I wouldn't blame you if you threw me the hell out of here. I should have known something was wrong. Knew it was, dammit." His face was twisted in disgust at his own incompetence.

"If anyone's at fault, I am." Gordon hadn't taken his eyes from Marvelita's face. "I was so damned wrapped up in what I was doing, I ignored my instincts." He walked over to Fletch abruptly, placed the briefcase next to the chair, and stood over him. It was a small space, and he was aware that he was taking up most of it. "Tell me what happened."

Fletch wrenched his eyes away from the bed. "After you and I spoke I went to find them. Goddamned fog was so bad I couldn't see a foot in front of me. When I got to the chiki hut I saw her on the ground. I never heard a thing, Gordon. No." He stopped himself angrily. "That's not true. I did hear something. Thought it was an osprey. It must have been...when..." He looked like he was going to be sick.

Gordon shook his shoulder roughly. "Never mind that now. You found her. Was Carmen there? Did you see anyone? Her attacker?" He was firing questions like bullets.

"No. Let me tell it." Fletch took a deep breath, frowning in concentration. "When I got to her I could already hear the sirens. A sheriff's car—not Fitz—and EMS came screaming in. They'd already been called. The paramedic said if they hadn't been, it…it might have been worse. I never saw Carmen. She must have called. Who else? Not whoever attacked Marvelita. Anyhow, the doc says they have to keep her ICU overnight for observation, but if she wakes up and all the vitals are okay, they'll release her to a room. Maybe even let her go home. Have to wait and see."

"Has Fitz been here?" Gordon demanded, picking up his briefcase.

Fletch looked around, as if startled. "He was here. I think he went to find you. Told him you were on your way in. He said something about arranging for protection. Hasn't he called?"

Gordon pulled out his phone. "Don't know. Turned it off once I got here." He powered it up. "Yeah. Three missed calls. Fuck him." He turned the phone off, put it back in his pocket. "He'll probably be back soon. Listen," he glanced around to make sure they were alone. "I don't want her to be alone overnight. Can you stay with her?"

Fletch looked at him, shocked. "Aren't you staying?"

"No," Gordon's voice was cold, hard. "I'm pretty sure I know who did this. I'm going to take care of him myself. By the time Fitz and his morons get through screwing around, he'll be halfway to Mexico. Meanwhile, I need you here." He opened the briefcase, took out the Luger, held it out for a minute, and slipped it into Fletch's pocket. "Cocked and locked. Can you use it if you have to?"

Fletch was looking at him in amazement. "Of course I can use it. What are you expecting here? In a hospital? You think he'll come back—and who are we talking about, by the way?"

"Unless I miss my guess, Costello," Gordon said briefly. "I thought it might be one of two others, but I'm certain it's him."

"How do you know? What did you find out?"

"She told me," Gordon looked over at Marvelita.

Fletch stared at him as if he'd lost him mind. "Gordon— she hasn't said a word. Doc said it would be a few days before she could talk. She could barely open her eyes just now. You read her mind?" His concern was growing.

"She squeezed my arm." Gordon said. Instead of explaining, he reached over and wrapped his hand over Fletch's arm; squeezed once. Thumb and forefinger.

"Son of a bitch," Fletch breathed, looking at Marvelita wide-eyed. He turned back to Gordon. "Costello would be crazy to come back here. Even if he did, he'd never get past the law. Fitz is planning to stay here himself. I've never seen him so worked up."

"That's what I'm afraid of," Gordon said in a chillingly soft voice. He let it sink in. "You're the *only* one I trust. Now do you understand me?"

"I hear you," Fletch said haltingly, "but I think you better fill me in. What the hell is going on? What did you find?" He put his hand in his pocket, drew it out sharply. "Jesus Christ, I wish I could smoke in here."

They were still alone. Gordon set the briefcase on the bedside stand and opened it up. Wordlessly, he took out the stack of papers, turning them over, one by one, on Fletch's lap, pointing to names, dates, dollars, addresses. About halfway through, he picked up the whole stack and handed him the last two pages, one with Marlene Flaherty's name on it, the other with her picture.

Fletch whipped a look of lightning comprehension at him. Before he could speak, they heard footsteps, the rattle of curtain rings. Gordon shoved the pages back in the briefcase and snapped it shut just as Sheriff Fitz drew back the partition.

Fitz gazed at Gordon over the bed in dumb misery. He looked like he'd aged twenty years in two days. He was having trouble figuring out what to say. "Never saw this coming," he finally managed. "You didn't either, did you? Or you wouldn't have asked me to stay out of it?" His eyes were searching Gordon's face, trying to read something, anything, in his blank expression.

"My fault entirely," Gordon said evenly, "As I was just trying to convince Fletch here. I should never have let her go alone."

"Why did you?" Fitz demanded. "What the hell was so important—" He stopped, aghast. "Sorry. I didn't mean that the way it sounded. It's just not like you, that's all." It was clear he was still waiting for an explanation.

"I had business on the island that seemed more important. At the time," Gordon said acidly. He put the briefcase down next to Fletch's chair. "You'll take care of that for me, then?" He said to his friend with a warning look in his eye. "A business contract," he explained to Fitz. "Fletch is going to drop it off at my lawyer's office in town when he has the chance." He was striving to keep his voice moderated. It took an effort. A change of subject would help. "Any idea who did this? Why?"

Fitz looked at him unhappily. "No. No one saw anything or heard anything at the marina. Fog was so bad they wouldn't have seen a helicopter until it landed on them. You have any idea yourself?"

"Only the obvious one. Marvelita said Carmen was afraid of someone or something. Someone meant to attack Carmen, got Marvelita instead. Thanks to the fog, most likely," he said bitterly. He looked at Fitz. "I can promise you one thing. If I find out who it is before you do, you won't need handcuffs, just the coroner's wagon." In case Fitz misunderstood the seriousness of his comment, he added, "And I resign, by the way. Officially and in front of a witness," he jerked a thumb at Fletch. "I'm no longer in your service as an indentured deputy or whatever the hell you made me."

Fitz didn't respond to this right away. The worry that lined his face deepened. "I know you're angry, Gordon. I would be, too, in your place. But you've got to let me handle this. We'll get this bastard, I promise you. You're only going to make matters worse if you take things into your own hands."

"Matters can't get any worse than they are," Gordon said angrily. "I tried it your way and the only thing that got me was a ringside seat at a hospital bed for the only person on earth I'd be willing to die for." This wasn't entirely fair but given the damning evidence lying quietly in the briefcase, he had to distance himself from Fitz. And the sooner the better. "You handle your investigation, I'll handle mine. If I come up with anything conclusive, you'll be the first to know. That's the most I can promise." There was some leeway in the term "conclusive," Gordon thought. Enough, anyway, not to make the statement a complete lie.

"Fair enough," Fitz said, but his tone was glum, dissatisfied. "Meanwhile, I'm going to stay here overnight with you. Between the two of us, she'll be safe." He looked down at the tiny figure motionless in the bed.

"I'm not staying," Gordon said, "But Fletch is. I don't want her to be alone."

"Not staying." Fitz repeated the words in slow disbelief. Then his voice hardened. "I may not know you well, Gordon, but I know you well enough. What are you up to? What's more important than her?"

"Finding out who did this to her," Gordon said. "I think the answer's back on Hogge, not here. I mean, the attacker may be here," he clarified, "but the motive's back on Hogge. Need both for a conviction. You handle the attacker, I'll handle the motive. Then we can hang the bastard."

Fitz clearly wasn't thrilled with this reasoning but, since he couldn't be in two places at once, agreed to it. "Fletch doesn't have to stay here. You might need him on Hogge— with whatever it is you're going to do."

"I don't need any help," Gordon said. "I told you, I don't want her alone. I know—" He waved dismissively. "You'll be here, but I want Marvelita to see a face she knows when she wakes up. Next to me, she knows Fletch better than anyone."

Fitz looked like he was about to object further when his radio crackled to life. "Let me get this. It might be important," he said and ducked out.

The instant he was gone, Gordon turned to Fletch quickly. "You fully in the picture now?" he said urgently. "If you have any questions, ask. I don't want to be here when he gets back. I want Costello."

"Won't you need this?" Fletch asked, touching his pocket.

"I think I can take care of Costello without that," Gordon said, with a grim smile.

"What if Costello has other ideas?" Fletch said pointedly.

"It's just a hunch, but I don't think he will," Gordon said slowly. "But if I'm wrong, the baton passes to you." He bent over Marvelita, whispered in her ear, and started to leave.

"How you going to find him?" Fletch called after him.

"I'm not," Gordon swept the curtain aside. "He's going to find me."

CHAPTER 39

Gordon left the hospital and headed back to Palm Point. Despite what he told Fitz, he had no intention of going to the marina. Instead, he drove past it, slowing down as he came to the streets with tree names. He was looking for Melaleuca Street, where Jackson Fitz lived. The fog was beginning to lift, but it was still hard to see. He saw the narrow lane, made a right and found number 24. It was a small Florida ranch, situated at the end of the paved road. Fitz's vehicle wasn't around, so he parked in the driveway giving some final thought to his plan. It was just before six o'clock—cocktail hour. If his luck was in, Marly would be home. He walked up to the door and rang the bell. Loud chimes echoed inside. There was a clatter of heels and an ugly bright green curtain drew back slightly from the bay window. Then, the sound of the door being unlocked. Cautious, he thought to himself.

Marly opened the door, eyes wide with equal parts surprise, wariness and whatever it was that she was drinking out of the glass she set down on the hall table. "Gordon, isn't it? Jacko told me what happened to your...to Marvli'a. Is she okay?" She was making an effort but nothing could disguise the slurred speech and bleary look that told him the drink was likely not the first by a long shot.

Gordon ignored the question. "I was hoping to catch Jackson at home. He wasn't in the office," Gordon peered past her as if expecting to see Fitz materialize over her shoulder.

"He's not here. I thought he was with you. He's staying at the hospital tonight. Marv'lia— Is it bad?"

"She had a close call but the doctors think she'll pull through. Won't know for a few days yet. I can tell you this, whoever did it won't pull through when I get my hands on him." Gordon didn't have to manufacture the anger that radiated from him. It was real, palpable.

A look of alarm flashed in Marly's eyes. "Do they know who did it?"

"No," Gordon said, "no one seems to have seen or heard a thing. Listen," he leaned on the doorjamb, looming over her. A musty whiff of gin and White Shoulders drifted up. "I have to get back to Hogge. Can you give Jackson a message for me? I can't reach him by phone—can't use them in the hospital," he explained, "but I figure he'll call you at some point to check in."

"Of course," she nodded, desperately trying to focus on what he was saying.

"It's important," Gordon looked at her dubiously, hoping she wasn't too drunk to be of use. "Tell him I'll bring him all the evidence he needs to wrap everything up tomorrow morning." He spoke distinctly. "I have most of it in my office. I'll have the rest by tonight."

"Evidence? You mean about Marvelita?" His statement seemed to have sobered her up a bit.

"Not just the attack on her. Everything that's happened on Hogge. I don't have all the names yet, but I'll have them by tonight. Can you remember that, Marly? I'll bring it all with me tomorrow morning."

There was no doubt at all now about her having understood what he said. She looked terrified. "You know...everything?"

Any doubts Gordon may have had about her involvement evaporated. "Not everything; I was real close and then all this happened with Lita. But by tonight..." He feigned a tone of bravado, "I'll have a stack of papers an inch high that will nail every one of the bastards to the wall. I can trust you, right? To tell Jackson?"

She got a queer look on her face. For a minute, Gordon was afraid she was going to make a confession or some sort of desperate appeal. He sincerely hoped not, otherwise, he was going to have to improvise. Some instinct for self-preservation must have kicked in.

She drew back in the doorway and picked up her glass. "You can trust me. I'll tell Jacko the minute he calls. It's...it's really great news." Her face said it was anything but. She gulped some of the drink. "I should get back to the stove. I've got something on," she said, suddenly in a hurry. "You're headed back to Hogge now?"

"Yeah. My boat's at the marina. Thanks." He waved over his shoulder and walked to the car.

Marly had apparently forgotten whatever was on the stove because she was still watching him from the doorway when he backed out, fear stamped all over her face. Fear and something else. Something that had nothing whatsoever to do with alcohol.

CHAPTER 40

So far, so good, Gordon thought, making his way back to the marina. He took his time. If Marly was going to tip Costello off—as he hoped she would—the man would need some time to get to the marina. And this was one confrontation Gordon didn't want to miss.

The marina was quiet. It wasn't a great boating day. He saw two determined fisherman tinkering with their outboard, but no sign of Costello. Gordon got in his boat, made a show of checking the oil, peering at the engine, dawdled as much as was reasonable. Still no sign of him. Maybe Marly had developed a conscience after all, just when he didn't need her to.

He finally left the dock, navigated the narrow channel into open water and motored at a steady pace, scanning the water intently for any sign of a boat following or approaching him. The weather was steadily improving. The water was still choppy but the sun was peeking through, a small haloed disc in the west. He picked up a few dolphins along the way, jumping in his wake, but that was it.

Maybe he was too late and Costello had already bolted. After all, his attack on Marvelita was an act of desperation. Once he realized he had the wrong person he may have decided to call it quits and take his chances on the run. It was a possibility, but Gordon didn't really believe it. Unless he had money stashed someplace, Costello wasn't going to last long on the run. And if he had already parked his money, Southwest Florida likely never would have seen him again to begin with, much less Hogge Island.

The real irony was not that Costello was a crook, it was that he had tried to go against his own nature and feign respectability. He believed his money could make him respectable, by the simple expedient of converting dirty funds into legitimate enterprise. It was an old story. Organized crime and financial charlatans had been at it for years. They were just much better at it. Their schemes were much bigger and there were more of them. Costello and his cohorts were small fry in the world of high finance even though, by Gordon's rough calculation, their finagling netted five or six million—that he knew of. Instead of continuing to live as crooks, they became businessmen, after a fashion, chained to money and its vast web of commercial enterprise: banks, ATMs, IRS regulations, credit. And now there was no getting away from it. Or living without it. They would have been better off following the late Jervis Pott's example and stuffing their ill-gotten gains under a mattress.

Hogge Island drew closer through the haze and before long he was docking in his slip outside the restaurant, no other vessels in sight. It was eerie, given the usual bustle of the place. The sight of the parking lot, empty, gave him another jolt. It reminded him of the post-hurricane days, the only other time in ten years that *Gordon's* had been closed. As he was tying off, he noticed a beat-up rust-colored skiff drawn up to the small cover around a bend of Mangroves. That in itself wasn't unusual—it was a popular spot for fishing or the occasional delivery of construction supplies. But the skiff looked very much like the one he and Fletch spotted on Okum's End, near Jervis Potts' place. Old skiffs did tend to look alike. Nevertheless, the sight of it heightened his senses.

Gordon stepped onto the dock and crouched down, fiddled with the bowline, tied it off at the cleat. To the observer, he was just a man tying up his boat, concentrating on the task at hand. He felt an almost imperceptible tremble in the boards under his feet, and tensed, ready to spring. There wasn't enough light to cast a shadow but some instinct in him, maybe the one that had kept him alive all these years, made him leap up, right arm flung out to protect his head, just in time. He caught a glimpse of a figure in a black fishing mask just as it swung at him.

The blow from a metal pipe aimed at his throat missed its target, hit hard on the muscle just above the elbow. Searing pain shot from his arm to his eyeballs. On a thinner man it would have cracked the bone. He grabbed at the pipe with his left hand and with his right, jerked the man's mask off. Costello. Lips drawn to his teeth, Costello aimed a vicious kick at his crotch. Gordon jumped back and the pipe came at him again. The threaded part caught him on the sternum, tearing his shirt and bloodying his chest. On the third swing Gordon lunged forward and grabbed Costello's arms. He shoved him backward off the dock and went in with him, letting his full weight take the man to the shallow bottom. He wrapped

Costello's neck in a vice grip from behind and surfaced, letting the man struggle with increasing desperation under water.

Gordon had every intention of killing Costello when he went in the water after him. He could still do that, he finally told himself, after he got the man to talk. He brought the choking, gasping Costello up for a gulp of air, then plunged him in again, this time longer. Costello flailed, kicked, tried to butt himself backward to break free, but he was no match for Gordon's height and weight. Gordon dragged him up again, increasing the pressure around his neck as Costello tried feebly to claw free with his good hand.

"If I have to put you under again, you're not coming up," Gordon warned him. He was breathing heavily, a combination of exertion and exhilaration. He started to take the man under again.

"Don't. No."

Gordon barely heard the hoarse croaks. Still gripping the man's neck, he turned him toward the dock, hauled his head out and bashed it viciously against the boards. The man went limp. Gordon heaved him up and flopped him on his back on the dock, climbed out after him. Blood ran from a gash in Costello's forehead and his right arm was sliced to ribbons from the barnacles that caught him on the way up. But he was alive.

Gordon picked him up, slung him over his back in a fireman's carry, and hauled him off to the restaurant.

Beni met him at the door, eyes alive and dangerous. "He is the one?" He asked.

Gordon nodded.

"He is dead," Beni said with satisfaction.

"No. Alive. Just. Get me some docklines. He might come to and I don't want to start in with him all over again."

Gordon dumped Costello in a chair in his office and held him upright until Beni came back with the rope. "Tie him to the chair," Gordon said, leaning back on the desk. "Then we'll clean him up and get him to talk." He looked down. His shoes were waterlogged and stained with the blood still dripping from his chest. He kicked them off and looked around for something to staunch the bleeding. The cuts made by the pipe thread were deep and likely needed stitches, but that could wait. Gordon peeled off his jacket, shirt and tossed them in the corner. While Beni trussed Costello up, he walked out and came back with a tablecloth. He wrapped it tightly around his chest. It would do.

They gave Costello some rudimentary first aid and waited for him to come to, if he was ever going to. It would be cleaner if he could get Costello to confess everything but at this point he had plenty of ammunition. It would be unfortunate if the man died, but not a shame.

Beni had no concern at all about whether Costello lived, died, or developed septicemia. Cleaning his wounds was a waste of time, Beni pointed out, because if the man did wake up, he planned to kill him. He showed Gordon the small revolver he had tucked into his chef's apron. "Marvelita gave me before she left," he said proudly. "To use if I had to. When he wakes up," he said conversationally, "I will shoot him."

"I tell you what," Gordon said, "If he comes to and won't cooperate, he's yours. But first let me see if I can get some information out of him." He found a pack of cigars in the desk drawer, lit one thankfully, and offered the pack to Beni.

About this time Costello started to groan, tried to lift his head. "My neck," he was still croaking in a hoarse whisper, "You broke my neck."

"That's a shame," Gordon said, stubbing out his cigar and leaning forward on the desk, hands folded in front of him. "Now listen. Here's the deal. You're going to tell me everything you know about Lopez, Hollows, Sharpe, Marly— the whole egg. Don't leave anything out, because I have most of the information right here," he pointed to his computer. "Then you're going to tell me how and when you killed those two men—"

Costello squawked something unintelligible at this.

Gordon raised his hand. "Or, if you didn't kill them, who did. And if you do that, if you talk, then I'm going to convince him," he pointed to Beni, who had his gun trained on Costello, "not to shoot you. He'll start on your kneecaps and work his way up from there." For emphasis, Gordon reached over and put his cigar out on Costello's arm, relishing the man's shriek of pain. "This is Hogge Island, Costello. You die here and no one will find your body until the next hurricane."

It took a while but eventually Costello talked. He prattled. He spilled. He sang like a two-fingered canary.

CHAPTER 41

The green and white Sheriff's boat was once again docked outside *Gordon's*. Two deputies whom Gordon didn't recognize were loading a handcuffed, bloodied Costello into the boat. Deputy Harris, who had gotten Gordon's call, was taking a statement in the office.

"No, there were no witnesses," Gordon was finishing up his recounting of the events. "He tried to kill me on the dock." He displayed his chest wounds. "We fought, he lost." He glossed over the next part. "He confessed to everything—after some persuasion." No mention of Beni, the cigar, or the gun. "He's the one responsible for the attack and was involved in the two killings out here. But he wasn't in it alone. Claims it was all Hollows idea. Alan Hollows. Fitz knows all the players and I have a ton of evidence sitting in a briefcase at the hospital." He paused. "It's a pretty complicated story."

Harris gave him a strange look. "So I understand. Your call surprised me. I thought you were working with Fitz." He looked at Gordon, questioning.

"I knew Fitz was at the hospital, guarding Marvelita in ICU." As excuses went, it was pretty thin, but he didn't elaborate. "I'm headed back there after you leave. I'll fill him in on everything."

Harris still had a curious expression on his face. "He's not there now. He's at the office. I radioed him when you called. He wasn't too happy about being kept in the dark. Better if you call him now," Harris suggested.

"I will," Gordon said wearily. He realized Harris was in a difficult position but bringing him into the picture now would only complicate things further. "Where you taking him?" He jerked his head toward the boat.

Harris wanted to pursue the matter of the sheriff, but didn't, seeing Gordon wasn't going to talk about it. "Hospital. Then city lock-up," he finally said. "He needs medical attention. He's pretty banged up. Looks like you might need some yourself," Harris advised.

"I'll get cleaned up when I get to the hospital. Looks worse than it is," Gordon said.

The deputy left and the Sheriff's boat got underway, leaving Gordon to consider his next move. Fletch was still with Marvelita at the hospital. It was unlikely Marly would try anything herself. She was in no condition to, for one thing. For another, she might be dishonest and conniving, but she wasn't cut out to be a killer. Besides, if he was wrong, Fletch was there to back him up.

He took out his phone and paced the floor, thinking. Eventually he had to speak to Fitz. But not on the phone. This conversation had to be face to face, no matter how unpleasant. He dialed.

"Gordon." The sheriff answered after one ring. It was obvious he was waiting for the call. "Done playing a lone hand?" He sounded bitter, but his voice was laced with uncertainty. "You'd better have a damned good reason for calling Harris and leaving me in the wind." There was hurt there, too.

"I did," Gordon sighed, "And I do. Meet me at the marina. I should be there in about half an hour. I'll give you the whole story. Jackson—" Some instinct made him use the sheriff's first name. "I had no choice, you'll see that. I'm sorry."

He told Beni where he could be reached, then came back and redid the makeshift bandage on his chest, sprayed more antiseptic on the cuts hoping he didn't already have blood poisoning. He put on his loosest fitting shirt and reluctantly slid into the damp, stained shoes.

This, Gordon thought ruefully walking down the dock, was how Lancelot must have felt just before he gave Arthur the good news. At least Lancelot had the benefit of a suit of armor.

CHAPTER 42

"Hard to believe a few days ago I was sitting in a hospital room with a Luger in my pocket ready to plug a sitting Sheriff," Fletch reached over and poured another whiskey. He had his own bottle, a present from Gordon, who was gratefully drinking bourbon.

They were sitting in Marvelita's bedroom back on Hogge. She watched them with a bemused expression, balancing a cup of tea in her hand. Against her wishes, Gordon had insisted on bed rest for at least a few more days. The livid bruises around her neck were healing, but her voice was still raw. Left to her own devices she would have been back in her kitchen, but Gordon said no, the restaurant could reopen the last week in August, just before Labor Day. Beni, who had installed himself upstairs on the living room couch when Marvelita came home from the hospital, agreed, with a new-found forcefulness that brought a surprised smile to Marvelita's lips. He had returned her revolver, but the aura of protectiveness he'd acquired during her ordeal was still very much with him.

Inexplicably—to Gordon at least—she didn't seem to mind it from him.

"I was hoping it wouldn't come to that," Gordon said, responding to Fletch's comment. "But to tell you the truth, for a few hours there, anything was possible."

"I still don't know everything," Marvelita complained hoarsely. "Only pieces. You said you would tell me everything when we were home. We are home." She sipped her tea, waited.

Gordon picked up his glass and leaned back. "Fletch told you at the hospital about the racket they'd worked, right?"

"Yes, Fletch showed me what you found. I do not understand it completely, but it was a lot of money?"

Gordon nodded. "From what I saw at least five or six million. Probably more if I kept looking. They all shared in the profits, like pigs at the trough. Everything was rosy as long as they could keep flipping the properties, cover up the trail. This was happening all over the country, you understand, but after the storm, Hogge was particularly ripe for the picking. Then in 2009 the bottom fell out. Real estate plummeted and the pipeline dried up. The bank found itself saddled with a mountain of bad loans and the regulators were circling. Worse, Lopez had roped in some pretty shady investors and they wanted their money. They made it clear his life was on the line. Lopez tried to make good, but eventually he needed more cash. So he started to squeeze Hollows and Costello for money, threatened to expose the whole scheme unless they anted up. By that time Costello had climbed into bed with Hollows as a silent partner. He regretted that later.

"But if Lopez turned them in he'd be exposing himself, too," Fletch objected.

"It didn't matter to him at that point. If he couldn't cover himself he figured being in jail was better than being dead. One way or another he was going down, and he wasn't going alone. Costello had the most to lose—his name was all over those documents. Hollows was cagier."

"He would be," Fletch said. "And just how in hell was all this high finance going on right under our noses? While we were living here?"

"Because we were all standing on our heads trying to repair homes, businesses, trying to survive without power, water. Who had time to wonder what the other guy was up to? I didn't," Gordon pointed out. "That hurricane was a perfect storm in more ways than one, from their point of view."

"Anyhow, Costello claims it was his idea to scare Max off with the attack. Hollows was livid when he found out about it. Old habits die hard," Gordon added as an aside, "and Costello acquired his a long time ago, during his dope running days. Unfortunately for the German tourist, they got their wires crossed on where Max was staying and Costello hit the wrong guy. Minute he realized it, he bolted. But that tipped Max off. He knew that attack was meant for him, and he knew why. He called Fitz. I'm pretty sure he was ready to give up the whole ball of wax, but we'll never know, because that night—"

"Friday night? The night of the power outage?" Fletch interjected.

"Right. You remember we heard that boat?"

Fletch nodded.

"Well, that night" Gordon continued, "Hollows told Costello he'd made a mess of things, and the only way to fix it was to take Max out of the picture completely. According to Costello, the power outage gave them a perfect opportunity.

Hollows got Max to the Club on some pretext and between them, they killed him and dumped him on the beach on the South end. Without Lopez in the picture, they figured they'd be safe."

Fletch frowned. "I get that, but how does Jervis Potts come into it? He couldn't have been part of their deal—he was about destitute."

Gordon sighed. "Potts got killed being Potts. Don't think we'll ever know how he got his hands on that watch, but being the scavenger he is, somehow he did. Took it off the body, most likely. If he lived in reality, or anything close to it, he would gone to the sheriff and saved everyone a lot of trouble. He'd also be alive. Instead, with his finders-keepers mentality, he tried to sell the thing to Hollows. He used to do odd jobs for the guy so I guess he trusted him." Here Gordon stopped, swallowed some bourbon, collecting his thoughts.

"Hollows wanted no part of it. He immediately assumed Potts knew everything and was attempting to blackmail him. No doubt because that's what he would have done. Costello claims Hollows killed him. You and I," he said to Fletch, "just missed walking in on his murder the morning we went out there."

He stopped, made a wry face. "The bitch of it is these killings were inept, ill-thought-out—men acting out of desperation. I suspect if Lattie hadn't thrown her wrench in the works, Fitz would have caught up with them pretty quickly. Her timing couldn't have been worse, and then she compounded it all by buying Potts off, ending up with the watch. At that point, Costello told me, he and Hollows figured they were off the hook. Costello was planning on clearing out and Hollows, well, for him it was going to be business as usual.

The thing they hadn't figured on was the maid, Carmen. Costello saw her the morning of the first attack and was afraid she'd seen him, recognized him by that hand of his. Then she vanished. I still can't figure out why she ended up back in the picture."

"And that part," Marvelita said straining to be heard, "is my story. I told you she looked familiar to me."

Gordon nodded.

"The day we met on the marina, before the puerco Costello tried to strangle me, she told me. Jaime—Max—was her half brother."

"I thought that was a possibility," Gordon broke in. "Fitz told me the half-sister's name was Carmella. I mentioned it to him but he didn't buy it."

Marvelita nodded. "She is the one Jaime called from the restaurant Thursday night. He was staying at the house next to the one the man was attacked in. She met him there and stayed until morning. They both saw Costello, she and Jaime, running from the house after he attacked the tourist. She thought Costello was gone so she went over to check on the man, but Costello saw her, before he got away in the boat. It was before the turtle lady got there. Carmen wanted to call the police, but Jaime said, no, he would do it, that she should leave the island, to be safe. So she did. She went to Miami."

"And disappeared," Gordon put in. "But why did she come back?"

"She worked for Hollows for two years, you remember. She spoke to someone on the island. When they told her about the murder of Max she thought it had to be Costello. She wanted to tell what she knew. She trusted me. We were to call the sheriff together, but then—" Marvelita coughed, drank some tea. "Then we know what happened next. But I do not understand how he knew we were meeting." She looked at Gordon questioningly.

"That was my fault," Gordon said looking down at his hands. "But by the time I realized it, it was too late." His jaw tightened and he continued. "I knew that Marly was mixed up with Costello years ago, you told me that," he said to Fletch. "But I figured that was over and done with. If I'd told Fitz about it from the beginning, instead of trying to spare his feelings, this," he gestured angrily at Marvelita's neck, "might never have happened."

"Then again, it might have," Fletch said cynically. "Love is blind and all that."

Gordon grunted. "Costello was getting pretty desperate. He knew Marly had married Fitz and started pressing her for information, convinced her that if the fraud was discovered and they went down, she was going with them. He said she refused at first, but he finally convinced her. He told her she was looking at least ten years in jail."

He leaned toward Marvelita and took her hand. "When I called Fitz and told him you were meeting Carmen, I didn't know yet that Marly was in the picture. Afterward, I prayed Fitz would have the sense not to tell her, but they were arguing when I called. I guess he figured if he shared his news, she'd stop fighting with him." He looked down at the little hand he was holding. "Men don't have to be criminals to be desperate. He knew there was something wrong but he didn't want to face it."

Marvelita squeezed his hand. "You could not have known."

"But you would have, I suspect. And I could have been smarter," Gordon said bitterly. He sat up. "After that I was. Once I knew she was in it, I was sure she was the one who tipped off Costello about your meeting. So I used her to set him up. At that point," he said to Fletch, "I honestly didn't know whether I could trust Fitz. He could have been in it by then. It was his wife, after all. And I believe he was really in love with her. I wasn't taking any more chances. Which is how you ended up with the Luger." He looked at Fletch, curious. "Would you have used it if it came to that?"

"Damn straight," Fletch said cheerfully. He looked at Marvelita. "I know you don't exactly approve of me, but I am very, very fond of you." He reddened slightly at this uncharacteristic admission.

"I approve of you more now," Marvelita said, her voice still hoarse. But there was an impish look in her eyes.

"How did it go with Fitz?" Fletch asked Gordon casually, pouring more whiskey in his glass.

Gordon didn't answer him right away, recalling that painful conversation. "It was pretty painful," he finally said. "I'll tell you about it one day." His face was impassive.

Fletch nodded slowly, changed the subject. "You took a hell of a chance facing Costello unarmed, you know." He shook his head. "What made you think he wouldn't just shoot you?"

"I might have been wrong about it," Gordon conceded, "in which case you'd be sitting here telling Marvelita all this instead of me. But all of them, the attack and the murders, were head bashings. I had a hunch Costello didn't like using a gun, maybe because he couldn't use one, at least not well."

Gordon held up his left thumb and forefinger, grinning. "I suspected Two-Finger Louie was left-handed. Turned out I was right. It was the last thing I asked him before I turned him over."

CHAPTER 43

Four days later Gordon was sitting in his office at the restaurant. It was still closed but he was using the unexpected free time to catch up on paperwork, letting the events of the past week recede from his brain. He'd just finished breakfast, a plate of ham and baked eggs and his customary bourbon, soothed by this small return to familiar routine. Marvelita, insisting she would be driven insane if she spent any more time in bed, was organizing her kitchen. The reopening was only a few days away. The marks around her throat were still fading but her voice had returned to normal. He could hear it drifting in from the kitchen now, in animated conversation with Beni.

There was a light knock at the door and it opened. Sheriff Fitz stepped into the doorway, and hesitated, waiting to be invited in. He had on his full uniform, neatly pressed for once, and was holding his hat, fingers working around its broad brim.

"Come in, sit down." Gordon said, indicating the chair. He looked around for some way to ease into this conversation. They hadn't spoken since that last devastating meeting at the marina on Palm Point. "You're looking remarkably put together," he finally said. Not a great opening, but better than babbling about the weather.

"Thanks," Fitz said, taking a seat. He gave a dismissive wave taking in his outfit. "Internal affairs review later this afternoon. Thought I'd better make a good impression, under the circumstances." He looked uncomfortable, more than a little self-conscious, and clearly at a loss as to what to say next.

Gordon grimaced sympathetically and decided to address the issue directly. "Internal review's on account of Marly's involvement? Is it routine or is this going to mean trouble for you?"

"Little of both, I guess," Fitz said flatly. "Having your wife turn up a crook is bad enough. It's worse when you're in my position. Sheriffs are elected here. Doubt I'll be reinstated. Not to mention…" He blew out a long, frustrated breath and looked up at Gordon. "You ever married, Gordon? What would you do in my place? I got her an attorney. Posted bail for her. The lawyer thinks he can make a pretty good case for coercion. Costello was pretty abusive, apparently." Fitz was making excuses and he knew it. "But," he had the hat in a white-knuckle grip, "even so, I don't think I could ever trust her again. If I could to begin with." He sounded bewildered and very, very sad.

Gordon, who had been doodling on a sheet of paper, looked up, considering how to respond. Fitz wasn't really asking if he could trust Marly. It was clear he could not. He was looking for absolution. That and some reassurance that the future would not always look this bleak. When your world blows up and takes your judgement down with it, hope becomes a very tenuous thing, as Gordon knew very well. As much as he loathed revisiting any past, especially his own, he felt he owed Fitz that much honesty, having been, in a way, the vehicle that caused the wreck.

He thrust the paper aside and looked Fitz in the eye. "You asked if I was married? I was. She's in prison," he said abruptly. Fitz, startled, opened his mouth to say something. Gordon held up his hand. "That isn't the worst of it. Hear me out." He forced himself to continue. "It was about thirty years ago. It started the same way for me: love, trust, all unconditional, never a question. She had a problem—alcohol and drugs. The weakness was always there. I saw it from the beginning, but I was sure it would go away. That I could fix it," he corrected himself. "Instead, it got worse."

Long dormant images started reappearing in his mind. He willed them away. "There were a few episodes—mostly her getting belligerent, loud, and me being too exhausted from long hours to deal with it. Always followed by remorse—she loved me, it would never happen again. She had a child when I married her. Cassandra. Beautiful little girl. For a while things were okay." He jabbed the desk with his pen, as if picking away at something. "But the older Cassie got, the worse things seemed to get. Sondra, my wife, started losing her temper more and more frequently. One day she got violent. Cut the living room couch to ribbons with a kitchen knife. Claimed it was because she got frustrated. I still didn't want to see it." He gave a grim smile. "She was very persuasive when she was sober. And she was very beautiful." He looked up at Fitz, who was watching him intently.

"One night I came in, beat. She started in about how much trouble Cassie was giving her, talking back—all the usual stuff you go through raising kids. I was tired, fed up. I told her I'd had enough, told to get out if she couldn't handle it." Gordon looked over Fitz's shoulder, silently bringing up the ghosts. "The next day I came home early. I guess I knew things weren't right on some level," he said bitterly. "Sondra was in the living room, still shaking Cassie with her hands around her throat. Cassie was dead. Sondra was still yelling at her, telling her to get up." He swallowed hard, went on. "I would have killed Sondra then. I wanted to. But she was pregnant."

"Jesus." Fitz sounded shaken. "You see a lot in this job. But you never get used to a kid. And your own—" He broke off.

Gordon continued. "When the police got there, Sondra tried to blame it on the neighbor. There was a guy who lived in the building, recent parolee, who was a little strange. She begged me to back her up. I couldn't." *But I thought about it*, Gordon thought mentally, reliving the scene. "Then her lawyer wanted to make a case that she snapped because I told her I didn't love her anymore, told her she'd be better off dead." He looked down at his hands, clenched into fists. "They almost got me to go along with it, but then she miscarried just before the trial. After that, I refused to testify in her defense at the trial. It's not pretty, but I didn't care what happened to her." He looked up at Fitz defiantly. "I still don't."

"What did happen?" Fitz was looking at the desk, not Gordon.

"They brought in a verdict of extreme emotional duress. The miscarriage went a long way with the jury. Gave her 25 years. She could be out by now, I guess. Like I said, I don't care.

"What if she comes looking for you?"

"Even if she did, she'd never find me," Gordon said. "After the trial I changed my name legally—it's not the one I go by now if you're wondering. Then spent the next thirty years a moving target. I came out of Iquitos as 'Gordon Strange.' I've been careful everywhere, even here. The restaurant, the house," he gestured, "all of it is in Marvelita's name. This is my last stop—end of the road." He threw the pen he'd practically bent in half across the desk.

Fitz looked at Gordon. It was hard to read the expression in his eyes, but there was sorrow there, and pity.

"I didn't tell you all this to garner sympathy," Gordon said roughly. "Point is, for me at least, I had to come to terms with the fact that Sondra may have loved me, but she didn't marry me for love. She married me so I could protect her—from herself. On some level I knew that and was fool enough to believe I could do it. I suspect Marly married you for the same reason. And we both know how well that works. Because the one thing you can be certain of in this world is that people don't change, not for someone else. Ever." He took a deep breath. "So in terms of trusting Marly, I think you know what the answer is. The real question is, do you want to accept it." He gave Fitz a long look, then abruptly shifted gears, trying to shake off the specters he'd called up from the past.

"Tell me where things stand at this point. I have no idea how everything came down after I left you at the marina."

Fitz shifted his weight in the chair. "They picked up everyone that afternoon. I turned the investigation over to Harris once I knew Marly was involved," he explained. "It'll take a while to sort out the charges but so far Hollows and Costello have been hit with the most serious of them; Marly with obstruction. Everyone lawyered up, of course, and

Hollows made bail. Hollows was ordered to stay in town. He won't be back here for a while."

"I'd expect his next stop to be jail," Gordon said, outraged. "I didn't think 'back here' was even an option. What gives?"

"It's a very complicated case," Fitz sighed, frustrated. "Hollows claims Costello was responsible for the attack and both murders and moreover, threatened to kill him unless he kept his mouth shut. Costello, of course, fingered Hollows as the architect of the whole scheme and claims Hollows murdered Potts. He weakened that argument by hiding out in Potts' place toward the end, so his DNA is everywhere."

"That explains how he was at my dock waiting for me the day he tried to kill me," Gordon said, enlightened.

Fitz continued. "Special investigations is going through the usual with a fine tooth comb—homes, offices, vehicles, computers—but it will take time. Meanwhile, we have almost nothing in the way of physical evidence for the murders. At least we have the pipe Costello slugged you with and his fingerprints from Marvelita's throat."

"Thank God for that," Gordon said sarcastically. "Not to mention Costello's confession."

"He says he was coerced, that you held a gun on him. Among other things." Fitz cut in, skewing him a look.

"His word, my word," Gordon said blandly. "I say he offered it voluntarily after he tried to kill me and failed." He was frowning. "What about that briefcase full of evidence I handed over?" he demanded.

Fitz brightened up a little at this. "That's more solid," he said, then grimaced. "But that's where it gets complicated. That investigation's been turned over to the feds—IRS and

FBI—because they prosecute mortgage fraud, tax evasion, all that." He waved. "Since the murders were directly related to the fraud, there's a fight over who has jurisdiction. Personally, I think it will end up a joint investigation."

"In other words, a complete cluster-fuck," Gordon said with disgust. "So you're telling me Hollows and Costello could be back out here in a few weeks picking up where they left off?"

"Not as bad as that. Case against Costello is pretty strong, for assault with intent if nothing else. He'll do time. Plenty of it. Hollows…" he hesitated, giving Gordon an unhappy look. "With him, it's going to be hard to make things stick. He was very careful on those documents. But the Feds have opened an investigation into all his finances. He'll be tied up with them for a very long time. I don't think you'll be seeing him back at the Hogge Island Club any time soon."

"I hope you're right," Gordon said. "I should have drowned both of them when I had the chance," he added.

"I'll just pretend I didn't hear that," Fitz said. He looked thoughtful.

"You didn't mention Sharpe," Gordon pointed out, "He was involved in the construction angle."

"He's part of the federal case. Insurance fraud is what I'm hearing. Seems he inflated invoices for the insurance payout, got kickback from the owners. It was quite the extensive nest of snakes you uncovered. The Feds are being pretty tight-lipped about it, but from what I hear, there may be a Vice President at Citizen's Insurance that won't be sleeping too well in the near future."

"That's not completely surprising." Gordon said. "I knew I'd find more if I kept looking. I ran out of time."

"One more thing," Fitz had gotten up, "I was furious when we saw each other at the marina. I was upset about Marly, didn't really want to believe it at first. But more than that," he was struggling, "I had a hard time with the fact that you couldn't trust me enough to put me in the picture. Thought I'd be compromised because of her. I said some pretty lousy things. I'm sorry for that. I see now that I would have done the same thing in your position."

"Maybe, maybe not," Gordon said, thinking of the Luger. "But I appreciate the sentiment."

"Anyhow," Fitz said, his hand on the door, "I believe I understand you a little better." He turned on his way out. "You suck as a deputy, by the way. But you'll do for a friend."

CHAPTER 44

After lunch, Marvelita ducked her head back in the door of his office. "Gordon—there is someone here to see you." She ushered in a woman, maybe ten years younger than herself and alike enough in frame and coloring to have been a relation. Her hair was swept up, caught in a tortoise-shell clip. She wore a simple black linen dress that emphasized her figure, the only spot of color a hand-painted silk scarf draped around her neck. Altogether, she was striking figure and considerably over-dressed, Gordon thought, for Hogge Island. He half stood, waved her in, and offered her a chair.

Marvelita hovered in the doorway for an instant and said, "I think you will be interested in what she has to say." With no more introduction, she left them alone.

"I came to thank Marvelita for risking her life for me," the woman said, sitting down. "And also to thank you, Mr. Strange, for finding my brother's killers. I am Carmella Duarte. Jaime, or Max as you knew him, was my half-brother."

Gordon looked at her with interest. "I was hoping we'd meet," he said, "and please call me Gordon. I'm sorry about your brother." He hesitated. "I'm afraid he was tangled up in a pretty bad financial mess. And picked the wrong people to do business with on top of it." He looked at her curiously. "How much do you know?"

"I met with Sheriff Fitz before I came here. He told me everything." She fingered her scarf. "Jaime wasn't a bad person, I mean, he didn't start out bad."

People seldom do, Gordon thought cynically, but said nothing, waiting for her to continue.

"He became bitter when he was very young. And it ruined him. He became obsessed with money. Money," she looked at him, eyes very dark, "and vengeance."

Gordon, who had been nodding perfunctorily at what sounded like a pedestrian story these days looked up, startled, at that last word. It had almost an old-fashioned ring to it and, given the circumstances that led up to Max's death, mystified him completely.

"That surprises you, I expect." She looked at her hands, then up at him. "Did you ever wonder why Jaime came to this island?"

"I always wonder what brings people here," Gordon admitted. "I had about convinced myself he found out about Hogge through you, since you worked here. Came when he saw an opportunity to cash in after the storm. But you're implying he came for another reason." He took out a cigar and offered her one, which she declined with a small shake of her head. "Look," he finally said wearily, "I'm lousy at guessing games and, to be honest, I've had enough of them these past few weeks. Why don't you just tell me what you're getting at?"

Carmella reached into the large black leather purse she had on her lap and handed him a short article, laminated in plastic, creased and wrinkled. Obviously old, obviously carried around like a talisman.

Gordon smoothed it out on the desk in front of him. The article was dated 1979 and was from a small newspaper in Maiden Oaks, FL. Pictured was a blackened structure damaged by fire. The headline read, "Arson Claims the Life of Local Mill Owner." He read the article through once, looked up at Carmella, who was watching him closely, and read it through again. It was a brief piece, essentially mourning the loss of the mill's founder, Eustace Cross, along with the mill—which had employed half the town—as a result of a fire attributed to arson. The arsonist was named as twelve-year-old Jaime Maximillian, as identified by Cross's grandson, Vanderbilt, who was nine years old at the time. Jamie was being sought for questioning, along with his mother, and half-sister but, as of that writing, there were no leads as to their whereabouts. The last paragraph gave highlights of the victim's illustrious life and details about his funeral arrangements.

Gordon handed the article back to Carmella and sat forward, folding his hands in front of him on the desk. "So, Max came here looking for Cross? He was bitter because Van Cross turned him in for the arson when he was a kid," he suggested. He looked at her doubtfully, recalling her earlier statement that her brother "didn't start out bad." If burning down buildings at the age of twelve didn't qualify as bad in her book, maybe they'd been fortunate after all on Hogge.

She seemed to know what he was thinking, gave a sad smile. "I know it sounds like my brother was a criminal from that article, but the point is," she sat up straight and spoke very seriously, "he did not set that fire. Vanderbilt Cross set it. And blamed it on Jaime." She looked at her hands. "Our lives there were over after that, ruined. Oh, it's true," she said seeing doubt in his eyes, "I saw it. I was there."

Gordon was frankly astounded. If he'd heard this story before Max's death, he would have immediately pegged Cross as the killer. Anyhow, it was all moot now. Max was dead and his quest for vengeance died with him. But some sort of validation was owed to the woman sitting across from him. "I appreciate your telling me this. Cross must have recognized your brother, which accounts for his behavior lately. He's been very erratic. Did your brother ever get a chance to confront him?" He was curious.

"Not directly. Let me explain it. You see," she spread her hands, "Jaime was smart, he worked hard, had good jobs. But he could not forget what Van got away with, how he destroyed our lives. It made him bitter. It made him mean. He became obsessed with finding Van and making him pay for what he did. He was able to track Van down and after that, he kept tabs on every job Van had, every town he lived in. Jaime used to send him letters, just a few lines, nothing threatening. Just to let him know he knew where he was, had not forgotten. Eventually, he found out that Van had moved here, to Hogge Island. Van probably thought he was safe here," she said, reflecting. "Anyway, Jaime found a way to make a lot of money, fast." Carmella gestured to Gordon. "You understand it was all for the same goal. So he decided to build a house on the island. It was Jaime's idea for me to get a job here, keep an eye on Van. About a week before Jaime was killed, he gave me a letter to leave on Van's doorstep. I did."

"So that's why Van became paranoid," Gordon said slowly. "The past few weeks he kept insisting someone was spying on him," he explained. "Guess he was right, in a way." He gave her an appraising look. "You must have been furious yourself to have gone to such lengths. It was a terrible injustice," he added.

She looked sad and a little distant. "I was angry, of course. We had to run away, to Miami. We struggled, my mother, Jaime, and I, for many years. But I really went along with the plan to come here because he was my brother and I loved him," she said simply. "And once I got here, I thought, maybe, this island would bring him peace. It's a very special place." She sat looking out the window. The afternoon sun was playing on the water. Pelicans lined the docks, basking in the warmth. "Maybe he could have healed here."

Instead, he died here, Gordon thought to himself. But even if he'd lived, there would still be the issue of his financial troubles. On the other hand, if he hadn't died, the whole scheme might have gone unnoticed, just another footnote in a larger financial cesspool. *Secrets wake up*, Marvelita had said. But even she couldn't have predicted this. He stopped ruminating and turned his attention back to Carmella.

"What will you do now? Do you have other family? A place to live?"

"I do in Miami," she said. "I'm opening my own place there, a small gallery. I have a lot of contacts with Cuban artists, and there's a strong market in that." She smiled sadly. "Insurance money came to me when Jaime…died."

"And what about Van?" Gordon asked.

"Van Cross knows the truth. Jaime may have been dishonest in the end, but Van is a coward. He will die a coward. I will leave him to his ghosts."

Her words sounded like a curse.

CHAPTER 45

The forecast for Labor Day Weekend was excellent: dry and sunny, every day a Chamber of Commerce ten. Hogge Island was full of tourists determined to squeeze out the last glorious days of summer vacation. Every seat was taken by 6p.m. at the grand re-opening of *Gordon's* on Friday night and the outdoor bar was three deep. Marvelita had outdone herself. In addition to a lavish raw bar, the special was *Feijoada Completa*, the slow-cooked Brazilian national dish that was a riot of meats, black beans, collards, farina, plantains, and rice. Beni was in charge of the kitchen. Marvelita, looking younger than Gordon could remember, floated from table to table receiving well wishes in a diaphanous dress of hand-painted silk. Her resemblance to the mermaid in Gordon's mural was never stronger.

Gordon himself had abandoned his usual post by the door and was presiding over a gathering of Hogge Island residents. He'd answered dozens of questions about the murders, Marvelita's brush with death, Fitz's tribulations, and recounted, in every detail, Carmella's damning revelations about Van Cross. At the point of exhaustion, he excused himself and wandered over to the small table that was reserved for him at the entrance. Fletch was already sitting there, reading a boating magazine.

"This is quite a crowd," Fletch observed, looking up. "Doesn't hurt, of course, that the Hogge Island Club Bistro is temporarily closed."

"Even if they were open, I suspect it wouldn't make much of a dent," Gordon countered.

"Never has," Fletch agreed, and resumed reading.

Gordon surveyed the lively scene around him with satisfaction. White lights ringed the dining room and extended out to the bar. The evening was hot, though comfortable, the wretched low front having finally heaved itself off to the north. For once, he was content to take a back seat to the action. He was pleased to see Marvelita out among the patrons. He was surprised when she turned over her kitchen to Beni, but not shocked. Beni had surprised both of them. And Marvelita had certainly earned her evening of enjoyment.

"Can I join you for a minute?" Jack Campbell had come over. He pulled out a chair and sat down. "I wanted a word with you privately," he said, taking a long pull from his martini. "I assume Fletch is already in the picture?"

Gordon nodded.

"If I read between the lines of what you were telling us," Jack said slowly, "it sounds like there's a chance Hollows might beat some of the charges. Again."

"Sorry to say, it's possible," Gordon said. "But he's not going to find it as easy to shake off the Feds. He'll be tied up for a long time, Jack. I understand family members have stepped in already to take over running the Hogge Island Club.

If you're thinking about that expansion, and the whole business with Lattie, I think that's history. Charges were never brought and Fitz seems to have developed amnesia as far as Lattie's confession is concerned." He grinned. "The island way, right?"

"Ah, the island way," Fletch put in, not looking up.

"Good," Jack was relieved. "What's going to happen to Fitz? I know he did nothing wrong, but Marly…" he shook his head. "Caesar's wife and all that."

"He's on leave right now for three months with pay while they sort out the internal review. I'm hoping they'll clear him." Gordon sighed. "If you have to deal with the law, he's not half bad. I'd go so far as to call him a friend. God knows what they'd send instead."

Jack nodded. "That story about Van Cross and Max was incredible. Powerful stuff. Think he'll change his attitude?"

"I wouldn't hold my breath," Fletch offered, turning a page.

"Shut up, Fletch." Gordon said good-naturedly. "Maybe with Max dead he'll stop being so paranoid. No more gun waving and ludicrous threats. As for the rest?" Gordon thought about it. "I don't think he's suddenly going to become a humanitarian. But it's taken him down a notch. Maybe we won't have as much sanctimony, as many ranting emails. For a while anyhow. People are funny. Without a visible irritant, they tend to revert to form."

He poked Fletch in the ribs with his elbow.

Jack laughed, finished off his martini. "Well, thanks. You've told me what I wanted to know. I'd better get back to the table. They're discussing the Hamboree—comes up in two months. Renee was pushing to do something different. She wanted to run some sort of ritzy murder mystery dinner, you know, like the ones they do on trains. Under the circumstances, we're going with a scavenger hunt. Besides, she's left us, anyhow."

"Renee's gone?" Fletch looked up, surprised.

"Vacation?" Gordon asked.

"Nope. Put her house up for sale and is going back to Naples. She says Hogge Island was too provincial for her, but personally, I think she wants to get clear before they start looking too closely at Hollows' finances—and associates." He gave Gordon a knowing look and stood up.

Piercing shrieks of laughter erupted from a nearby table.

Jack rolled his eyes. "One more weekend," he said. "Take heart. September is almost here." He turned and stumped off through the dining room.

Gordon brushed some ash off his white linen blazer and swirled his bourbon contentedly. From behind him, he heard an unfamiliar voice; female, brassy with assurance.

"That's what I'm trying to tell you. They're all in witness protection. He may own a restaurant now, but that's just a cover," the nasal voice intoned. "He was the head of some mob family back East—I can't remember which one. I mean," the voice dropped a decibel, "look at the size of the man. Does he look like a businessman to you?"

It took Gordon a minute to realize they were talking about him.

A male voice broke in, annoyed. "That's just ridiculous, Mabel. Where do you get these stories?"

"Marty, you were there," the woman said, exasperated. "The captain told us yesterday, the one who took us out fishing. That one," her voice dropped to a stage whisper, "sitting over there reading."

Gordon looked at Fletch, bug-eyed, and snatched the magazine out of his hands. "What's wrong with you? Witness protection? Haven't we had enough excitement without a rumor like that starting up?"

Fletch grinned up at him, a glint in his eye. "Tourists like stories. It adds to the allure of the place. Give 'em what they want, I always say." He reached for his glass, raised it.

"Besides, Marvelita says it's good for business."

ABOUT THE AUTHOR

 Karen Sirabian was formerly Director of the Manhattanville College's Master of Arts in Writing program. She was one of the founders of Inkwell, Manhattanville's nationally acclaimed literary journal, and served as its faculty advisor for many years. Prior to her involvement in the college, Ms. Sirabian spent ten years in the publishing industry.

Her short stories and poems have been published in a number of literary journals and other venues, including *Writer's Forum, Kalliope, Cimarron Review, The New York Times, The Madison Review*, and *Runes: A Review of Poetry.*